I0654446

Covert-Ops: The Extraction

Steve Barker

FIRST EDITION

Published in 2024 by

GREEN CAT BOOKS

19 St Christopher's Way

Pride Park

Derby DE24 8JY

www.green-cat.shop

Copyright © 2024 Steve Barker

All rights reserved.

ISBN: 978-1-913794-65-1

All rights reserved.

No part of this publication

may be reproduced in any form or by any means without the prior written permission of the publisher.

This book is sold subject to the conditions that shall not, by way of trade or otherwise, be lent, resold, hired out, or otherwise circulated without the publisher's prior consent in any form of binding other than that in which it is published and without a similar condition including this condition being imposed on the subsequent purchaser.

ACKNOWLEDGEMENTS

Thank you to
George James
Simon Munnery
Derek Barker
George Holland
Joshua Standen

for their help with this book

Contents

Chapter One – San Juan

Intense rays of sunlight beam across the balcony and through the glass patio doors into the stateroom, bouncing off the quilt-covered body next to me on the massive double bed. Apart from that, the cabin is quiet, except for the ship's near-silent humming and the gentle vibration as we travel through the Caribbean Sea to San Juan in Puerto Rico.

I lay wide awake, staring at the ceiling and still buzzing about last night's incident on deck 7 after Lucy retired. I thought about waking her and keeping her abreast of things but decided it could wait until later. Besides, several more puzzling questions are starting to rotate in my mind regarding the call from Simon a week ago.

First, why did the person request our initial meeting at the old Fort Castillo San Cristobal in San Juan? Second, how did the two people we need to extract become involved in what can only be described, going on the knowledge we know so far, as a well-organised militia?

Before I can think too deeply, Lucy's arm appears from beneath the covers as she moves close, pressing her body against mine.

"What time is it?"

"Time we get dressed and head for the Garden Café for breakfast," I say, sliding out from under the quilt and sitting on the edge of the bed.

In a quiet, half-asleep voice, "Five more minutes."

"No problem, I'll grab a quick shower, then head up. I need my morning gallon of coffee. You can meet me in the café."

"Sounds like some plan to me, Steve. Won't be long."

We have been together a while now, so I know that when she says five minutes, she means 20, like most women. So I have plenty of time for my hose down and down a few mugs of caffeine before she arrives.

Arrive at the Garden Café as the enormous cream-coloured metal doors swing open. I'm confronted by three young Malaysian ladies and the words, 'washy, washy'. I recognise the lady as Karen, who welcomed Lucy and me to the steakhouse last night. Sure she is related to the Duracell bunny because, just like yesterday, she greets all of us early risers with a smile and enough enthusiasm to make you sick, this time in the morning.

This isn't my first visit to the buffet restaurant for breakfast on this cruise, so I know what I want — English bacon. None of the hard crispy crap the Americans call bacon and the rest of the world call pork scratchings. With far too much food piled up on the plate, I head for one of the tables opposite the vast windows surrounding the café on three sides, to wait for Lucy.

Because it's still early, the joint isn't busy. The only other people are the usual culprits. Most of them have been sent by their partners to reserve a spot close to the window. They are easy to spot by how the table is laid out for two people, including some beverage stewing in white china cups.

I love watching these men as, within minutes, they are making like nodding donkeys as they slip backwards and forwards back into sleep; a place the brain is telling them that's where they should still be. But for a peaceful life, they're doing as they are told.

The kind waitress has just brought over my fresh coffee when, out of the corner of my eye, I glimpse sight of Lucy entering the Garden Café. Thoughts of letting her wander about the joint until she finds me flash for a second around my head. Then, as fast as a bar waiter seeing an empty glass, I realise I'm not that brave, so I stand up and walk over to fetch her.

"Morning, honey, I'm sitting over there," I point toward my half-eaten breakfast on the table opposite the window.

I'm greeted by her usual beautiful smile, which is something that always amazes me. Even though she is a trained killer, she is always smiling.

"Let me grab some brekkie, and I'll be over to join you," she declares, heading for one of the omelette cooking stations.

Peering out the floor-to-ceiling window, watching the white caps appear on the water as waves crash in on themselves, and sipping on the lukewarm coffee, my mind wanders back to the meet with our contact.

A person sitting in the chair on the other side of the table brings me back to the moment.

"So what are you thinking about," comes the soothing voice of Lucy, after downing half a glass of fresh orange juice.

"Not much, just about the meeting point for our potential next mission. I've been to this fort once before; from what I can remember, the place only has one way in."

"Is that an issue then?"

"Could be, as the only way up is via a steep tunnel which opens up to the first courtyard. It's the ideal location for an ambush. This will be a perfect place if we are walking into some trap. With nowhere to go, would make the ideal killing zone."

"Think you're letting the part of your PTSD, where you trust nobody, run around in that tiny head of yours."

"You are probably right, Lucy. Besides, we have time to recce the area after we meet up with the boys later today at the Sea Drop hotel in Old San Juan," I reply, after finishing my brew.

I chose this place, as I remember from my last visit, the terminal is across the road. However, after I confirmed the reservation, I learned that the bloody cruise line embarkation and disembarkation were carried out at Pan American Pier, located on the other side of the bay. This will teach this numpty not to read all the small print before booking. Never mind, just an expensive transfer.

I peer down at Mickey on my wrist, which tells me we only have one and a half hours before we arrive in Puerto Rico and this holiday ends. Unlike many numpties who insist on carrying off their bags, we placed ours outside the cabin last night for the house elf to unload this morning.

After finishing what food remains on my plate, I glance up, "We will be getting off soon, so better head back to the stateroom and pick up our hand luggage, and double-check we've packed everything."

"I'm ready when you are. What time are we meeting with the rest of the team?" asks Lucy, after drinking her coffee.

"They should be staying in the same hotel, so once we have settled into our room, I'll call them and have them meet us in the lobby, but knowing them idiots, more than likely be the bar."

Back in the cabin, I check every nook and cranny to ensure nothing is left behind, while Lucy places the two carry-on bags next to the door. The only thing to do now is wait for the voice in the ceiling to tell us we can disembark.

There are still about 45 minutes before our disembarkation time, so plop our arses down in the atrium close to the purser's desk. I love this spot on the final day of the cruise, as you can overhear all the excuses from cruisers about why they don't want to settle their onboard account.

I feel sorry for the staff. They must face all the same crap after every voyage. My philosophy is that if you buy or use any service, pay up. Anything medical, that's what your travel insurance is for.

Finally, our disembarkation colour is called via the tannoy. Grab our carry-on bags and head for the gangway, which, by the look of it, has seen far better days. Mind you, it matches the terminal building of battered old corrugated sheets, complete with the obligatory rust patches. Once off the ship, it's a short stroll through a series of portable metal railings laid out to form some route to the terminal's entrance and our waiting luggage.

The interior is as unimpressive as the outside, just a vast empty hanger with massive grey A-frame beams holding up the roof. When you walk inside, the bags are lined up in front of coloured boards that match your suitcases' labels on your left. Then, some organised chaos, with everyone pushing and shoving to enter the sheep pens that mark the lanes to be the next to have their faces scanned and onto customs.

It brought back some memories of my army days, and I couldn't help but start chuckling.

"Go on, share the joke, idiot," Lucy says, after elbowing me in the ribs.

"Not much; when I was a young soldier, my first posting was on some old airfield with several hangers, and we were forced to sit on the floor in lines to simulate being on an aircraft. The tightfisted idiots in charge wanted to practice airlift for some exercise in Germany."

"That made you laugh like a deranged numpty on drugs?"

"No, what came next did; located in the corner of the hanger near the offices, some music-playing device, I can't remember exactly what. One of the boys broke loose and played..." I start laughing again.

"Tell me what or shut the fuck up," comes the sarcastic words from Lucy.

"He put on 'You're in the Army Now', by Status Quo, a big hit in the '80s."

By this time, we arrive at the US customs as Puerto Rico is part of the US. I am about to remove my passport from my jacket pocket when the officer asks a few questions about food and drink, to which I lie and say no. He waves us through with no checks. He didn't know my bag contains several bottles of spirits, ready for customary pissup before we start a new mission.

Outside the terminal, our transfer from 'GO' is supposed to be waiting for us, but after 20 minutes of nobody showing up, I turn to Lucy, "Can't be arsed to hang about any longer. Let's grab a taxi."

"What if the driver turns up once we've left?"

"Not our problem, leave the arsehole to wait around."

I can't stand people who can't be bothered to show up on time. It was a habit picked up in the army where you needed to be there five minutes before the parade. And as the saying goes, it's better to be 30 minutes early than one minute late.

The ride is short, with us arriving in under a quarter of an hour, with no comms with the driver as he said he didn't speak English! It's funny how he understood 'take me to the Sea Drop hotel' and 'how much?'.

The entrance to the building is down a small side street. This consists of enormous green framed glass sliding doors which lead into the lobby area. Of course, this being part of America, the porters jump at carrying our bags inside for a tip.

Some trick I learned a while back is to fold a one-dollar bill so the $1 is facing inwards, preventing them from realising this tight arse only gave them a dollar. Besides, we won't meet them again after we leave the hotel.

The reception desk is off to the left, tucked behind a small wall that juts out from the doorway, where two young ladies in their early 20s are busy checking guests in. The system must work well as we soon find ourselves standing at the counter talking to Ruth; I read her ID tag.

"Hi, I have a reservation under the name of Barker," handing her my booking confirmation.

"One moment, sir, while I check if your room is ready," comes the reply.

Lucy keeps her in conversation while I recce the rest of the ground floor. Off to my right is a red-carpeted double staircase that turns into a single one leading up to the second level. Beyond that, another lady is sitting behind a smaller desk beside an electronic screen, which scrolls through different tours available to purchase from the hotel.

At the far end, a long teak wooden table about waist height occupies one-half of the room, with several stainless steel stools tucked underneath. An orange sofa and a small coffee table fill the rest of the room.

By the time my scanning of the room is completed, Lucy is handing me a room key.

"We're on the fourth floor, room number 400. The lifts are over here." she points behind me.

As rooms go, it wasn't bad; I have slept in a lot worse than this. It will do us for now. When you enter, the bathroom is in front of you, and a reasonable size. At least the room is equipped with a shitter and a shower. Off to the right is a vast white quilted double bed on which Lucy has now spread herself across.

Along the far cream-coloured wall, a desk with a kit for making a brew and a television hanging precariously from a bracket attached to the wall.

"Sorry, honey, you can't go to sleep, we have things to do," at the same time, launching the cases in the corner.

"Who said anything about sleeping!" Lucy replies with a knowing wink.

"That would be tempting if we didn't have to meet the others. I'll take a rain check on that, though."

"Your choice, Steve," as she drags her skirt erotically up her leg before getting up and heading for the shower.

Take this opportunity to grab my mobile phone and dial Simon's number. He answers it within a few rings. After a short conversation, I hang up as Lucy re-enters the room.

"Lucy, I called the boys while you were in the bathroom; I'm right. They are in the boozer near here as the hotel bar doesn't open until 17:00. I Told them we would meet them in 10."

From the outside, the local establishment appears to be a little rough. Plus, for some reason, the place has a familiar look, as though I've been here before.

The exterior is painted a pale yellow with three sets of green wooden slatted doors that open onto the street, exposing the interior. Off to the right, tucked into the corner, is a long marble-covered counter where two men sit on stools, drinking beer and chatting with the young lady behind the bar.

Beyond her, stacked in neat rows, lines of a vast assortment of the usual culprits of spirits are divided by a giant mirror that takes the central stage on the cabinet.

The rest of the room contains several old, battered-looking tables and high-back chairs. Two are occupied by couples sipping on drinks and, from what I could tell, talking in Spanish.

To my front, a substantial concrete post painted the same colour as the rest of the joint, a pale yellow. Behind are a few more tables at which the boys sit, occupying a couple of bench seats on either side of a five-foot rectangular table.

"Here come the lovers, just entering the bar, Simon," says George, pointing towards mine and Lucy's direction.

When we walk closer to join them, "Nice for you to show your fat ugly face, Steve. Great to see you again, Lucy. hope you're well?"

"Fine, thanks, Simon. Have you been here long?" Lucy asks with a cheerful smile.

"The boys and I decided to come several days earlier than planned to spend a few days on the piss."

After sitting on one of the benches facing George and Simon, "So where is Derek? Didn't he come with you?" I enquire.

"He's over at the bar getting yours and Lucy's drink. You walked straight past him, you blind bastard," declares George, shaking his head.

At that moment, Derek joins us, "Put that down your neck," placing two drinks on the table.

"Cheers, mate. Have you three idiots recced the area, particularly the fort, or have you been on the lash the whole time?"

"Been on the piss the whole time. Waiting for you and Lucy to show up. No point going to a planning meeting without the planner, Steve."

"So true, Derek. If our recce troop, aka Simon, has anything to do with it, he would probably have you at the wrong fort," I say, trying not to laugh too much.

"The only thing I have to say about that, you green numpty, is the second word is off, try to guess the first one," replies Simon, putting his empty beer glass on the table.

"How was your cruise? I hope it all went well with no issues?"

"Went fine, thanks, George...."

I'm interrupted by Lucy, "What about the fucking idiot who walked about the ship with t-shirts saying he is a member of the real Irish Republican Army, and wearing different tops promoting the fact he supported them?"

"About that...! I did think about telling you earlier, but it slipped my mind."

Lucy gives me one of those knowing stares only a female can provide.

"OK, what the fuck did you do," asks George, after taking a swig of his beer.

"Nothing important. After Lucy fell asleep, I started to feel a little peckish...."

"No change there then, fat boy," comes the response from Simon.

"As I was saying, I just finished talking to Kyle, the art auctioneer and Daniel, the cruise director, when I saw the scumbag pass me, heading towards the stairs. Grabbed some food from the 24/7 eatery, then headed to walk along deck 7 to stare out to sea," take a huge gulp of beer.

"Keep going, Steve. Now you have all of us wondering what happened."

"Just getting to that, Lucy. I am minding my own business, when who would appear giving me loads of mouth? Yep, our terrorist friend. So I did what the cruise line failed to do."

"What did you fucking do?" asks Simon, with a half-knowing look as though he guessed what came next.

"Only did what any of you would have done, and carried out what our training said we should do to these idiots. After five minutes of me taking loads of shit, I snapped and launched at him, knocking him back towards the ship's railing. Before he could resist, in one swift movement, I rammed the handle of the spoon I was holding through his right eye until I heard the squelch of it entering his brain, and blood started to spurt from his eye socket."

"What the fuck, Steve? What did you do then?"

"Took a leaf out of your book, George, and threw him overboard. Tell you what, the fat bastard must have been overdoing the buffet, he weighed a ton."

"Take it the man was dead when you launched him over the side, and nobody saw you?" Derek enquires.

"Sorry, I didn't take time to enquire about his fucking health. But if he wasn't, sure, the sea would finish the job. And yeah, no problem with anyone seeing me, mate. They are probably still looking for him, to throw him off the ship."

"For your sake, Steve, let's hope he is. You know the rules, always check your kill before leaving the scene; I wouldn't like him to be a pain in the arse later. We have enough trouble with the idiots from St Halb," George says, shaking his head.

Lucy squeezes my hand hard, "We will discuss your communication skills when we return to the hotel."

"Anyway, moving on, who's round is it?" holding up my empty beer glass.

"After that revelation, yours, so off you pop," declares Lucy.

"I don't mind fetching the drinks. Same again, everyone?" I reply, standing up from the bench.

I had only walked a few feet when a short, plump, local-looking man in his mid-50s approaches me from the other side of the bar.

Out of habit, I clench both fists, and my body tenses up, ready for a fight if it occurs. I'm about to say 'excuse me, you're blocking my way to the bar', when the man stops and stares straight at me.

Before my brain could even think about my mouth working, he utters, "Mr. Steve, amigo, welcome back."

"I think you may confuse me with someone else, mate. I've never seen you before."

"You forget me already? Remember two years ago, you got very drunk here, my friend, and when a couple of local men from the town attacked a young woman, I think she came from the UK, you beat the shit out of them with one of the chair legs, and I called a taxi to take you back to your hotel. My name is Andrei."

"Yep, sounds like you, Steve," George says, over my shoulder, where he's been ready to cover me if needed, when he saw the man approach.

After some time, it comes back to me; I thought I recognised the place. Plus, I also remember returning to the hotel in some pain. The men had got some punches of their own in.

"Now I think of it, I remember you. Fancy a cold beer?" I ask, patting him on the right arm.

"No, thanks, amigo, but you behave this time."

"Of course, I'm a quiet, gentle person who wouldn't harm a fly."

Turn around to catch George spitting his drink across the table, nearly gagging.

"Say that a-fucking-gain, you're what, Steve?" says Simon after his fit of laughter.

"Fuck off the lot of you; I can be caring when I want to be. I don't show it often. And that's a waste of fucking beer, George."

16

The drinks and conversation flow as the bar becomes packed with more locals. Plus, from the look of it, tourists also frequent the place, judging by the appearance of souvenir bags and even more stupid t-shirts with some logo someone thought might be funny. We still have work to do before we drink too much alcohol and become shitfaced.

"Sorry to kill a drinking session, folks, but before it gets too late, we better make a recce of the fort and tomorrow's meeting point. The last thing we want to do is to walk into some trap. I told Lucy that on the ship, when I visited the place before, I only found one way in and out via a long, narrow tunnel. It's a perfect killing field. We must find out if we have an escape route if it all goes wrong."

"You're right as always, mate. Come on, you idiots, drink up," Derek says, standing up and downing a half pint of beer.

Without saying a word, everyone does the same and finishes what remains of their drinks.

"Come on, Steve, lead the way, as you've been here before, and the boys and I couldn't be arsed before you two showed up," says George, heading for the door.

Ten minutes later, we arrive at the entry point from my previous visit to find a vast locked metal gate across the entrance, and the building used to purchase my ticket is closed down.

"And you were slagging off the recce troop earlier; it appears like the green numpty got it wrong!" states Simon, as I receive a slap around the back of the head.

"Don't fucking blame me, blame the stupid Yanks," I protest.

After a scan of the area, Lucy points to a black signboard hanging off a brick wall. "According to this sign, the entrance is this way, follow me, gents. Would hate for Steve to become lost again."

"What the fuck is this? Have a go at me day?"

"Yep, so shut up and follow Lucy," comes the instant comment from Simon.

Past the ticket office, we enter a vast courtyard surrounded by thick stone walls, with the wall to our front stretching up about 40 feet. Let's hope the entry point isn't the only way in or out.

On the left, a series of openings lead into rooms now used to house exhibits of Spanish soldiers, back when the fort was built to defend the island from the land and sea.

Off to the right, leading away from us, more of the same. Plus, a ramp-up to the next level. At our 12 o'clock, a small archway with a stone slope. At a guess, this goes to the upper level as well.

I turn to Simon, "Where is the meeting taking place?"

"According to my contact, we must go up to the second level via the ramp. At the top, we must keep left and follow the wall to the end. We will find a round guard tower. This is where our contact should be," Simon replies, leading the way.

"Good idea, mate, let's check the meeting point first before looking for an alternative way out, and OP's overlooking the area, where you lot can monitor the area and warn Simon and me as we meet the contact."

"With you on that one. Plus, I brought some tiny earpiece radios with a range of about 300 metres in a clear line of sight with me," says Derek, pulling a small box out from his backpack he'd be hauling around all morning.

"A Green Jacket saves the day again," I say, grabbing one from Derek.

"About time you green numpties were good for something," says George with a stupid grin.

"Shut the fuck up, George, and if you're a good boy, maybe we will let you do your guard bit and stand in one of the sentry posts," Derek responds.

"Do one, twat," George grunts.

At the top of the ramp, it opens into another enormous space extending far to our right. Again, the leading edge comprises a high ten-foot thick stone wall with triangular wedges cut out to provide some gun emplacements. Following the outer wall to our left, we soon come across a concrete structure that stands out, as it's different from the rest of the fort. The Americans built it for use in the Second World War. The plaque attached to the left of the doorway explains why.

Inside a square room with a slot looking out to sea; in the right-hand corner is a hole in the floor with a ladder leading down two levels.

"At least we have one escape route," I point to the open gap.

"Might make a good position for Derek to hide during the meeting; it's close enough for his radios to work to overhear the conversation. Plus, if you and Simon are in trouble, he's nearby to assist."

"Brains and beauty, Lucy," says Derek, raising the thumb of his right hand.

The guard tower we are to meet in is located at the far end, and only just big enough to squeeze two people in. "I don't like the look of that, Simon. We can become trapped. I'm changing the rendezvous point to opposite where Derek will be."

"Me neither, Steve; besides, the contact will know it's us if he's done his homework," replies Simon.

"What about George and me? Suggest we walk around this level making like dumb tourists," says Lucy.

"Makes sense to me. All we need to do now is locate our escape route. If Derek and I head down the ladder and find out where it goes while you three head off in that direction, we will meet just outside the entrance in half an hour."

Thirty minutes later, Derek and I exit the fort. Simon, Lucy and George are already there, sitting on a small old brick wall.

"You find a way out?" I shout as I approach.

"Sure did, Steve; at the end is a spiral staircase leading down to the first level. What about you?" George replies.

"Same, the ladders come down here. We may only have an issue if this is the only way out. Let's hope everything goes to plan."

"Fingers crossed, hey, Steve. How about we head back to the hotel, and you can devise a plan of action while we four have a few cold ones."

"I'll drink to that, Simon," says Lucy, jumping to her feet and heading down the hill.

On the way back, I formulate a simple plan to cover all areas, including an emergency rendezvous point. We still need to obtain weapons for the task, depending on how the meeting goes and where the mission will occur. Our standard play equipment is back in the UK due to idiots at Customs not letting me bring my bang-making kit onto a plane. And I'm not taking a stick to a potential gunfight.

By the time we arrive back at the hotel, I have some plans formulating, so time for our customary pre-mission piss-up.

Chapter Two – The Meeting

It's hot outside, and the air conditioner hums faintly. The room is comfortable, with a window letting in the dawn light. As I lay in the soft, plush bed, I glance to my right and see Lucy, with her long blonde hair and beautiful naked body scattered across the white sheets.

It will take all my willpower to focus on the meeting, which isn't far away. The briefing will take place in old Fort Castillo San Cristobal, where we recce'd yesterday, and the tension is costing me well-needed sleep.

I try to put it all out of my mind and close my eyes to catch at least a bit of kip as our pre-mission pissup continued until the early hours.

The room is silent except for the gentle hum of the AC, which breaks the silence. I'm uncomfortable and toss around in the bed. But I must have gotten a quick five-minute shuteye; when I turn to face Lucy, she is nowhere to be seen.

Wonder for a moment where she might be, but then detect the sound of the shower being used, the noise of water cascading down the drain, and her humming to herself.

A couple more minutes pass before I drag my sorry arse out of bed, somewhat refreshed and energised after getting at least some sleep. Walk towards the bathroom door and push it open. She is standing there, steaming and dripping wet. We've been together for a while now, and seeing her naked still makes my heart skip a few beats.

Step into the shower and feel the soothing water dripping down my body. I could now release the stresses that weigh down on me. Stand behind her and begin to seductively wash her neck, sliding my soapy hands down to her shoulders and onto her ample breasts. She tilts her head back, and I witness the serene expression on her face as the water drips down our bodies. She closes her eyes in pure bliss, enjoying the calming sensation. Leaning in and kissing her softly, Lucy turns her head to kiss me on my lips.

I wrap my arms around her and hold her in a tight, warm hug as the water continues to wash across us. My heart rate quickens as I begin to lose myself in the moment. Our embrace is nothing new, but the way we move together and the sounds she makes drive me wild. So, lift her and wrap her legs around my waist. Take her with intense passion that burns within us.

For the next few minutes, I wash her body slowly as we explore each other with our hands and lips. The steam continues to rise, and the water in the shower rains down around us; our bodies twist and turn, losing our intensity and all sense of everything going on around us, like standing under a waterfall in some rainforest.

"Better get dressed, Lucy. We need to meet the boys down for breakfast at 07:00, and it's now 06:55," I say, picking my clothes up from the pile I'd thrown them in sometime during the night.

"Be right with you, Steve, give me five minutes."

We are already running late when we arrive for brekkie.

Upon entering the diner, you are greeted by a freshly brewed coffee aroma filling the air. The restaurant is an ample, open space with floor-to-ceiling windows letting in the bright morning light. The room is decorated with neutral tones in a sleek and modern design. The walls are lined with art pieces from local artists, giving the joint a personal touch. The tables are arranged in a semi-circular formation, affording each guest a clear view of the stunning ocean.

When we enter, the rest of the team is seated around a white table at the rear of the room.

"The lovers have arrived," Simon teases as Lucy and I sit down.

"Don't know about you idiots, but I'm starving; time for food," Derek proclaims, as he stands up and heads for the breakfast buffet line.

With that, we join him, loading our plates with eggs, bacon, and piles of pancakes. Once back, the conversation turns to the events of last night.

"Anyhow, what time did we call it a night? I've got a mouth like a camel's flip-flop," I say, after downing a full glass of fresh orange juice.

"About 02:00 this morning, I think. It wasn't long after George decided to do the dance of the flaming arseholes around the bar," states Simon, looking up from his breakfast.

"Bollocks, don't remember that," George says, with a reddish glow on his cheeks.

"Yep, I do, you fucking idiot; that's when the bouncers suggested we go to our rooms. We would have been pissed as we took their advice and left."

"Must have been intoxicated, Derek, for us to leave without an argument," replies Lucy, after sipping her fresh coffee.

Only a few people are still eating on the other side of the room. So safe enough for the conversation to turn to our meeting at the fort.

"OK, here is the plan for the meet-up with our contact at 13:00 today. Once we have finished stuffing our faces, collect anything you need from your rooms. Then we head off around noon, giving us plenty of time to be in position..."

"Shall us three," pointing to George and Derek, "go ahead of you and Simon?" Lucy interrupts.

"Good idea. We will leave here at 12:15; gives you numpties time to be in situ."

"Roger," comes the reply from Derek, placing his earpiece receiver on the table and now busy checking it over. "Give me the radios so I can do a final check over them."

After everyone's completed their task, we will meet in the lobby at 11:45, ready to head for the old fort.

Bang on 12:00, Lucy leads her team out of the enormous green framed glass sliding doors, turning left as they exit. The next 15 minutes seems to stand still as Simon and I remain sitting on the orange sofa, waiting our turn to leave. With only one more minute to go, I stare at Mickey on my wrist as the third hand ticks around the clockface until the last agonising second ticks onto the 12.

"Come on, Simon, let's make a move and head for the fort," I stand up and walk out of the building, with Simon walking by my side.

It's mid-March in Puerto Rico, and the sun is over the city. The sky is painted with vibrant shades of red, orange, and pink. So, if nothing else, the walk will be a pleasant one.

We already know the route, so before long, we arrive at the entrance. I turn to face Simon, "You ready, mate?" He gives me a thumb-up.

No other people are standing waiting to pay in the booking office, so I take a shortcut bypassing the rows of posts and barrier tapes that mark the lanes leading to the cashier sitting behind a high teak-looking wooden counter.

The young lady must have been in her early 30s, dressed in a recognisable grey shirt, green trousers and a distinctive American National Park Ranger hat.

"Good morning," I glance at Mickey.

"Hi, sir, how can I help you?" she says through a forced smile.

"Two tickets, please."

"No problem, that is 20 dollars each. With this ticket, you can also visit the Castillo San Felipe del Morro, about a 15-minute walk away."

"Thanks, but just this one today," as I hand over the correct amount.

Inside, Simon and I go up to the upper level. At the top, the open plaza is surrounded by massive stone walls, some with cast iron cannons still perched atop them. The view from up here is incredible; the city stretches below us like a patchwork quilt of red and white tiles; something we overlooked the previous day, because finding the meeting point and an escape route took centre stage in everyone's minds. It is something inexcusable and a rooky error as you should always check all your surroundings. But we can't let our guard down even a second on this mission.

The fort is now a popular tourist spot with its stunning views. One thing different from our last visit stands out like a spare prick at a wedding. It lacks people and is somewhat quiet. Unusual for this time of the day. So everyone is on alert as we move with utmost care towards the rendezvous point, where our contact is meant to be waiting.

In the meantime, Derek hides in the small structure identified yesterday, watching and listening for any signs of danger, ready to take down anyone who poses a threat to the meeting. George and Lucy disguise themselves as tourists and keep an eye out. They disappear into the small crowd of people wandering around the place, and no one suspects a thing.

I check the time on Mickey. It's almost 1 p.m.; the contact [conact?] is supposed to meet us by 1:15 pm, so I scan the area again before seeing a figure approaching us from a distance. A tall, muscular man with a short, thick beard and piercing blue eyes wearing a dark grey suit; it must be our contact.

On reaching our location, "Good to see you both. My name is Bear," he says in a deep, booming voice.

"Likewise, this is Simon, and I'm Steve," I say, shaking the man's hand.

Not wanting to waste time on general chat and pleasantries, "What's the deal with the job you want us to do?" I ask, getting straight to the point.

"Our intel indicates a drug cartel has been handed two young people by a corrupt Customs official at the local airport, when they were caught smuggling a tiny amount of heroin. They're being held for ransom," the contact explains.

"A man in his early 20s called James Rapson, with short brown hair standing about five foot seven inches, from America. And a woman about 30 years of age and six feet tall with long black hair, from Peru. Her name is Ana Martinez.

"They have been taken to a small makeshift camp in a rainforest on a nearby Caribbean island. Your task is to rescue them and eliminate any cartel members in the area. They are led by a very unpleasant and violent man called Aron."

Bear hands us a thick brown envelope, "You will find all the paperwork here, including photos of the two people you must bring home. Sure you're professional enough to destroy the folder once you've read its contents."

"Of course," taking it from him.

After I finish flicking through the information inside, I pass it to Simon, who doesn't waste any time pulling out the map and starts going through the main details. Meanwhile Derek is still monitoring our surroundings constantly, and Lucy and George continue their undercover observations.

"Any more questions before I leave," Bear asks.

"A few. First, why are the governments of the two individuals not involved?" Not that I give a flying fuck, as I'm getting paid.

"That's an easy one; they don't want government involvement as the penalty for drug smuggling in Peru is execution. So, you can understand why they aren't."

"Second, a matter of our fee, which will be one million," staring straight at him, to make him uncomfortable.

"Won't be a problem; the families are financially secure with plenty of money to pay for this type of employment, as long as it's completed on time with both parties being returned unharmed."

"That's acceptable, half up front and the rest when we hand over Ana and James," I say.

"Done."

"My last question is, what is your involvement in this escapade, and why are we meeting here?"

From the expression, he is a little set back by this, as though it's none of our business.

"Let's just say, James is the son of one of my nieces. And here, because our conversation can't be overheard, and I have a private plane waiting for me at Isla Grande Airport, which is over there," he points to a tarmac runway.

"You got any questions, Simon?"

"Just one, Steve. Any idea how we travel to this island?"

"Took the liberty of arranging a boat with one of my contacts. He will be taking you over from the docks in San Juan; I've marked the location on the map. It's about a three-hour ride. You'll have a small window of opportunity to be in and out before anyone realises what's happened. Can you handle the job?" Bear replies.

"I think we can manage it," I say, with conviction that hints at the team's years of experience in the field. "If all goes to plan, we'll leave tomorrow."

Bear nods, then turns and walks away, his muscular gait betraying his confidence in the team and me.

Once Bear is out of my line of sight, I touch the tiny earpiece to transmit, "OK, task complete; RV back in the hotel lobby."

Turning on the heels of my feet, I quickly walk back towards the exit with Simon close by, still clutching the envelope given to us by our contact. We travel in silence until we are out of the fort.

Once outside and standing on the black tarmacked footpath overlooking the ocean, I turn to Simon, "Thank fuck the meeting went without a hitch, didn't fancy fighting our way out."

"With you on that one, mate. Suggest we go through all the information in this when we arrive back at the hotel," holding the envelope in front of him. I nod in agreement.

The area is alive with the hustle and bustle of tourists and locals alike. The narrow footpaths are overcrowded as street vendors hawk their wares, and musicians serenade the crowds with steel drum beats.

As we walk, the hotel receptionist's warning echoes in my mind, for some reason, a dire reminder of the real danger of local gangs lurking in these back streets. So I keep my wits about me as I navigate through the complete chaos, because amongst the excitement and buzz lurks a sinister threat that hangs in the air like a heavy fog.

Then, out of nowhere comes the distinctive sounds of gunshots, which grow louder and more frequent, echoing off the ancient brick walls and bouncing back at me like a warning. My mind tries to convince me the noise is only cars backfiring, but I have been in too many firefights not to recognise gunfire.

While my brain has been running away with me, Simon stops at a stall at the end of the street.

"What are you buying?" I enquire.

"Bought you a small gift."

"Thanks, Simon; what is it...?" He hands me a packet of pegs, chuckling to himself.

"We all know you like to make things go bang; I thought these would be useful."

"You're right, but you are still a fucking idiot. Come on, we better get a move on."

After what appears to be hours of weaving through the chaos and my PTSD starting to kick in, I spot the sign of my hotel.

When we enter, Lucy and George are sitting at the long wooden table, drinking from white china cups.

About to ask where's Derek, when a voice from behind me calls out, "Sorry, I'm late, just following the Green Jacket motto, first in, last out." Derek just entered the lobby.

"Whatever, idiot, plonk your arse down next to us and let's go through the paperwork while the lobby is empty," says George, scanning the room for any CCTV cameras which might overlook the place we are sitting. There aren't any.

Undo the clip holding the package closed. Then, scatter the contents onto the tabletop, spreading them out so everyone can see.

"Right, you know your tasks, so go through this and concentrate on your areas of expertise. Make any notes; then, later, I can use the info to form a basic plan away from any nosey bastards who might be showing any interest in our activities."

The team huddles together, heads bent over the papers scattered before them. The information we have been given is impressive, with maps and satellite imagery. Grabbing a handful of maps and photos, I look at the overall mission and try to assess the terrain and everything from this point forward. I start formulating a course of action from landing on Saint Ann to the rescue itself and our route back here to hand over James and Ana. I will leave Simon to work out our transport requirements.

Looking up for a moment to rest my eyes and ensure nobody came in while we all concentrated on the task at hand, I attract Simons's attention.

"Have you called Katie yet about any weapons?"

"Already done. You can meet someone in the old district who will have what we need. I'll give you the details once I've found out about flight schedules and other travel options to Saint Ann, as something doesn't seem right with me about our contact arranging our crossing. Plus, I'm checking for any requirements to transport us from the landing point through the rainforest to the camp and back."

"With you on that one, we will only use the prearranged boat if you can't find anything else," I reply, as I glance over to find out what Derek is doing.

In front of him is a stack of white paper with what appears to the untrained eye like gibberish. However, it must be something to do with testing frequencies and ranges of radios we need, ensuring our communications equipment would be crystal clear when needed.

At the end of the table, Lucy is deep in concentration, reading the files of the two hostages they plan to extract: James and Ana. She is committed to finding any valuable details that would help the team.

George is hunched over a separate map, studying the rainforest surrounding the enemy's encampment. He is planning where to position his and Lucy's sniper positions, analysing every potential line of sight and escape route.

As we work, our area starts to bustle around us. Hotel guests chat and laugh. We were so engrossed in what we are doing that we didn't notice all the people entering the lobby and taking up residency in the other half of the room.

"Better call it a day on the pre-planning, as there are now too many people in here; any of them could be listening to our conversation. Anyway, we must go into town to get some equipment as most of ours is back in England. Suggest we split up to cover more ground quicker."

"Good idea," says Lucy.

"Lucy and I will make first contact with the arms dealer once Simon gives me the details of when and where. Derek, you're the only one familiar with what radios are required, minus the stuff you brought. So, can you head off and locate what you need? There's bound to be something available in the old town. Leaves George and Simon to go and find us all some clothing for the rainforest."

"Would be handy if everyone could give me your sizes. Not yours, Steve, already know your measurements, fat bastard," says George, with a pen hovering over a blank bit of paper.

"So true, George, one size smaller than you."

"Here you go, Steve, the name of the person you are to make contact with is Phillip. You are to meet him at Café El Mercado at 18:30. Which gives you about one hour and 30 minutes to find the place. I've marked it for you on here," Simon hands Lucy the map.

"Roger, we will all rendezvous back in the bar on the third floor at 20:00. If there are no questions, suggest we make a move," heading for the door with Lucy.

The roads of San Juan are still busy with tourists as we walk down the narrow, cobblestone streets. My eyes scan through the crowds of people for any threats—something my bloody PTSD always has me doing, no matter where I am.

The sun is still blazing down. The humidity leaves a layer of sweat on the skin. We make our way through the colourful buildings that line the streets, some with balconies and others with elaborate, ornate ironwork. The bustling noise of chatter, car horns, and the scent of local food and exhaust fumes mixed with the aroma of saltier air from the nearby ocean attack our senses.

A few minutes later, we reach the spot outside a cosy café tucked away in a quiet corner of the old district. Fronted with huge windows, the café stands back five metres from the road, with lace curtains hanging down from every window. Several tables out on the street are decorated in the same fashion, with laced tablecloths draped over them, on which sits a small china vase complete with fresh flowers. This is where the arranged meeting with the dealer will take place.

Still another 15 minutes to wait, according to the timepiece on my wrist. We can't afford to draw attention to ourselves. Lucy goes inside and orders two iced coffees while I take a position at one of the tables. This is unknown territory, so we need to remain alert.

"Here you go, Steve, one caffeine fix," Lucy hands me my drink before sitting beside me.

Scanning the area for our contact, I sip on the iced coffee as I wait. Lucy checks her phone for the umpteenth time, ensuring all the contingency plans are in place, which consists of calling the rest for any help.

Moments later, the person we have been waiting for comes into view, just as Simon described him. He is a tall and muscular man with a shaved head and a scar running down his cheek. He's walking towards us, carrying a grey bag.

Moments later, the man is standing on the pavement outside the café. We stand up to confront him, and I'm about to say something when the arms dealer greets us both with a nod.

"You must be Steve and Lucy," he says, his voice deep and gravelly. "Katie told me to expect you. My name is Phillip."

Out of habit, I look the person up and down, something my training always has me doing when someone I don't know enters my comfort zone. He appears trustworthy enough, but as everyone knows, appearances can be deceiving.

"We need to put our hands on some weapons," I say.

He grins. "Follow me."

He enters the café. Inside, Phillip strolls to the back of the room and sits at a small table in the corner. He reaches into his bag and pulls out a sheet of paper with some items written on it, his eyes flicking back and forth as he talks through the details before handing me the list.

The comprehensive list contains all we will require: five 9mm Browning pistols, two L115A3 sniper rifles and three L119A1 CQB Carbine. These are British special forces equipment, so where did he buy them from? But it's best not to ask too many questions in our line of work.

After weighing the pros and cons of each weapon and some haggling over prices, bringing them down to a manageable cost, we come to a price we all agree on and settle on the deal.

"So where can we pick up our purchase, and when?"

No need to worry, Mr Steve, I'll bring them to your hotel later. Where are you staying?

"Tell you what, Phillip, to protect us all, why don't we make the exchange about 23:30 tonight down on the seafront, close to the cruise port?"

"No problem, I will be in an old warehouse, which you can enter via a disused alleyway opposite Muelle 4. It's easy to find, as there is only one."

"OK, see you then with the money," shaking his hand and walking away with Lucy.

Meanwhile, Simon and George walk through the narrow streets, bustling with market vendors hawking their goods, locals bargaining in rapid-fire Spanish, and tourists looking slightly lost. Their eyes scrutinise the colourful array on sale for anything that could be of use in the rainforest. The air is thick with the mingled scents of spices and smoke and music and laughter.

Simon wipes a bead of sweat dripping from his forehead and squints up at the sun. He scans the stalls, mostly seeing bright-coloured items and trinkets that would do nothing to help them in the rainforest. They need to hurry if they are going to find something that will work.

George, the meticulous one of the two, begins to survey the various fabrics and materials each vendor offers. They soon discover that finding durable clothing won't be as easy as they think, even though Puerto Rico has a rainforest. Most garments are made of flimsy, sweat-soaked material which would fall apart in the unpredictable climate.

Walking deeper into the market, they find an old, dirty-looking building a short distance from the road, specialising in outdoor and adventure equipment. A small, unassuming shop set back from the road on the corner of two cobbled streets. It gives the impression that it's been here for decades due to the dirty exterior.

Making their way through the store, scanning the racks of clothes as they go, Simon is drawn to a set of green camouflage fatigues but soon realises their price tag is far beyond their budget. Ever the bargain hunter, George starts to haggle the price, in English, with a weathered old gentleman with a thick Spanish accent. The man eyes George and Simon up and down before nodding in approval.

"You two would appear like you're on a mission," he says with a crooked smile.

They explain that they and some friends are planning a camping trip to Saint Ann for a few weeks. After hearing their needs, the storekeeper begins to rifle through the racks, looking for something to fit them both. Simon appreciates the owner's expertise as he comes out with five durable sets of clothing for their task.

"These clothes are lightweight and breathable, perfect for the humid climate of a rainforest," the storekeeper says, handing them to George.

The dark colours mixed with browns and greens would help them blend in with the surroundings. They dig deep into their pockets and pay the store owner for their purchases before returning to the hotel.

While the others complete their tasks, Derek stomps through the cobblestone roads, the hot sun beating down on his face. He wipes the sweat from the back of his neck as he navigates towards his destination. The streets in this part of town are similar to the rest of San Juan and are alive with locals and tourists alike.

The district has a vibrant and colourful labyrinth of colonial-style buildings painted in pastel hues, and an array of local shops and vendors selling everything from handcrafted trinkets to exotic fruits. Derek can't help but take note of the city's beauty, but he can't let himself be distracted by the sights and sounds of the bustling area.

His task is straightforward: find rugged radios to assist his team on Saint Ann. Walking deeper among the crowds, he cannot ignore the eerie feeling that someone is following him, which trails his every step.

Despite the eeriness of the place, he presses on, his eyes scanning for any sign of the communication shop he is seeking. When he rounds the next corner, he stumbles upon a street vendor selling cold coconuts that glisten with condensation. He can't resist and buys one. The vendor's smile is infectious, bringing a brief respite from his tension.

As he continues walking, he becomes more cautious as he is on his own, unlike the rest. Noting the surveillance cameras on the nearby building walls, the suspicious glances from locals, and the occasional suspect-looking vehicle parked in the shadows, all of these make him believe he might not be alone; someone or something is watching his every move.

The alleys turn and twist, sometimes leading in circles, some opening up into small plazas or abandoned courtyards filled with overgrown plants and crumbling fountains. The relentless sound of street music and children playing in the distance is overpowering. He tries to pay little attention to them and pushes them to to the back of his mind and concentrates on the job at hand.

Moments later, he spots the sign he's been looking for, 'Radio Shop,' written in faded letters above a storefront that appears as old as the surrounding architecture. His pace quickens as he moves towards the store, all senses on high alert.

Inside, placed in rows on metal shelves, is an assortment of radios; some appear ex-military. Perfect, he thinks to himself, just what we need.

"Can I help you?" comes a vocal sound from the far end.

He turns in the direction of the voice. Standing behind a small battered wooden counter is an older man, about five-foot-four inches tall with a white beard and hair and wearing a blue shirt.

"Yes, please, I'm looking for rugged radios that will work in rainforest mountain terrain, plus they must have at least a 30-mile range," Derek replies.

"You are in luck; a shipment of Dewalt DXFRS800 returned from a customer this morning. They are brand new."

"What's wrong with them?"

"Nothing, the customer ordered too many. I'll give you a great deal if you want them, as it helps me out."

"Could be interested if they are small enough to be carried; my mates and I are going on a camping adventure, and each of us needs one."

"They are very rugged and have a range of about 38 miles. Got them in green or yellow," the man says, placing them on the counter before him.

"How much for all six green ones?" Derek enquires.

"Normal price would be $1,400, but you can have them for $1,000."

"Done, if you throw in some earpieces, too!"

The man agrees and places the equipment in a canvas bag, "You can have the holdall free."

With all the radios purchased, Derek heads back to the Sea Drop hotel to catch up with the others.

Chapter Three – Trip to Saint Ann

The whole team have arrived back at the hotel, loaded with the purchased equipment, and are now in my room.

After making everyone a brew and sitting on the bed, "Did everyone manage to obtain everything without any issues?"

"Simon and I managed to buy some waterproof combat clothing that should fit everyone, but you better try them on to make sure they fit."

"Thanks, George, will do in a moment. No idiots follow you?"

"Nope, all good," replies George.

"What about you, Derek?"

"Purchased the radios," he empties the holdall onto the bed, "these should be suitable for what we need them for. As for being followed, I had this strange overwhelming sense someone was watching my every movement."

"We faced the same problem," Lucy adds.

Take a swig of my coffee, "The good news is we met with Phillip, the arms dealer Katie put us onto and sorted out the weapons; he has what we want. We will meet him in some derelict warehouse near here at 23:30."

"That sounds a little iffy to me. We could be walking into a trap," says Simon, grabbing a set of clothing from the bed.

"I agree, but we don't have much choice. That's why only me and Lucy will go into the warehouse while you keep a lookout from the roof of this building. You have a great view if it's where Phillip says it's located. While we are inside, Derek and George, if you conceal yourselves outside near where we go inside. If everyone is ready, let's get moving."

The heat is oppressive even in the middle of the night, with the humidity making it feel like we are walking through a sauna. The air is thick with smoke and the scent of gunpowder as we make our way down what appears to be an abandoned alleyway towards the secluded location near the cruise port. The concrete walls of the alleyway are cracked and crumbling, ivy overtaking some of the nooks and crannies.

Lucy and I move with stealth towards the entrance of the building, something we have learned over years of doing this type of work and the specialist training we both received in the army.

On reaching a rusty door on the side of the warehouse at the end of the alley, we hesitate before entering. The inside lights give off barely visible light, flickering lights casting shadows across the rusted walls.

Phillip, the arms dealer we are here to meet, is well known for being notorious, ruthless and unpredictable—something Katie should have mentioned on the first call. But after a call again with Katie, she informs me that Phillip is the only one she knew in the area in the short time frame we gave her.

I've dealt with his type before, and know from experience I will need all of my training and skills to walk away from this deal unscathed.

While Lucy and I enter the building, Derek and George conceal themselves outside the warehouse in case of any trouble. Derek perches on a fire escape across the street while George hides behind a nearby dumpster. Simon is on the hotel roof overlooking the entrance, covering our movements and anyone who might come along later, such as the police.

The warehouse is an old one, with peeling paint and rusted walls. Metal shelves and abandoned machinery litter the space. Crates are piled high with various goods. There are five 9mm Browning pistols, two L115A3 sniper rifles, and three L119A1 CQB

Carbines, plus, boxes of ammunition for all the weapons on a long table in the centre of the room—an arsenal fit for an army.

We both approach the table, fingers itching to inspect the goods.

"Show us the merchandise, Phillip," I say in a firm voice.

Phillip stands at the head of the table, his arms crossed over his chest as he monitors our approach. His face is indifferent.

With a nod, Phillip signals for us to come closer. The three of us huddle around the table as Lucy and I inspect the weapons.

"Do you have the money?" Phillip asks in a gruff voice.

I nod, pull out a large brown envelope, and hand it to Phillip. But before he could even open the envelope, the echoing sound of dozens of footsteps echo down the hall.

Without warning, the front door to the warehouse bursts open, revealing three armed men aiming their weapons directly at the three of us, shouting.

"Hit the floor, arseholes, and don't fucking move."

Lucy and I launch towards the table; as several rounds fly past our heads, our two hearts pounding, we grab two of the rifles. We are in luck; Phillip has loaded them, probably to be safe because he had only met us once for a moment earlier today.

At the same time, Phillip picks up one of the pistols and fires back at the people in the doorway.

Diving behind one of the crates for cover, I take three deep breaths before standing up and firing three shots at the man closest to me, hitting him in the head. His body slumps to the floor, blood pouring from the massive hole in the back of his head. At the same time, another person drops to the deck. I turn to look at Lucy. Her arms are outstretched, recoiling from the round she sent into the body of the remaining attacker.

A quick area scan confirms that Phillip has done a runner with the third man.

"Where the fuck did they go?" I shout, turning to face Lucy.

"Don't fucking know, but Phillip's run off with the money."

At that moment, there is the sound of a commotion outside, "Come on, Lucy, follow me."

By the time we exit the warehouse and are back into the alley, Derek and George have a person on the floor, kicking the crap out of him. The man lets out several loud screams as another foot strikes his head.

"Don't kill him yet. We need to know who the fuck he is," I yell.

While Derek releases his foot from the man's neck, George and I grab his arms and fling him against the dumpster. Seconds later, Lucy is inches from his face, screaming at the top of her voice. "Who the fuck are you, arsehole, and why did you come after us."

There is no reply, so Derek lands a powerful punch to the man's stomach that makes the man double up in unbearable pain.

"If you don't want to talk, that woman is going to put a bullet in that tiny head of yours," Derek whispers in the person's ear.

"I'm telling you fucking nothing," the guy replies in broken English, with a Spanish accent that gives him away as a local.

"No point in you being here then; move away, boys."

Before the bloke can react, Lucy puts the rifle against his head and pulls the trigger and the back of the man's head is scattered across the dumpster, spraying blood and brain matter everywhere.

"Leave him there; let's collect the remaining weapons and ammo before the local constabulary turns up. As we can't take them to the hotel, suggest we stash them somewhere and pick them up in the morning. Take the pistols with you."

Five minutes later, we have collected all the equipment and are heading back to the hotel room. On the way, I touch the small radio in my ear.

"Meet us back at the room, Simon."

"On my way," comes the reply from Simon.

Fifteen minutes later, everyone is back at the hotel and gathered in Lucy's and my room.

"After what just occurred, the big question is, were the idiots after Phillip or us? One thing is certain: we will need to be more alert and be in mission mode from now on," I say.

"Think we all agree on that one, Steve, but do they have connections to our contact, or even the people who arranged to take us to Saint Ann? I, for one, think we should make our own arrangements," says Lucy, sitting on the bed.

"I'm inclined to go with you on that one. If our transport guy can find another way across, we will go with that. We will not cancel the boat, to be safe and keep people guessing. What time are we supposed to be there, Simon?"

"According to the paperwork, we need to be there before 09:00. I took the liberty of planning several ways across earlier. The best one is a local helicopter firm. They say they can take us to our proposed LZ, but there is a catch!"

"You all know I love going in boats! So what is the catch, Simon?" George enquires.

"Only a small one. There is nowhere to land where we have chosen to be dropped off on the island. They can drop us off about five miles away, and we walk to the LZ. Or they can hover about 10 feet above the ground, and we can jump," Simon continues.

"You want me to jump 10 feet? You're fucking mad, mate,"

"No need to panic, George—you will bounce, you fat fucker."

"What do you know about this company, Simon? Do you think they can they be trusted?" I ask.

"Think so, as it's a one-person outfit; the pilot's name is Butch, ex-British Army Air Corps. I spoke with him when we were looking over the information."

"Call him and see if he is available later today."

"Already done that. All we need to do is call and give him at least two hours before we need him."

"That's settled then. Make the call, Simon, for him to be ready for about 07:00. This gives us five hours for everyone to sort their kit and grab some sleep," grabbing my Bergen and emptying the contents on the bed, ready to pack what I need for this operation.

I didn't sleep much for the rest of the night. The scenario of getting the ride to the island and then plotting a route from the drop-off point played over in my head. One advantage is that I know where the company operates, as I walked past it on my last visit.

For some reason, it remains stuck in my head. It might be because of the tranquil walk I took along the seafront last time I was here and not having anything to worry about. Like, who wants to put a bullet in me? Mind you – this is never far from my mind these days. Good job I have the team with me, four people I can trust. Not easy with this bloody PTSD.

Time to stop this thinking lark, as the alarm on my phone is singing it's head off. Turn to Lucy, who is also awake, crawling out of bed and heading for the bathroom. Make use of the time and dress in the new jungle gortex outfit provided by Simon and George. Pack what little equipment I have with me into my Bergen. Luckily for me, out of habit, I always carry my basic kit no matter where I go. If there is anything else we will need, we can purchase it on the island of Saint Ann.

With Lucy out of the bathroom and packing her kit, I grab a quick shower. It may be the last for some time. Through the water cascading down me, I hear the room phone ring a few times before Lucy answers it. It's now 05:00. No doubt the boys are ensuring we're up, as no other idiots would call this early in the morning.

Want to leave and be in position at least 40 minutes before the agreed time with Butch. The planned time to depart with the rest is at 05:30, so there is still time for a decent brew before we head out.

"Fancy a coffee, honey," turning to face Lucy, who is now sitting on the bed, checking the pistol from the warehouse last night.

"Yes, please."

One final thing to do is grab everyone's mobile phones, smartwatches and anything with a computer chip inside. These need to go in my Faraday pouch to prevent them from being tracked by government officials or criminals. From now on, we will only use the radios Derek purchased yesterday for all communications.

Drop mine and Lucy's in the bag. "I'll be back in five minutes; just going to fetch Simon, George and Derek's electronic equipment," heading towards the door.

Walking down the corridor the short distance to where the boys are sleeping, I'm aware of the silence of the hotel; with only the noise of people snoring so loud, they could wake people up in a rock concert, breaking through the darkness. Reach the room and knock twice before I detect the sound of the door being unlocked from the inside.

"Morning, gents, give me your phones and other electronic equipment. You need to place them in this bag. I will leave it in the hotel safe while we are away. Plus, I've spoken to the hotel manager, and he is letting us leave the stuff we don't need in the baggage storage area."

"We are coming back this way then, Steve?" George says from the other side of the room.

"That's the plan, unless our transport guy has other ideas," I point to Simon.

"Not made any yet; if I do, you will be the last to know."

"Cheers, Simon, I love you too. Once you are all ready, meet you downstairs. Want to be out of here by 05:35 at the latest."

I leave the room and return to mine to collect Lucy and my bag. We are the first to the lobby, which has just enough light for people to see what they are doing. More than likely, the hotel is pretending they are protecting the environment. But in reality, they are trying to save on their energy bill. Out of the darkness comes a voice from the direction of the reception desk.

This takes me by surprise, as in my experience none of the staff are normally here this time of the night. They are usually around the back, catching a few minutes of sleep.

"Good morning. What brings you two to the realms of the hotel this time in the morning?" It's a young lady I've not seen yet since staying here.

"Morning. Me and my friends have an early start, as we are going on a camping trip up in the rainforest for a few days," I lie.

"Have a good time. Is there anything I can help you with before you depart?"

"Was going to ask if we could leave this bag in the hotel safe," I hold up the Faraday pouch, "for a week, give or take a few days? Plus, I have an arrangement with the hotel manager to leave our baggage in your storage area."

"Sure, no problem, I'll do that right away for you."

I detect the swishing sound of the lift doors opening from behind me. Turn in time to witness Simon, Derek and George walking in my direction. Once we are all ready, I signal to depart and get the operation underway.

It will look stupid if we take up our normal tactical formation. So exit the building and cross the main road to the footpath running along the coast in a group. The only other people around, as we walk towards the pickup point, are a couple of idiot runners getting their daily exercise in the cool air of the early morning. Apart from the sound of them pounding the pavement and a few passing cars, the area is silent.

It isn't long before we arrive back at the rear of the warehouse to collect the weapons. We stashed them here, as it is unlikely that somebody would return in the short time frame between us dumping them and our return. We were correct. The place is quiet, with no one around, not including the dead bodies that still litter the building. Pick up the rifles and share out the ammo.

Within 30 minutes, we are walking past the seahorse statue and the footbridge to the park at Muelle 8, where, with luck, Butch should be waiting one hour from now. Stop short of the curved footbridge that crosses the inlet.

"OK, ladies and gents, the helicopter pad is close to the harbour wall in the far right-hand corner. We need to be on our guard, due to the fact we were jumped by some unknown attackers at the warehouse. So, George and Derek, once over the bridge, turn left and follow the path, keeping the building and public toilets on your right. It shouldn't take you long. From the bogs, you will be able to scan the pickup location. Stop short and radio us."

"No problem," Derek confirms.

"You two," I point to Lucy and Simon, "wander around the park looking for anything out of place. If you witness something, radio it through. I will continue to the corner once you are all in position."

While the others move into their positions, I sit on a green cast iron bench near the bridge. They say the best location to hide is in the open. At the same time, I listen to the tranquil sound of the ocean hitting the harbour wall, while watching a cruise ship sail close by. I'd only been there 10 minutes when the message I'd been waiting for in my earpiece came through.

"In location, eyes on the target." It's George.

Seconds later, Lucy's voice comes over the airwaves, "In situ, waiting for orders."

Press the transmit button of my radio, "Stay fast and cover me. I'm going to the pad to recce the location."

Check the time on Mickey: 06:20, before getting up and following the footpath. The place is in darkness, and the entry to the pickup point is protected by a high mesh fence about seven feet tall. Inside is a small wood-clad building, painted blue. Since no lights are on, I would guess there is yet to be anyone here. Over to the left is a vast tarmacked area with the compulsory 'H' in giant yellow painted in the middle.

I turn to walk back into the park when, overhead I hear the distinctive sound of helicopter blades chopping through the early morning air as it approaches our location.

Still need to be cautious, so go back about 100 metres, take up a concealed vantage point, and watch as the craft lands. Once the blades stop spinning, a single man alights and walks to the building. Seconds later, the white illuminations break through the window. This must be Butch. Still not taking any chances, the team remain in position for a further 10 minutes, observing.

Only when I'm positive he is alone do I transmit the message, "All clear, RV on my location."

By this time, the man opens the locked gate, returns to the helicopter, and checks it. Once we are all together, Simon walks up

47

to the figure while the rest of us stay back, just in case this isn't the person we are waiting for.

"Morning. Take it you're Butch?"

Butch stops what he is doing and turns to face Simon, "Yep, that's me. Take it you're Simon, the one I spoke to on the phone? You on your own?"

"No, the others will be here in a moment. Are you still on for dropping us off on the island of Saint Ann? No questions asked."

"Not a problem. I haven't done anything like this since my army days. Remember what I said. Where you want to be dropped off, I can't land, so you will have to jump?"

"Shouldn't be an issue. I'll kick them out if I have to," Simon laughs.

By this time, the rest of the team assembles around the helipad, dumping their Bergens on the floor.

With no time to waste, I introduce everyone. Then, getting straight to business, "How long do you think it will take us to reach the drop-off point?"

"My baby here, this Eurocopter Dolphin helicopter," he taps the sides. "Travelling at 200 km/h should take about one and a half hours for the 300 km trip."

With that, equipment is launched in the back, and everyone clambers aboard, taking seats at the aircraft's rear. I climb into the front righthand seat with my maps to confirm with Butch the LZ.

The crossing goes without any hitch, on radio silence most of the way, with occasional air traffic control contact. We have a good man here, as he tells them he is on the way to an airfield near the town of Hyde. The time goes fast, and we are almost there when my brain, which never shuts the fuck up, is already planning the return journey to San Juan.

Decide to take a chance, "So, Butch, you may have surmised... we might not be on a camping trip. Thinking that we are leaping from a helicopter might have given it away. So here are my thoughts..." I pause for a moment to let what I'm saying sink in.

"Yeah, sort of guessed that," Butch replies.

"Well, here is the thing—any chance you might be open to picking us up? Can pay you the same as we gave you for the way here."

"Tell you what, Steve, add an extra 200, and you have a deal. You need to contact me the day before to arrange the time and place," comes Butch's reply.

"Cheers, mate."

"I wouldn't worry about a pickup yet. We have 10 more minutes to your dropoff, and the weather radar shows it's pissing it down. Hope you lot brought some wet-weather gear." Thank fuck George and Simon managed to obtain them.

With only a couple minutes to go, Derek slides open the rear door after putting his pack on first. While the rest approach the door, I clamber out of my seat and head for the back. "Tell us when to jump, Butch."

"Get ready. We are over the LZ," Butch shouts from the front, as the noise with the door open makes it difficult to communicate.

A few seconds later, we are about 12 feet from the ground and hovering in position. Someone yells 'GO', and Derek is the first to leap out; Lucy is next. Hesitant George stands in the doorway, finding it hard to leap from a perfectly good aircraft. But soon, with the aid of Simon's boot, he leaves shouting,

"You bastard," as he plummets to the deck. Not long after, we all have taken a dive into the unknown.

The sound of the rotors echo through the trees as we land and quickly scatter amongst the dense undergrowth. After checking myself, I turn to check on the rest of the team as my attention turns to ensuring we all made it unharmed and ready for the next part of this rescue mission.

"Everyone OK? Where is George?" I can't see him straight away.

"He's over there in that crater the fat bastard made when he landed," Simon says, pointing and trying to stop himself from laughing too loud.

"Did you kick me out, you lanky stream of piss?" George whines.

"Sure did. Now bring your arse over here with the rest of us."

As we collect our bearings, the sky becomes a deep shade of black as the rain hammers down nonstop, making it difficult to see clearly, with the sound of torrential rainfall pummelling through the dense foliage which echoes across the rainforest, illuminated by the occasional bright flashes of lightning.

Once the helicopter is out of range, the forest comes alive with the sounds of exotic creatures. The rustling of leaves under the weight of predators prowling the undergrowth, the distant howls of some unseen beast, and the croaking of early morning amphibians all mix in an organised symphony of danger.

With everyone gathered around the map, "Right folks, we are here, and we need to be here," I point to the village of Barbles, five clicks from here. "Looking at the terrain, it should take, at most three hours to reach. This is unknown territory to us all, so keep looking for dangers lurking in the forest. It's unlikely, but we may still have people on our trail."

From here, we take up our usual patrol formation, with me leading Simon behind me, double-checking that I'm going the right way. Close behind him is Lucy, followed by Derek, with George taking his usual position at the rear. Unlike the Yanks in Vietnam, even in this dense rainforest, we still ensure there is a gap between us. Enough so you can still see the person in front without being up their arse and therefore not giving anyone in an ambush an easy kill.

We have been going for about half an hour, when the brain and the sounds of the rainforest start playing their usual tricks. Even the slightest noise is now a potential threat. In the distance, the sound of something moving grabs our attention. The rustling grows louder as we push on, making our own noise to add to the symphony of the rainforest with the crackling of branches underfoot. Every snap and creak echoes through the confines of the forest, warning of our presence to anything or someone close by.

After two hours of struggling to navigate the dense foliage, sweat soaks through our clothes as the humidity intensifies. We become aware that we are not alone. Everyone is now on alert as we weave along a dark path that mingles through the rainforest, down a steep, muddy ravine towards the sound of rushing water.

At the bottom, we come across a 40-foot waterfall peering out of the tall trees, crashing and roaring as it cascades over the rocks, emptying into a massive pool at the base before it spills into a smaller one and disappears into a fast-moving stream bubbling over rocks. Use this time to take a break and refill our canteens with fresh water via our filtering systems, which we all carry. And take a well-earned rest.

"From my calculations, we should only have an hour until we reach our RV for the night. From here, we can plan what to do next," I say, looking at the map.

"Roger that, mate," says Derek, pouring the contents of his canteen over the back of his head to try to cool himself down, as the humidity has risen since the rain stopped.

Break over, we pick up our kit and move deeper into the forest. We soon come across a small open space amidst the dense trees, only 30 minutes from the falls. On the edge, I stop, hairs on the back of my neck standing on end as, without warning, a growl can be heard coming from the darkness beyond the clearing.

Turn instantly and signal the team to circle up, huddling together and closing ranks. We can hear the sound of something creeping closer. The atmosphere is electric, as the team get ready for the fight of our lives, all our senses engaged. At this moment, amidst the dense jungle and the sounds of exotic wildlife, everyone understands they will need to rely on everything they know to survive the next few minutes.

A long agonising minute passes before, out of the undergrowth comes the distinctive large, round heads, short legs and a stunning coat dotted with dark rosettes and spots of a jaguar. These cats are renowned for their fearless nature. They are not afraid to take risks, so we are not taking any chances. Everyone stays perfectly still, with rifles in the aim just in case it attacks.

"Didn't think they lived in a tropical rainforest," Lucy says, over the sights of her barrel.

"Me neither, but there is one standing in front of us. It might have escaped from somewhere," I reply.

"Want me to place a bullet in its head?" says George, taking up a kneeling firing position.

"Only if it runs this way, mate. Otherwise, let's wait and find out which way it goes."

"You're the boss, Steve."

"No, I am," Lucy laughs quietly.

Our friendly jaguar sniffs around the open space's edges and disappears into the forest.

"Must have smelt you, Derek, and decided it didn't fancy rotten meat," Simon says, throwing something at him.

"Don't panic, Simon. If it comes back, I'll throw it a bone, the one inside your leg," Derek's retort comes.

Wait five minutes before heading off towards the RV. After taking a compass bearing and aligning it with the map, I locate a track on the other side of the open ground that leads in the general direction of the way we want to go.

"Come on, you lot, and keep your eyes and ears open for the pussycat, as it went this way as well."

"OK, I know you green numpties like walking into danger, but can't we find a way that doesn't follow the cat?"

"Nope, this way, Simon."

After another hour of following a muddy track through the densely packed trees, crossing small streams and winding our way up and down inclines, finally, we come to the spot where we will be setting up camp—a clearing on the edge of the village of Barbles.

Without anyone saying anything, the team spread out and take up defensive positions surrounding the central point. I picked this location due to its proximity to a body of running water and available cover, and from the looks of it, the place will be easy to defend if it comes to it.

I can't detect any sounds or movement in the local vicinity, so keeping low, walk past each person and tell them to make camp. Within minutes, the place is a hive of activity with everyone apart from George, as he draws the short straw and is on sentry duty. It isn't long before we have a home-from-home among the green floor canopy.

We are soon sitting around a fire pit I've dug into the floor after scraping away the foliage, so Simon can start on the all-important brew. The hole in the ground is suitable for hiding naked flames but doesn't do much about the smoke. With any luck, this will blend in with the steam rising from the ground.

While Simon is doing that and George is on stag, Lucy, Derek and I start constructing bamboo beds off the forest floor. First, attach a long pole across the gap spanning two trees before attaching two longer bamboo shafts on top. Join the two furthest ends into a point with some vines hanging from a tree. Then, raise the end and rest on a short pole knocked into the earth.

The next task is to stretch more vines and leaves between them to form a bed. Above all, we attach a poncho to keep any rain off. I watched a survival programme on TV once where the person smeared tree sap around the parts of the bamboo that enters the ground, and the base of the trees, to stop you from sharing a doss bag with biting insects. I might as well give it a go.

Chapter Four – Saint Ann

Once all the beds are constructed, our attention turns to the weapons. Before we need to fire them in anger, we better ensure the round lands where we point the damn things. With George being one of the two weapons experts, Derek relieves him on stag so Lucy and him can go a short distance from the camp to find a place to make a makeshift zeroing range. The location has to give at least a 25 metre clearance, and the forest, as best it can, must muffle the sound of rounds being fired. In the meantime, Simon and I break out the rations to prepare a hot meal. It might be our last.

"Found a perfect spot not far from here," says Lucy, sitting beside me.

"In that case, we will check all the weapons two at a time once we've all finished eating."

"Suggest Lucy and me as the snipers go first, as the rifles may be needed for a long shot if we come across any open spaces in this damn forest," replies George, grabbing a plate of Simon's chuck-in stew.

With food out of the way, and everything else packed away, everyone readies their equipment, ready to fire on the range. I confirm that my magazine is full by pressing down on the rounds; they didn't move, so it must be full.

Over at the makeshift range, George has the L115A3 sniper rifle in the aim and pulls his index finger back, taking up the first pressure, and starts to control his breathing, preparing to fire the first round.

"Fire when ready," says Lucy, looking at the massive piece of peeled-off bark acting as the target through a pair of binoculars.

A moment later, he squeezes the trigger. Simultaneously, the firing pin strikes the base of the brass casing, causing an explosion as the bullet twists in the barrel as it leaves, heading for the target. It lands slightly just below the centre.

"Up one inch," Lucy calls out.

He makes the necessary alteration to the sight, aims, and fires again. This time, the round hits the middle of the piece of wood. The rifle is zeroed, so they swap places, and Lucy takes aim with her sniper rifle. She follows the same procedure as George until she hits the centre of the target.

To conceal the noise of firing rounds, we leave 30 minutes between the next two and myself checking our weapons. Plus, this allows us time to react if someone comes investigating. This gives me time to review all the information again and triple-check our route to Barble, fixing all the waypoints in my head. You can't mark them on the map in case it becomes lost for some reason. Somebody, if found, would know our intended target and how we plan on getting there.

After getting everything straight in my head, I call Simon over, as he will be confirming the route to help keep us all pointing in the right direction. Take the next 20 minutes going through all the details with him. Once he understands, we explain it to the rest of the team. It's vital everyone in the team knows the objective, the direction of travel, and, far more critically, how to leave the island if the mission fails, incase someone gets killed.

Time is getting on, and we still need to erect our defences. From a glance around our surroundings, any possible attack would come from the rear along the trail we came in on. This is where I will put the punji trap.

I make my way back the way we came. Locate the ideal spot about 40 metres away. Leave the dirt track, head into the dense undergrowth to my right, and go to the place opposite, where I will dig the pit. While I'm doing this, Derek prepares one of the radios to work with a trip wire to be placed out the front of the sentry post.

Take out my trowel and make a hole about two feet down and two feet square. Sharpen the six short bamboo sticks with my knife to a sharp point. Push them into the bottom and pack the soil I've removed hard around the bases. This is to ensure they remain standing upright with the points facing skywards.

Grab a handful of small twigs and leaves and cover the hole, taking care I don't apply too much pressure. The last task is to layer a loose covering of dirt from around me so it blends in. The trap is now ready for some idiot who isn't looking at where they are going to stand on, therefore, letting out an enormous scream and alerting us.

At the other side of the camp, Derek passes Simon, who has now taken over stag duty. Bending to speak close to Simon's ear, "Going about 50 metres to your front to place the tripwire. Don't fucking shoot me."

"Will think about it," comes the reply.

After finding the ideal spot, Derek fastens one end of the fishing line to a tree and then leaps across the track to another on the opposite side. He ties a short length around the base just below an offshoot, to stop it from riding up, then through another, he makes further up about head height.

He returns the wire to the first one and connects the radio before concealing it. Now if some smart arse walks this way and spots the bottom one, then think they are outwitting us and jump over the lower one, they will strike the top line, setting off the switch, which will transmit to the person on guard duty. If this wasn't a covert operation, the wire would be connected to a claymore or some form of explosives.

On the way back past Simon, "Thanks for not putting a bullet in my backside."

"No problem, Derek. Would have been a waste of a perfectly good round."

Now that all the required tasks are complete, there is nothing else to do apart from continuing the stag until first light tomorrow morning. All of us take a two-hour stint. Everyone makes the most of the time to carry out their personal affairs, clean weapons and catch some shuteye.

One thing about being in the dense rainforest is that it becomes dark early, something I must consider when planning each part of the mission. Finally, the fading luminescence disappears, the place is in darkness, and the wild nighttime chorus warms up its vocal cords. I drift into sleep, my loaded pistol by my side.

When I wake up, the first task is to ensure the rest of the team is up as we need to move from this location as soon as possible. With the first light of the day breaking through the canopy, and the sun starting to heat the entire forest, the heat is stifling. Sweat runs down my forehead and trickles down my spine. It had been a humid and sticky night, preventing anybody from getting a good night's kip.

I spend the next few minutes dismantling my makeshift bed, scattering the bits over the rainforest. We must do this so anyone who knows what they are looking for comes this way, they will be unable to ascertain our morale, such as the team slept well, therefore alert. The same goes for any rubbish; we will take this with us. Again, people don't know if we are all well-fed. You will be surprised by what intelligence can be gathered from what people leave behind.

Simon is already getting the brew going when I finish and return to the fire pit. I hand him my black mug, which he fills with coffee from the pot heating on the gas stove.

"Here you go, Steve, get this down you; far better than a cold drink this morning, even with this heat."

"Thanks, Simon."

Soon everyone is sitting on small logs to keep their arse off the forest floor, so they are not bitten by the hundreds of ants that have decided to build a highway through our RV.

"OK, folks, while we are enjoying the hot beverages, the plan for today is to make our way to the village of Barble. Here, we can stock up on supplies for the next part of the journey to this location," I point to the splash map I've stretched out on the ground before me. "According to the information given to us by Bear, we are to meet a local who can give us more info on the camp James and Anna are being held."

"When do you want to leave?" Lucy asks.

"Might as well make a start if everyone is ready, as making our way through this shit only gets harder from here," I wave my arm toward the undergrowth.

"Roger that, Steve," says Derek, downing his drink and putting his cup away in his Bergen.

Once packed, I lead the team through the dense rainforest that blankets the tropical Caribbean island. The humidity is high, and the sounds of the forest fill the air.

The map is in my hand, but it's useless as the foliage is too thick and the vines tangled. So, I'm forced to rely on all my instincts, years of experience and determination to make our way to today's destination.

Simon follows me, double-checking the compass to ensure we stay on the right track. Lucy scans the surroundings, looking for any indications of previous human moments, such as footprints or discarded items. Derek is listening and observing for any movements in the dense undergrowth, especially those that could pose a threat. Finally, George keeps an eye on the rear, securing our flank and watching the trail behind us.

The village of Barble is our next objective; we are only a few kilometres away. Getting there is far from easy, weaving through the underbrush, pushing aside packed vegetation and leaping over tangled roots. Each step brings a new challenge - a twisted tree root to avoid, a dangling vine to sidestep, or a thorny bush to skirt around.

The sun sears through the treetops, making the air humid and sticky, weighing us all down like a heavy blanket. The tropical forest stretches as far as the eye can see, with its tall trees serving as a natural ceiling, shielding the worst of the hot sun; with its dense undergrowth, with ferns, nettles, and parasitic plants clinging to any surface that supports them.

In the near distance, I detect the sound of water cascading and crashing into rocks from a nearby waterfall, and the aroma of cooking fires fills my nostrils. We must be getting close. My heart races with anticipation, as we emerge from the greenery and find Barble standing before us, a location that appears to exist outside of time.

The houses are built entirely from bamboo, as though modern technology forgot to visit. Roosters and hens roam in the dirt streets. The local children look on with curiosity, following our every move as the team checks out what's around them, wondering what kind of people live in this isolated place.

Something about this seemingly tranquil village feels dangerous, and we can sense that trouble is brewing. As we delve deeper, our senses are alive.

We are more aware than ever of the danger as a group of villagers gather on the verge along the edge of the road, their colourful garb alerting me and the others that this is a location of intrigue.

Without warning, George's hand grips Lucy's arm, and he points her to a few men sitting on the grass by the side of the street, looking at us curiously. Their expressions are grim, and they appear solid and agile.

Deeper in the village, we come across a row of dirty grey buildings. One building is set back from the rest, with old wooden tables constructed of broken pallets outside. Behind one stands an older woman wearing a black dress and is cutting the heads off several fish with a bone-handled chopper. Her eyes are on both what she is doing and us.

To the left of an open doorway is a second, this time containing a variety of fresh vegetables. A dim light is coming from inside what appears to be the local store.

"This might be a good place to purchase supplies," says Lucy, once she reaches my location.

"Why don't you, Simon and George go inside and see what they have while Derek and I remain here? Something is making me uneasy," I say in a low voice.

With all the Bergens by our feet, I stare across the road at a group of young men on the floor under a massive coconut tree, talking and looking in our direction. At the same time, we witness an older man pushing a child in a pushchair past our location before returning five minutes later. But this time, there is a different kid in the pram.

On the other side of the street, one person dressed in green shorts and a black and white t-shirt has relocated further down the road and is watching our every move. Another has done something similar but to our left.

Turn to Derek, "See what's happening here? Think they are ready to try to rob us."

"Think you're right, Steve, better watch them closely. I've seen this situation before on St Halb," Derek replies.

Reach inside my jacket and check that my pistol is easily reachable. I don't want to use it. But if I have to, I will. Several more minutes pass, and the group of friendly locals are getting braver. They now all start to stroll in our direction, reaching the edge of the road seconds later.

Derek and I clench our fists, ready for a fight. No way am I letting these idiots get the better of us. They have now reached the middle of the street when all of a sudden, they come to a halt. From behind me, I detect the voices of the other three as they come out of the shop.

"Looks like we have a scrap on our hands," says George, punching one hand with the other clenched fist.

As the locals move forward inch by inch, a new wave of bravery seems to have come over them.

Seconds later, the person who appears to be organising this attack lunges at me, holding a long knife. Stand firm, not flinching a single muscle until he is at arm's reach. Grab his arm, turn and pull it across my shoulder. Throw him to the ground. Press firmly on the thumb of his right hand in which he holds the knife. He drops the weapon as he lets out a loud, ear-deafening scream of pain.

The others are about to rush at us when a yellow Toyota Hilux screeches around the corner, stopping in front of us. A youngish man in his early 30s with long dark hair, dressed in blue jeans and a black shirt, the logo 'Making Tracks Adventures' printed on the back, clambers out.

Within minutes, the people who were about to make this an exciting day, including the idiot lying on the floor by my feet, ran off, disappearing among the houses.

Our rescuer comes over and shakes my hand, "Sorry about that. I'm Jayden, one of the community leaders around here. Not many Westerners come here. So they fancied their chances of robbing you of your backpacks," he points to the pile of Bergens.

"Good job you showed up, or this could have turned into a shitfest," I say, picking up my bag.

"Where you lot off? Can I give you a lift anywhere?" Jayden asks.

"We're on a hiking and camping trip, making our way through the rainforest. And no thanks for the ride. Would defeat the reason we're here," I lie.

"In that case, I wouldn't hang around the village too long as they may come back," Jayden says, strolling back to the Hilux.

"One last thing before you go. Is there anywhere we can rent a vehicle in Hyde? If we don't fancy walking back?" Simon says.

"There isn't a car rental place.... However, there is an ATV business that might rent you some bikes. The company is on the edge of town. Can't think of the name, but it will be easy enough to find."

"Cheers, Jayden, sure we will locate it. Stay safe."

Once the Toyota disappears up the road and is out of the line of sight, "Think we should take this man's advice and fuck off out of here. Did you find any supplies in the shop, Lucy?"

"Got some stuff that will do us for the next few days, Steve."

Within 10 minutes, we are leaving the sleepy village and about to enter the forest, when my ears become aware of a commotion behind me, and I turn, thinking our friends are following us, to see George chasing several chickens through a cloud of dust and feathers. Moments later, you hear the death rattle of a chicken, and he emerges holding a hen that hangs lifeless from his hand.

"Well caught, mate, fresh meat is on the menu tonight. But no more fucking about, we need to put some distance between us and this place. Besides, I want to make camp on the outskirts of Hyde before we call it a day."

"Better move your fat arse then, Steve," comes the remark from George.

We trudge through the dense undergrowth, sweat mingling with the humid air for about 200 metres into the rainforest before I stop and go to the ground. The rest of the team spread out in a circle, all weapons pointing out while everyone watches and listens for any signs that someone from the village is tailing us.

Stay this way for the next 20 minutes. Rising to a standing position, I take out my compass and take a bearing of the track to my front. We have a choice to take our chances on the trail, which will be easier- but this brings an added danger of being seen by anyone who might be following- or proceed on a direct course through the tightly-packed forest. This would be safer, but there is no way, on my calculation, we will reach Hyde before nightfall. The whole team will have to decide.

After a short discussion, we take the first option and follow the track, keeping well apart in case of ambush.

We've been tracking through the unyielding rainforest for about an hour, and traversing through steep and rocky terrain when we detect the sound of rushing water. We slog through the underbrush just off the trail. In front of us is a raging river that spans 40 metres to the opposite bank. What we found made me curse out loud.

We walk close to the edge of the riverbank to assess the situation. Time is of the essence, and we need to cross. With the rest, we scan along the riverbank in both directions, trying to find a way to traverse it safely. There is no going back the way we came as the objective is on the other side. There is no way across.

"OK, folks, I'm open to ideas of how we get our sorry arses across," I say, hoping the river may be fast but shallow.

"Why not throw the skinny bastard like a log with a line attached? He can pull us over," says Derek, pointing to Simon.

"Good idea, numpty, apart from one thing. Anyone got a rope?" Simon responds.

That's when Simon spots several vines snaking down from a nearby tree. "How about we quickly fashion a makeshift one out of the long, green vines?"

"Fuck me, Simon, that tiny brain of yours has kicked in. Not a bad idea," as I walk over and yank down one of the trailing plants.

Thirty minutes later, with each member playing their part, and after many failed attempts, a fifty-five-foot natural rope is constructed.

"Any volunteers to go first," I ask.

"Yep, I volunteer… you," says Lucy, picking up one end and tying it around my waist.

"In that case, I will need the two fat boys, George and Derek, to hold the other end as an anchor."

I can't afford for all my gear to become wet, so strip down to my underwear and place the clothing in the plastic bag in my Bergen. It may be cold now, but I'll soon warm up once I'm on the other side and put my clothes back on.

Not being the world's biggest fan of swimming across fast-moving rivers, I start to inch my way, feeling the spray of the freezing water churning beneath me. Take one step at a time, ensuring my foot is firm before taking another action.

All goes well for the first part, as it only comes up to my waist as it rushes past. Take a short break behind the eddy of a vast boulder near the middle.

"Come on, chunky, we haven't got all day," comes the encouragement from Simon on the bank.

Take several deep breaths and continue to cross. I only take a few steps when the river deepens, and the gushing ice-cold water surrounds my neck.

At last, I reach the other side and collapse in a shitty heap on the ground. The coldness has taken my breath away, so I am gasping for air. I soon get control and quickly dress.

While I am getting my kit back on, Simon secures his end to a tree that overhangs the river. Now I need to fasten this end to something solid to make some sort of rope bridge, so the rest can come over to join me. Find a coconut tree that will be ideal for the anchor, but it's too far from the bank. The only other option is a huge rock that juts out of the river.

"Come on, you lot, strip off and drag your butts over here," I yell, trying to make my voice heard over the gushing water.

Lucy is the first to undress. Doing so in front of the boys didn't bother her; she's been on too many missions with us to care and she's seen everything we're packing.

With me now on the opposite bank, Lucy steps forward, her knuckles white as she clings to the makeshift rope. Once on the other side, she repeats the same exercise as me and gets dressed before shouting for the others to come across.

George, Derek and Simon follow each other, inching their way through the river, the vine digging into their skin. Soon, the whole team is across, kit on and ready to make a final push toward the town of Hyde.

"There is no way we are going to reach our planned RV. The crossing has taken far too long. So we will aim to be at least three-quarters of the way there," I point to the map.

"One question, Steve, were we not supposed to meet a contact in the last village?" asks George.

"Yep, but nobody showed up. Will try to call them once we set up camp for the night."

With everyone ready, we move swiftly back into the forest and through the dense foliage until we pick up the trail again. Glancing down at my map, my mind slips back to the meeting with Bear. From what I remember, he said that Aron's drug cartel is often seen in the area and, beyond doubt, in the town of Hyde. Better travel with even more caution than usual. The last thing we need is a gun battle on our way to our objective.

We've been walking for around two hours, with the sounds of chirping birds and buzzing insects filling my ears, and the rustling of dead foliage underfoot echoing throughout the dense rainforest. The winding path leads us deeper into the wilderness.

Tall, towering trees spread out before me, their thick, gnarled roots reaching out of the ground like tentacles. For some reason, it appears more prominent and intense than the forest on the other side of the river. The occasional rustle of leaves in the distance draws my attention and reminds me of our encounter with the big cat.

Through the gap in the treetops, I see the sky starting to darken; we will lose the light soon, so look for a suitable point for us to RV for the night.

It takes another 15 minutes before we arrive at a small clearing in the tightly packed undergrowth. This is where we will make our RV.

"OK, you lot, it will be last light shortly. Better set up camp here. Lucy, can you take the first stag while Derek and I arrange the perimeter defences? Shouldn't need a sentry as the forest itself should provide enough cover, but better put one out just in case," I say, dropping my Bergen to the floor.

"Sure, you got anywhere in mind," Lucy replies, throwing her Bergen under a bush.

"Somewhere facing that direction, leave it up to you."

Like last night, Derek sets up a trip wire on the track behind us while I dig another punji pit on a smaller trail off to our right. It's only a short time before the campsite is up and running, with Simon getting some chow and brew on the go. The night routine runs as usual for the next four hours. Soon, it is my turn to relieve George at the sentry post. Pack away all my gear in case we are attacked while I'm on stag, then head off to locate George.

"OK, mate, I'll take it from here," I whisper in his ear.

"Cheers, Steve. I'm just going a few feet off to your left for a shit; I would appreciate not obtaining a second arsehole."

I lie still in the humid tropical rainforest, with my rifle pointing along the track. I feel the damp soil beneath me. I am in awe of the sheer magnitude of this place; it's a living, breathing ecosystem and the raw, natural power pulses through every inch of it.

The cacophony of sounds surrounding me suddenly intensifies. This lush forest's thick, dense foliage creates a cocoon around the RV, muffling the rustling of animals and the cry of an unknown bird.

My senses are on high alert as I strain to listen for sudden movements, the crunch of twigs or the crunch of a leaf. Listening for the distant sounds of footsteps, the chatter of voices and whispers, and the sound of others moving through the dense forest.

I'm broken out of my mini trance of appreciation when, about a hundred metres away in the darkness, I detect the sound of what my brain is telling me: people are creeping around. Every snap and crackle is amplified through my bones, adrenaline pumping as I hold my breath, waiting for whoever might reveal themselves.

Questions appear in my mind: Who are they, how many, do they know we are here, or are they just passing through? The questions are soon answered as the sounds get closer and more intense. Out of the pitch black appears a man standing on the track just in front of me, holding an AK-47. This can't be anyone else but the cartel's people.

Wait until he gets closer to me. Take out my knife; this person needs to be dispatched quietly. With my body tense, I launch at him, knocking him back a few feet. Press down hard on his frailing torso, making it impossible for his weapon to be fired. Reach up with my left hand and cover his mouth.

The last thing I want is for him to make any more noise. At the same time, I drive my blade into the right side of his neck behind the windpipe and pull forward. I keep my hand over his mouth as thick red blood oozes from the large gash where his throat used to be. Not long before any movement ceases, the body lay motionless on the floor. Blood runs into the sandy trail, drying quickly as it is absorbed.

Turn and run back toward the RV to warn the others, we are under attack. When I arrive, Lucy is busy slicing the throat of another attacker while Derek is smashing a man's head in with a giant boulder. Over in the distance, I can catch the sound of a commotion followed by a single shot. Fuck, I hope that isn't George being killed.

With the rest of the team working, Simon collects everyone's kit and piles them in the middle, ready for people to grab.

George emerges through the trees, blood dripping down from his left arm and falling off his hand as he rejoins the rest of us.

"You OK, George?" I yell.

"Yeah, it's not all mine," comes the reply.

Minutes later, silence returns to the RV. "Come on, everyone, we need to bug out and put as much distance away from here," slinging my Bergen on my back.

"Right behind you, mate," George shouts.

Leave the rendezvous point at high speed, pushing our way through the dense foliage to a vantage point overlooking the way we came, about a click away. We stop to ensure we are not being pursued. Stay here for the next 30 minutes to be sure.

Before we go, Lucy walks over to George, "Let's look at that injury for you."

She takes his jacket off as George flinches in some pain. There is a four-inch gash in his upper arm that is still bleeding.

"Need to stitch that up," says Lucy.

Without thinking, Lucy reaches down, grabs a giant leaf-cutter ant, and places it on the wound. The moment the insect bites through the skin, she snaps its body off, leaving the head in place. This action closes the gash. She repeats this several times before placing a field bandage over the area.

Once Lucy's finished, we carry on towards Hyde.

Chapter Five – The Town of Hyde

Last night, we trampled for hours through the forest, trying to put as much distance between us and the remains of the people who attacked us earlier, until we couldn't go any further as the terrain was making it too dangerous to continue.

Awake under the cover of a small green bush, where I collapsed the previous night as it became far too dark to set up a proper RV. Besides, at best, we would only be here for a few hours.

Lucy is beside me, still in the land of nod. I shake her, trying to do it in such in a way that she doesn't come around and try to kill me.

"Time to wake up, honey," I say, as I clamber off the floor to join Derek, a couple of feet away, checking his rifle.

George and Simon crawl out from the foliage to my right, dragging their Bergens. With his hands stretched out, reaching for the sky, Simon lets out a huge yawn and comes over to us.

"Morning idiots, anyone fancy a brew?" he says, taking the gas stove from the backpack's side pocket.

"Come on, Simon, you know I need my morning gallon of coffee. Remember what the head doctors at Combat Stress said about routines," I say while fetching my black mug.

Everyone is drinking their brews, so I call our contact on the pay-as-you-go phone I'd purchased in San Juan for this purpose, as our electronic equipment is in the hotel safe. With any luck, they will fill us in on the latest details regarding the drug cartel's camp and its up-to-date location.

The phone rings several times before a female voice on the other end says, " Who's this?"

"Yes, morning. It's Steve here. Am I speaking to Tennille?" I say, reluctant to give her any more information; it might not be her.

"Hi, Steve. Bear said you would be calling. Where are you now?"

"Not far from the town of Hyde," I'm not giving my current location to someone I don't yet trust.

"In that case, can you meet at the Forest Retreat at, shall we say, 11:00 today? I will be upstairs on the veranda, looking at the rainforest beneath. So you know it's me, I will place three empty glasses close together on the table," she says.

"No problem, see you then."

When the call ends, I take out the map to align it to the terrain to double-check our position. We were moving at some speed last night; I only made a rough guess on the way we ought to go. I needed to use all the tricks I'd learned over many years to get us to this point.

Learned along time ago that one of the best ways to find out how a trail meanders through the rainforest is by looking up at the gap left at the top of the tree line. Plus, of course, checking the stars. Earlier, I'd noted which ones were above the direction we need to go.

Call everyone over, "Now, If everyone takes a gander at the map, it is only about three clicks from this location to the edge of town. It shouldn't take us more than an hour to reach if we stay on the track and out of the bush. So when you're ready, folks, let's make a move," I place the map into my jacket pocket.

With me leading and the rest in their usual formation behind me, we head along the trail towards our meeting point with Tennille at a bar called Forest Retreat.

As we start to come closer to our next objective through the dense jungle, the heavy humidity hangs in the air like a wet blanket.

Sweat drips down our faces, and mosquitoes and other insects buzz around us. The sounds of exotic birds and rustling leaves fill our ears as we cautiously move down the worn dirt path leading to the town of Hyde.

Eventually there is a break in the dense undergrowth as we arrive at a point closer to the town; a massive open clearing of short wild grass which stretches out in front of us for about 200 metres. We glance across to the other side, where several different-coloured timber-clad homes are running along a compacted track that lines the outskirts of Hyde.

Beyond that, dilapidated structures that make up Hyde appear like they've been abandoned for years. The buildings are small and made of timber, with thatched roofs, several of which have holes in them. The wooden steps leading up to the porches are rickety and look like they are about to collapse.

The scent of old lumber mixes with mildew, and the steam rising from the pavements after the rain hangs around in the air. The sounds of creaking boards and the whisper of leaves swaying in the wind were punctuated by a strange insect's occasional chirp or buzz.

"This place is worse than the one we left behind. Gives me the creeps," says Lucy, as she steps out from the forest cover.

"With you on that one, Lucy, but this is where our meeting with Tennille will be held," I say, joining her on the open ground.

The time now is 10:00, one hour before we meet with the contact, soaking wet and covered in mud. We cross the town's threshold, heading for what appears to be the main drag through the centre, running in a straight line away from us all the time, watching for any sign of danger lurking in the shadows.

What is strange is that the time is just after 10, and apart from a few people wandering about and the occasional car, the place appears abandoned, until we walk deeper among the many streets. It opens up in a vibrant townlet with people buzzing around, darting in and out of buildings. There are more vehicles on the road. It's as though someone has taken a massive axe to the town and divided it into different parts. The contrast between the two is unbelievable.

The only thing out of place now is us, dressed in our wet, muddy combat gear. Not knowing what type of built-up area we are walking into, we had the sense to conceal our Bergens and rifles in a hide 200 metres back in the forest and away from the track. Easy for anyone who knows what the markers we left mean, but hard enough for any numpty to find. I confirm that my 9mm is still within reach and out of view before walking deeper into Hyde looking for the meeting point.

As we navigate the streets, our footsteps echo against the worn pavement. Every person we pass stares in our direction; unsure if this is to do with five strangers walking through their town or the fact that we are covered in mud.

Continue for another 15 minutes before I stop and glance at the map, indicating we must turn left down the next road on the right. It's a narrow street with beige stone-coloured houses lining one side. Some residents sit in the doorways dressed in old t-shirts and ripped trousers. On the other, the local market with several stalls selling fresh produce, from vegetables to fish caught by the local fishermen. Beyond them, on the beach, are rows of traditionally painted fishing boats in a multitude of colours.

This appears like the poor part of town, so I'm not surprised when an old gentleman wrapped in what can only be called rags walks out between the stalls, trying to sell me a fish. Either that or he is a good businessman who doesn't want to miss an opportunity for a sale.

Stop and turn around to witness Lucy handing him money for the fish, "What the fuck are you going to do with that, Lucy," laughing out loud.

"Not got a fucking clue yet. Probably give it to the next local who looks hungry," she says, smiling.

Ahead of us is a small crossroads. The location for the meeting should be on this corner. From here, we must move carefully, so indicate the rest to follow me onto the beach.

Once we locate a suitable place where we can not be overheard, "Right, the bar is just up here. Lucy and I will go inside to meet Tennille while you locate some spot out of view; keep an eye out for any cartel people who might enter after us. We can communicate with the earpiece radios."

"I'll take the road behind if anyone comes that way."

"Good idea, Derek. I will leave it up to you two to find a good location," I point at Simon and George.

Give it a few minutes before leaving for the Forest Retreat, a rundown bar notorious for its illicit dealing, according to the brief given to us by Bear as one of the possible meeting points with Tennille.

About 10 feet away when a group of men emerge from the front door, their faces obscured by the shade given off by the building. From what I can see, they are carrying weapons. They make a half-hearted effort to hide them but stick out like a dog at a cat show.

We wait until they stagger off down the street and out of our line of sight. Then, without saying a word, we enter the Forest Retreat, our pistols out of view but ready in case we need them.

The Forest Retreat is awash in shadows, and the scent of cedar and smoke hits your nostrils when you walk in. The tavern goes almost silent as I scan the room, looking for Tennille. A lone patron sits at the long wooden counter clutching his gin and tonic. For some reason, I can't shake the sensation that Lucy and I are being watched. Keeping our composure, we make our way to the back, where the room curves into alcoves, half in darkness.

Not seeing what we hope for, we purchase two drinks, stand in one of the alcoves, and monitor the doorway to see if anybody followed us inside. After we are confident nobody did, we head upstairs.

On the veranda at the far end of the bar, a ray of light lands on a woman's face. In front of her, I can make out three empty glasses on a square table covered with a red and white chequered tablecloth. The signal is that this is the person we are here to meet. She is an older woman in her mid-40s, a little overweight for her height, around five feet six inches. Tennille sits on a teak-coloured stool, staring into her bulky-looking laptop.

I sit facing her, while Lucy monitors the situation from the other side of the room.

Wait until Tennille glances up, "What's the plan?" as I lean against the backrest of the chair. Tennille reaches for her drink and sips as she scrolls through some data on her computer.

"From what my sources tell me, the people you are to bring out of the rainforest are still being held in the camp," says Tennille.

"That is good news," I say, leaning in closer. "Do you have the new location, or is it in the same place? Bear said you can update us," I say, peering over her computer.

"Yes, they haven't moved the base of operations yet. Some information has come to my attention. They are planning a move sometime in the next two weeks. So, you only have a short time frame to rescue them."

At that moment, Tennille's phone rings, and she frowns as she answers it—a sense of dread twists in my gut.

Tennille finishes her call and then glances up. "Something is wrong. We have an issue. Aron, the cartel leader, is visiting his men for a week," she says, putting the telephone down on the table.

"Is that going to be a problem?"

"Not for me, but for you; it means he will travel with his bodyguards, a group of ex-government forces. About six of them, I believe."

"How many people are guarding the prisoners now?" I ask.

"At present, there are only around 9 or 10 guards at the place, but as I said, in a few days, you will have additional men to deal with, and these are ruthless people who will shoot anyone just because their boss says so."

"Three final questions before I leave, Tennille."

"Can you give me that up-to-date map you have half-tucked under your laptop, and are any roads or trails that will assist us in arriving at a point closer to the camp quicker?"

She takes another long sip of her drink, closes the computer and pulls out the map.

"Thought you may ask that, so I've marked a route for you, along with a derelict home about two kilometres away from where the hostages are being held. You might want to make the most of this place as a springboard for whatever you have planned."

"Next question, how do we know we can trust you, and you will not update Aron of our movements?"

"I'll just say this, Steve: Ana, one of the hostages, is a family friend. What's your third question?"

"You can probably guess from the aroma, I stink. Do you know anywhere in Hyde where I can shower?"

Tennille laughs, "You're right. Wait here for a few minutes, and I'll ask my sister, who runs this bar if you and your unit can use her facilities."

"Thanks."

With that, she stands up and walks downstairs. Now that she is out of the way, I approach Lucy.

"You catch all that."

"To get our arses moving, rescue these people ASAP. But after the shower," sniffing her armpits.

About to give up on the hose down when Tennille reappears, "Spoken to Gabriella, she says she has a few rooms round the back they rent to tourists. You and your team can use the showers here."

"Thank you," I follow her down and around the back of the bar. The moment Tennille leaves, I call everyone to join me.

About 50 feet from the primary building are two square stone-built structures painted white with one vast window overlooking the gardens. Inside is basic, with a double bed in the middle of the room flanked by two small cupboards. Over in the corner is a set of drawers matching the rest of the decor. More importantly, as far as we are concerned, a separate room houses the refreshing shower we all badly need.

Within a few minutes, everyone joins me in the first of the two rooms. "Suggest that at least one of us stands outside as a lookout, just in case friends of Aron show up."

"Good idea, Steve. If you take the first one, that means Lucy can have a shower in peace."

"Thanks, Simon. You heard the man, Steve, off you pop, go on stag," Lucy replies, heading towards the shower.

"Not a problem, but remember not to use any scented soaps in the shower. Don't want anyone smelling like a whore's armpit and giving away our locations," I reply.

Plonk my arse down on a battered old wooden bench at the end of the garden facing the exit. Take the time to start formulating a route and plan to get us to the next RV, which will be the rundown house Tennille mentioned. The planning for entry can wait until we are closer and get our eyes on the building. Now, I need to concentrate on getting us there.

The idea of the ATV is a good one, but since Simon came up with it, a few questions have been rolling around in that space between my ears.

First, for all we know, Jayden could have said something without thinking, to be overheard by someone connected with our friendly drug cartel. They could now be waiting for us to show up.

Second, this is a bike tour company, and they are bound to have trackers on them. Again, if thugs from Aron's lot put pressure on the owners, they will soon find out where we are and might set up an ambush.

Our safest option will be to continue trekking, this time following a route close to the road that, according to the map, goes more or less straight to where we need to be. With that in mind, getting to the house should take another day.

At this point, Lucy walks over and sits beside me, "Go on, stinky boy, grab a shower. I'll take over until the boys come out."

The lush, warm water cascades over my body, releasing the tension and aches from the last two days. I feel some weight lifting as the caked-on mud dissolves off me and runs down the drain. I could easily stay here for the next few minutes, enjoying the moment, but I hear the door of the bathroom opening.

"Come on, Steve. You don't have that much of you to wash. Besides, more than four strokes of your dick is classed as a wank, and that's my... job," says Lucy, holding a towel.

Take the towel from her and walk naked into the other room. Lucy is lying spreadeagled on the bed. Standing in the middle of the room, drying my hair, she clambers off the bed and walks over and grabs my cock, "Shame we don't have time for this, but we need to make a move," she says.

There is no better sensation when on a mission than getting a shower halfway through, even if you're wearing the same dirty clothes. So refreshed, I grab my gear and return to the garden to rejoin Derek and Simon.

A few minutes later, George and Lucy come out to join us. "The good news is, the next RV is only days away...."

"Come on then, let's have the bad news," enquires Simon.

"The ATV idea of yours was a good one, but thinking it through, we are faced with too many risks," I outline my concerns.

"Fair one, mate. We better go back and collect our equipment and start walking," comes Simon's reply.

To keep confusing anybody who might have been observing us, we take a different route back to our weapons dump, moving carefully through the deserted streets of the old town of Hyde.

The dilapidated buildings loom overhead, casting long shadows across our path; all the time, we keep our eyes peeled for any signs of danger. We had already encountered several armed guards leaving the Forest Retreat, so we know drug cartels are in the area.

Soon, we are at the edge of the rainforest, after pausing for a few minutes to watch and listen for any sounds different from the usual sound of birds, insects or the wind blowing through the trees.

Hopefully, none of Arons's men are in the vicinity. But if, for any reason, anyone is near the arms stash, we must take them by surprise. With that in mind, Lucy, Derek and I take one way in while Simon and George take another route about 50 metres away.

The tension is intense as we edge closer to our destination; moving with stealth, acting like ghosts, blending into the shadows as we progress. Every time we detect any noise, we freeze, communicating with hand signals.

Two armed men appear about 100 metres away, scouring the forest for something. Shit, are they looking for us or our weapons? Whatever they are trying to find, we can't take the chance. Place my hand on my head, signalling the other two to close in on my location.

In a whisper, "We have people near our kit. You make your way around to the other side, Derek. I will approach from here if you take the right, Lucy."

Without another word, we move into position and then wait a few minutes for everyone to be ready.

Take my pistol out from my jacket, and then, with one movement, I leap up and rush the person in front of me. Before he has time to react, I fire two quick shots, the second hitting him in the face. He drops to the floor, blood spurting in all directions as he falls.

Turn to charge at the next one when Derek emerges from the undergrowth and kills the other with a single shot. With adrenalin still pumping about my body, I scan the clearing to confirm that the area is clear.

"Think that is all of them," I say to Derek as he approaches.

I am about to put my 9mm away when a third attacker springs from under a bunch of green foliage behind Lucy and swings his arm around her neck, gripping her tight while putting a pistol to her head. This isn't Lucy's first time in this situation, so she plays compliant.

When I move closer, I can see the attacker's eyes glinting eerily in the light and a wicked, twisted smile spreads across his face as he pushes his weapon hard against Lucy's head.

"Come with me, and don't make a sound," he whispers into Lucy's ear, his voice dripping with malice. His only thought is getting out of there alive, forcing Lucy to walk deeper into the rainforest back towards the town.

"You harm her in any way, there is no place on earth where you will not suffer unbearable pain before you die," I yell, as I ease my way towards him.

I sense Derek grab my arm, "Wait for a sec… look to your left," he whispers.

Off to my left, a glint of metal catches my eye as George emerges from the shadows about 40 feet away, his pistol drawn and pointing straight at the foe.

Uttering a warning growl, the attacker raises their weapon for a second, then moves away step by step, creating a deadly standoff.

For a few tense moments, the air becomes electrified, and the accompanying sounds of the rainforest appear quiet as George and the man holding Lucy stand their ground, each waiting for the other to move.

Then, the sound of a single gunshot emanates from the skies. The aggressor collapses to the floor with a gaping hole in the right side of his head, releasing Lucy as his limp body slumps to the deck.

Even though the man is dead, I empty two rounds in his head. Turn to face George, "Cheers, mate, a good shot."

"That's why we have snipers in the team," replies George, walking over to retrieve his kit from the stash.

At the same time, Simon searches the man for any information that might come in handy for the rescue. In the man's jacket pocket is a large envelope, which Simon passes to me. Inside is a sketch of the layout and location of the camp. But why would he have this, unless he has some authority among the group? What I pull out next has me going numb as I freeze, motionless.

"What's the issue, Steve?" says George, coming over.

While shaking my head, I hand him a white envelope with a blue line running from top to bottom near the left edge.

"Not those fuckers again. One day, we are going to have to wipe these people out. Come take a gander at this, Simon," states George, getting angry.

For the benefit of Derek and Lucy, I explain that this type of envelope has kept popping up since our job on Saint Halb and is connected to Henry and his family of drug dealers.

Once all the equipment has been retrieved and everyone is ready to leave, "Folks, Aron and his men might know we are in the vicinity and coming, but the big question is, did they find out we are in this area, or are they just lucky? If they did, who told them?"

"Sure we will find out soon enough, Steve."

"You're right there, Derek. Better make a move, as we need to be at the camp to rescue Ana and James, and we only have a few days to do it, in case they try to relocate them, and they know we are here."

I lead everyone back into the forest, heading for the road Tennille had pointed out on the map.

Chapter Six – The Camp

Meanwhile, at the location, Ana and James are being held hostage, the dense jungle is a surging wall of green, swaying in a fierce wind that screams through the area. The sun beats down without mercy upon the makeshift prison campsite.

A helicopter lands outside the perimeter fence in a thunderous roar of dust and gravel. Stepping out from the rear door, Aron, a man of few words who conveys an aura of power. It took him only a few years to make his way up to the ranks. From a foot soldier at 16, he quickly became an enforcer before moving up to running part of the organisation. By age 25, he evolved into one of the most infamous drug lords in the Caribbean.

Aron has arrived, bringing his entourage of ex-special forces bodyguards, sleek and dangerous as a pit of vipers, to his makeshift prison in the heart of the tropical rainforest. Surrounded by dense foliage and the calls of wild animals, a six-foot barbed wire fence encloses the base.

After a brief stop to talk to the two men carrying AK-47s standing at the main entrance, he proceeds to a large building made of the same material as the rest of the camp, bamboo, just to the left of the compound and enters.

Inside is basic and consists of a sitting area containing several old brown leather sofas, looking worse for wear, and a table. Off to the right is an improvised kitchen with dirty, used cups and plates. At the far end of the room is a wooden desk and chair on which sits a woman in her late 20s, dressed in a beige top. In front of her is an AK-47 and a plastic bag containing white powder.

The moment Aron enters, everyone in the room rises to their feet. "It's OK, everybody, relax," Aron says, walking to a separate room at the back. This is his private room; nobody dares go in there when he isn't there because of the fear of reprisal.

In contrast to the other room, this one has a brand-new green leather couch along the back of the room next to a teak cabinet on which several crystal decanters of whisky sit. Plus, there is an array of other bottles of spirits.

A vast dark mahogany desk with a red felt top inlay is up against the far wall. Behind that is a plush executive chair. To the left is a five-foot high biometric safe that needs Arons's fingerprint to open.

With Aron is Ryan, his right-hand man, an ex-special forces officer. His job in the outfit is to carry out any executions Aron requires and maintain discipline and order in the camp.

When they are alone in the room, "Close the door and take a seat," indicating with his arm for Ryan to sit on the sofa.

"What's on your mind, boss?"

"After we complete the inspection and put the frighteners on the hostages, you need to ensure the men receive their wages," walking over to the safe and placing his right index finger on the control pad.

With the door open, Ryan can see piles of 100 dollar notes filling the bottom three shelves. Each bundle contains $10,000. With both hands, Aron removes five bundles and gives them to Ryan.

"Can you sort this, please? I must make a few calls to the families of our guests to inform them they have two weeks to pay up, or you will execute one of them every four days," states Aron, moving back to his desk.

"No problem. When do you want to do a walkabout?" Ryan replies.

"Might as well do it now. Better make the cannabis stash our first stop. Want to make sure none of our people have been robbing me."

Walking around the compound, Aron scans the camp, looking for any weaknesses - nothing escapes his trained eye, not even the tiniest flaw- with Ryan by his side, silent in the shadows, watching everything happening, including how the men act and behave.

The store is inside the perimeter fence under the front left watchtower for security reasons. Standing outside are two men with rifles across their shoulders. One is smoking, the red glowing end moving up and down after each drag. When he witnesses Aron and Ryan approach, he throws it to the floor, stamping it out with his right boot.

"Open the door," Ryan barks.

One man fidgets with the keys, walks to the 40-foot container, and opens the door. Aron takes time to talk to the other one.

"How are you? Are you getting down to Hyde much? "

The man responds, "I'm doing OK, thanks. I was down there a couple of days ago and went to the Forest Retreat with four others for some beers. "

"Glad to hear that. Ryan will pay all of you before we leave later this week," says Aron.

On his way to the top, he learned to look after the people working for him; that way, you're less likely to be shot or stabbed while you sleep. Of course, that didn't work for his last boss, as this is how he came to run the outfit.

The container contains two banks of metal shelving from floor to ceiling, running the entire length on both sides. Each shelf has several blocks of cannabis, each wrapped in hessian and weighing one kilo, with a street value of over $7,000.

Within, Aron strolls along the rows, stopping every couple of feet and checking that there are no empty spaces, indicating someone is robbing the organisation he has built up over time.

When he gets to the end, he spins around and makes his way back, examining the other side.

He turns to Ryan, standing in the doorway, "When is the next batch due out?"

"Sometime today."

"Excellent. I want to talk to the transportation guys when they arrive," Aron replies.

Once the container is secure, they head to the watchtower along the back fence to speak with the people there. After a brief conversation, their attention turns to the men's accommodation.

There are a total of four buildings within the perimeter. Two are the guard's lodging, one is the canteen, and the other is where the hostages are held. All are built using local materials, with the walls and roofs constructed from bamboo and lined with large leaves from palm trees, which grow in abundance in the area.

Inside the first of the guard's quarters are several improvised beds with the guy's kit thrown across the blankets. At one end is a table complete with wooden chairs, on which sits empty beer cans and the remains of last night's dinner. A small opening on one wall lets in the natural light.

The canteen building isn't much bigger than the other rooms. One half contains the kitchen, where a woman dressed in chef's whites is stirring something in a large metal saucepan on top of a four-ring gas stove. Around her are several counters full of cooking ingredients and equipment.

"So what do the men have to eat tonight?" Ryan asks.

"We have cooked green bananas with rice and chicken. Followed by fresh fruit salad," the chef replies.

"I'll be having some of that."

One thing Ryan brought with him from his time in the military was that if you keep the men's morale up with good food and an excellent place to rest,they are more likely to fight when it comes to it and not run away the moment the first round is fired. They are doing both, so he has a fighting unit ready to take any required action.

At the other end of the room are two six-foot tables with long wooden benches on either side. Several bottles of hot pepper sauce are sitting on them, along with a box containing eating implements.

With the camp inspection over, it's time to check on the four people being held captive. Aron and Ryan stroll over to the final building.

As Aron and Ryan approach them, the hostages can only scrutinise their every move, praying for a miracle to free them from their imprisonment.

Ana, James, along with Eliza and Ralf have been in captivity for two months. They had been handed over to their captures by a corrupt customs official, whom the cartel paid for each person they sent to the cartel.

Since they have been here, Ana and James had nothing to do but reflect on why they had agreed to smuggle a small quantity of drugs through the airport. It wasn't because they needed the money. Their families are wealthy, and they had plenty of cash when stopped.

If they were honest with themselves, it probably had more to do with the thrill, and believing they knew how to beat the system after watching several airport security programmes on television.

They didn't know how the officers knew they were carrying illegal narcotics. The moment they approached customs, they were taken to one side. Suppose somebody had set them up, but who was it, and why?

Eliza and Ralf were in the same predicament. They had also been stitched up and asked to take some drugs to a man on the island. They were promised 5,000 dollars each for bringing it in and handing it to someone they would meet in a café in the town of Hyde.

The four are being held in a tiny 10-foot square room constructed of bamboo, with only blankets to sleep on, and are provided with a small ration of food twice a day. They are surrounded by guards that proclaim their contempt for them on a daily basis. They are all stuck in a damp and rotting room, huddling together, trying to stay dry and warm during the cold nights. The harsh conditions are taking a toll on them, with their health and spirits deteriorating fast.

In the distance, the town of Hyde glimmers like a faint beacon of hope. A full day's walk away. For them, it might as well have been on another planet. They are cut off from the world, trapped in the heart of the dense rainforest, at the mercy of their captors' whims.

Through the ambient noise of the camp, the four can hear the thud of boots becoming louder as each step along the bamboo veranda gets closer to the small room where they are being held. Moments later, the door is flung open. Two men carrying weapons are in the doorway, shouting for them to follow them outside. James is the first to exit. The moment he does, he is seized by the back of his collar and tossed out the door, losing his balance and landing on his knees. Once Ana is out, she helps him to stand up, and they walk into the yard; following a few steps behind are Eliza and Ralf.

They are now standing in the middle of a bare, open area, brown soil beneath their feet. The bright sun is hurting their eyes as this is the first time they've been outside for a month, apart from one person emptying the shit bucket each morning. The room they are in doesn't have any natural or other light, apart from a sliver of light through a crack in the bamboo. Their faces are pale in the glow of the merciless sun.

Aron shoots a vicious glare; his eyes narrow as he surveys the prisoners, shuffling toward him as they line up in the centre of the yard in front of him. This is the person who, at this instant, has the power over the life or death of the hostages.

Without saying a word, he strolls around them, scrutinising each of them, watching their movements as they stand, shaking with pure fear. His breathing is low and harsh. For an awful moment, the four believe he is choosing who will live and who won't.

The tension grows unbearable as Ryan ambles towards the prisoners and brandishes his weapon, pointing at each of them. They know better than to make eye contact. The last time one of them did, they received a rifle butt to the stomach, so they avoid even the slightest interaction.

Tears run down Eliza's face, believing her time has come, and whispers the Lord's Prayer to herself as Ryan rests his rifle on her forehead. A few agonising moments pass as she waits her turn to die. Then Ryan lowers his firearm and walks back over to Aron, who's been watching the whole thing play out with a vast smile.

At that moment, a green Land Rover drives into the compound and stops before Aron. A well-dressed man in a grey suit wearing a hessian sack that covers his head is thrown from the back, landing in a shitty heap on the floor. His hands are bound with a nylon rope behind his back. Two men lift him, drag him over to Ryan, and force him onto his knees.

The man, trembling, says, "One more week, and you'll have all your money. Don't kill me."

"Why shouldn't I? Give me one good reason, and you may live," says Ryan, giving the man some false hope.

"I will have what I owe you for the last drug shipment in seven days. You kill me, and you will not get anything, and my people will start a war on your cartel." His smugness starts to come through, believing he is winning the battle for his life.

"Fair point," says Ryan, walking until he stands a foot away from the man, his pistol outstretched in his right hand.

Then, without warning, a gunshot echoes through the forest as Ryan squeezes the trigger and puts a bullet into the man's head. His body slumps to the ground, blood oozing through the sack and seeping onto the floor.

The two people who brought him here dragged the dead man back to the vehicle.

The four hostages crowd together, shaking with dread and bracing themselves for what might come next. Yet, instead of executing them, Ryan shouts, "Back inside! Now!"

They flinch, imagining the worst, fear forcing them to obey. They understand Aron and his men are unpredictable and have just witnessed it first-hand, and they don't dare test their limits. Once back in their cell, they huddle in a single mass of bodies, listening as the guards grow quieter with each passing moment.

And then silence. No footsteps, no orders being shouted, nothing. The hostages crouch on the floor, tense and frantic, trying to listen for any sign of what is occurring outside.

They detect more shouting, screams, and the unmistakable sound of another gunshot from their cell. Something is happening. They scramble towards the peephole in the bamboo wall, straining to see what is occurring outside. But the only thing visible is their captures moving around the camp, a chaotic scene that they can't decipher. The hostages cling onto each other, in the hope that their torment will end someday.

Over at the front watchtower, the man on guard had seen a wild boar come out of the rainforest and shot and killed it with a single bullet. Its dead, limp body is now lying in the foliage, blood oozing from the small hole to the right side of its head. Two men are running around to collect it before something big and hairy emerges from the forest and takes it away. This unfortunate animal will be tonight's feast.

In the meantime, Aron and Ryan have walked back to the drugstore and are watching the operation of checking the drugs for shipment, ready to be loaded into a truck when it arrives. His men are preparing a massive shipment of narcotics that will soon be heading to distribution points worldwide.

They all go about their business in silence, checking the product quality by sampling bundles from the store at random, ready to be shipped out. The aroma is overwhelming, a pungent mix of chemicals and sweet perfume.

Five guards surround them. The drugs are in the open, making them vulnerable to rival gangs and law enforcement raiding the camp. The cartel's profits will be astronomical, but only if everything goes according to plan.

Just because they are in the heart of a tropical rainforest, a land of fertile trees and the sound of the forest all-encompassing, with monkeys chittering in the distance, they can't lower their guard, even in this tranquil place.

In the distance comes the sound of an approaching vehicle cutting through the cacophony of the forest. Aron turns and faces the main gate, to see a truck coming down the dirt path towards them. The vehicle moves with caution as it approaches the two men standing on either side of the entrance.

With its canvas cover over the cargo area, the three-ton lorry pulls up and stops for a few seconds before the guards recognise him and open the gates. The driver drives up to where Aron and

Ryan are standing and halts. From it emerges a man they know well; it's Paco, the head of the distribution arm of Aron's cartel, responsible for the worldwide dispersal of the drug cartel's products. He approaches Aron.

"What took you so long?" Aron asks, his voice low and menacing.

Not flinching a muscle, "I had to be careful; as you know, we are not the only ones who operate in this business."

Aron nods. "True enough, Paco, you have never failed to deliver."

The truck is backed up close to the store, so the drugs don't have to be out in the open for an extended period, just in case the local authorities are flying a drone in the area on the lookout for cannabis plants growing in the vicinity. The rainforest protects them from the air, but the cover isn't 100 per cent.

Everyone turns their attention to the work at hand. The product is loaded, and every package is moved carefully so none is split while loading. It's a delicate operation, but the cartel's reputation depends on going off without a hitch.

Finally, the last packet is in the back of the truck. Just before he leaves, Paco passes over a brown leather briefcase to Aron, then jumps back in his vehicle and drives off, rumbling down the dirt path he came in on and out of site.

"They will be onboard the cargo ship heading for America by nightfall," says Ryan, catching up with Aron as he walks back to the main building outside the gate.

"More important, my friend, we have this," he lifts the case in his hand.

'No need to ask what is inside', Ryan thinks. He already knows — cash from the last shipment.

In Arons's private office, he ensures the door is secure before putting the briefcase on the desk and opening it. Within are bundles of used 100-dollar bills. Takes the counting machine from the shelf to ensure all the money is there, and starts placing each stack through to both count and check that no forgeries are hidden among them. He's been at this game far too long to take someone's word.

Once everything checks out, he turns to Ryan, sitting on the couch sipping on a glass of whisky he took from the drinks cabinet. "It's been a good week. Better get this in the safe before we discuss what we will do with our prisoners."

With the money secure, Aron sits opposite Ryan after fixing himself a drink.

"So what is the latest? Have the relatives been in contact and arranged payment for their return, or do we start executing them one at a time until the message sinks in?" asks Ryan.

"Two of the families have agreed on a sum. We are waiting for the bank transfer to be completed. This will be concluded by the end of the week," says Aron, between sips of his whisky.

"Are we going to let the other two go when we have the funds, or will we kill them anyway?" asks Ryan.

"We should hand Eliza and Ralf over when we receive the money. This will send the others a message: there is some hope that their loved ones will be allowed to go free. You can shoot them where they stand if they don't pay up. Doesn't bother me either way."

At that moment, there is a knock at the door, and a voice calls out, "I have your dinner, boss."

With the door unlocked, two men carry two large trays piled high with cooked meat, rice, and fresh vegetables. All are prepared by a first-class chef. Aron keeps her on his payroll and she travels with him, cooking all his meals. He doesn't do this out of kindness to the woman. It has more to do with him knowing his food is safe and hasn't been poisoned.

After the meal has been laid out on the mahogany table with the silver tableware, they sit down to eat. One man stays behind to serve them fine wine. As the glasses empty, he tops their glass when required before backing off and standing with his back to the wall.

Back over in the bamboo structure holding the hostages, the four detect the sound of footsteps getting closer. Seconds later, they stop outside the door. The hostages freeze, their hearts pounding with fear, remembering what occurred earlier in the yard. The door creaks open.

A man shouts, "Chow time, pigs," while opening the door a tad and sliding two large wooden bowls across the floor. One contains cooked rice, the other chicken, and several water bottles.

As the days go by, they all begin to feel the effects of their imprisonment. Their stomachs growl with hunger; their throats crack from dehydration, due to the hot temperature inside their prison cell from the scorching sun, high in the sky. Even though the food is terrible, they have no choice but to eat whatever comes their way.

Not having any cutlery like they are accustomed to at home, the four have become skilled at eating with their hands. Even in this environment, they must maintain hygiene standards to help stop them from becoming ill. This is the last thing they need as they fear that rather than give them medicines, they will kill them instead.

To this end, every person scoops out a little of each and places it on the floor before them, after using a little water to clean the area.

Once their meals have been eaten, there is nothing to do but sit in the near darkness. The only light source comes from a couple of slits in the bamboo. With the unsanitary conditions, they were handed one bucket to use as a toilet, which they can only empty every morning, so, the aroma of urine and faeces hangs thick in the air.

They wrap themselves up in the thin blankets given to them when they arrived, hoping they are still alive tomorrow and rescue comes soon. Especially for Eliza, her health is starting to fade faster than the rest. She does her best to disguise it when the guards are around, but the time will come when she can't hide it anymore.

A magical transformation begins as the sun starts to dip below the horizon. Earlier bright green and vibrant forest floor turns a deep shade of blue, as the ominous presence of twilight replaces the ever-dwindling light. The once-bustling canopy now takes on a unique and mystical aura, the flickering lights of hundreds of industrious creatures gradually fading into obscurity.

As the sunlight fades, the sky is awash with hues of crimson and orange, as if fire dances in the heavens. At the same time, the sounds of the rainforest crescendo into a symphony of life. There is a gentle rustling of leaves as they catch the breeze.

Animals settle in for the night, while the low hum of insects fills the air, as if the surroundings are taking a deep breath and slowly releasing it. Crickets chirp, adding a soothing element to the tropical soundtrack, their repetitive song almost lulling you into a trance. In the distance, a whoop of a monkey breaks the silence, shattering the illusion of serenity.

As the last light filters through the trees, it casts a warm glow, highlighting the intricate details of the tree's leaves and the vibrant hues of the delicate flowers. The canopy becomes a kaleidoscope of greens and yellows as the sun's rays penetrate the maze of foliage.

As twilight turns to darkness, the rainforest evolves into a stage illuminated only by the glimmer of the stars and the moon. The dark cloaks the forest in mystery, making it almost impossible to see beyond your immediate surroundings. The cacophony of sounds continues as the nighttime creatures come out to play. The buzz of an insect, the low rumble of distant thunder, and the unmistakable sound of green monkeys fill the air.

As though the rainforest is alive, breathing in time with the rhythm of the night, past the lush greenery and enchanting symphony lies a more profound beauty – the rainforest's ability to sustain life. This magical place hosts countless species of plants and animals that have adapted to survive in this harsh yet nurturing environment.

Chapter Seven – Windover Cottage

Last night went without a hitch; after disassembling the RV and ensuring no signs of our presence at the location, we set off for our next objective.

Today is one of the hottest days we have experienced on the island. The sun is beating down on the overgrown rainforest. The humidity is almost suffocating. Sweat drips down our faces and soaks through our clothes as we trudge through the dense undergrowth. Today's mission is to hike towards an abandoned building on a hillside overlooking the drug cartel's camp.

As we hike, the tropical forest provides endless greens, browns, and yellows, with tall trees covered in vines and lush vegetation. Everyone does their best to stay cool in their heavy gear, and not slow down the pace. We move faster now, our gait quickening as we sense we are running out of time for the rescue to be successful to grab Ana and James. We know there is no choice but to reach Windover Cottage by nightfall.

After hours of hiking along the muddy rainforest floor, there is suddenly a distinct aroma of hemp wafting through the air, being carried on by the gentle breeze coming across the valley. We ease off on the pace, listening for any signs of trouble.

What we catch sight of a short distance away stops us in our tracks. To our front is a massive field of tall marijuana plants with easily recognisable jagged leaves. An array of green, yellow, orange and purple flowers are lined up in neat rows stretching as far as my eyes can see. The scene looks serene, with the sun shining on the bushy crop.

But our initial fascination quickly turns into dread as we realise the area must be tendered to by individuals linked to Aron's notorious drug cartel. Being so near our day's objective, the last thing we need now is to be seen.

From the periphery of the treeline where we have taken cover, in the distance, patrolling along the edge of the fields, a group of five people make their way towards us, stopping now and again while one person checks inside the woods.

Shit, if we stay here, there is a good chance we might be spotted. Signal the team to close up on my position, by placing my hand on my head.

Once everyone is together, "Take a gander to the other side of the field, a body of men is closing in on our location. Due to their proximity to the crop across the track, they must be part of Aron's drug cartel, protecting their assets. We have several options: Go back into the forest and risk making a noise; there is a good chance they will detect our movement. Or hide in the dip in the ground about 100 metres to our front among the marijuana and hope the patrol wouldn't spot us."

"Agree. Our best bet is in the field," says George.

"We don't have time to cross one at a time, so all go together, keeping a short space between us."

Crouch low with our heads below the height of the crop. We sprint across to the depression in the undulating land. Once there, we press our bodies against the stems of the fragrant plants. We try to obtain as much cover as we can underneath the foliage. You can feel the sticky sap on your exposed skin. Praying we won't be discovered, not that we would run from any battle, but for the sake of the mission and a surprise attack on the camp, we must stay hidden.

Not long before the patrol approaches our location, the sound of boots crunching on the dirt gets closer. The team hold their breath, hearts pounding, trying to remain as still and invisible as possible.

Seconds later, one of the cartel's patrolmen stops abruptly, his gaze sweeping across the field.

The situation is intense, as we all prepare for the fight that might come our way, but we hope it doesn't. Several minutes pass until the man turns his back and rejoins the group, and we all breathe a silent sigh of relief. This is short-lived, as once more the same person spins around again, his suspicion piqued. He is now walking deliberately towards the team's location, his rifle in the firing position.

Only one thing for it. We remain motionless. He is a mere few feet away. I can hear his breaths coming in shallow, sharp bursts. If he gets any closer, we might have to break cover, tackle him to the deck, and silence him.

Time appears to stand still, waiting to see how events play out. Our luck must be in as he comes to a halt, turns, and re-joins the rest of his patrol, now about 200 metres away, further down the edge of the field.

Stay where we are until they are gone from our view before heading back into the woods, going a short distance, and then stopping close to a clearing among the trees. The only sounds to be heard are the forest's chorus of birds and insects.

From here, I take a bearing. The direct route takes us straight through the crops. We can't take it, as we will be discovered this way. The only alternative is to skirt along the edge of the field, keeping just inside the treeline for cover. Make a snap decision to go the way the patrol came from, assuming they will not return that way for some time.

Signal for the team to follow as I lead off again, heading for our objective. After an hour of moving with stealth around the marijuana fields, we are back on our original bearing. Sixty minutes later, once clear of any signs of Aron's people, we stop for a well-earned break close to a fast-running stream.

"Take a quick 10 minutes, folks," I say, dumping my Bergen on the ground.

The rest do the same, dropping their kit before removing water bottles and drinking the contents, then refilling them from the creek through their filtering systems.

"How much further?" asks Lucy, who has joined me.

Take the splash map from my jacket pocket, shake off the access water and orientate it to the terrain. "We are only a few clicks away now, so we will be there soon. I can't wait to arrive at the house and pour some coffee down my neck."

"With you on that one, honey," says Lucy.

"As we are stopped, we might as well go through a quick outline of how we enter Windover Cottage to ensure we aren't surprised. Just in case some of Arons's people are inside."

"So, what's the plan, Steve?" asks George, coming over to join Lucy and me.

"Normal standard operating procedures, mate. You will protect us from a vantage point once we locate it, and give cover while we four go in and clear the gaff.

"After the area is cleared, we will set up camp there and rest before planning to recce the target to collect more info on the base, how it's guarded, etc. We will communicate via the radio."

"Sounds like some sort of a plan, Steve. I suggest we make a move. It gets dark here early, remember, and George can't see fuck all; never mind lay down protective fire if needed when we require it," says Simon, picking up his pack.

After another hour of trekking through the forest, we arrive at a point where our objective is not too far away in the distance. After the near miss in the field, everyone is vigilant as we approach the abandoned Windover Cottage, only two kilometres from the camp.

"Remember, the enemy could be hiding inside, waiting for us to make a mistake," I remind everyone.

As we push through the dense, green foliage, the sounds of exotic birds and insects fill our ears. When we stumble upon a clearing, the long-forsaken house is in the midst of it.

Stop on top of a ridge that overlooks the property. The rainforest appears to encircle the grounds. From here, we scrutinise the area, looking for any movements in or around the target area. A quick scan confirms that the best place for a sniper is where we are.

"This seems to be an excellent location for you to set up your position, George," dropping my equipment, which will be a hindrance during the house clearance.

The rest do the same while George sets up. We will return for the stuff later when we are sure there isn't anybody about.

To make things worse for the approach, the rain starts to pelt down, making the leaves rustle and the undergrowth squelch with each step the team take. This is useful in one way, as it hides the sounds of us trudging through the dense foliage. It is harmful in another way, as the rainfall will also conceal any noise anyone makes.

Once George is ready, we divide into pairs: Lucy and me forming one team while Simon and Derek make up the other and advance towards the cottage. We need the element of surprise in case some arsehole is waiting for us, so move with the agility and grace of panthers on the hunt. As we approach the building, we scan the area for hidden traps or people lurking in the shadows. Every step is taken with caution, each breath steady and measured. Any mistake now could get someone killed.

Entering the grounds, you can see the white-washed walls have been battered by years of exposure to the elements, causing the paint to peel and flake away. Ivy and creeping vines have wrapped their tendrils around the weathered wooden boards, seeking any crack or crevice to wedge their way into the interior.

Once sturdy and thatched with palm leaves, the roof has long since caved in, leaving only fragments of the leaves scattered on the ground.

Outside, the surrounding vegetation encroaches on the space, rendering it almost invisible. Small gardening tools lay rusted and discarded, a child's broken toy car is half-buried under some nearby ferns, and a garden path, now overgrown with plants and weeds, leads to the side of the cottage.

As you step closer, the aroma of must and decay hits your nose. The air is thick with the scent of saturated wood and damp earth. The door is wedged open, hanging on a single hinge, allowing us to peek inside looking for any signs suggesting human life may have been here in the recent past.

The cottage's interior is dark, with shadows cast by the trees above. Cobwebs cling to the room's corners, and the musty odour overwhelms you. The few remaining pieces of furniture lay in ruins all around, covered in a thick layer of dust and debris. Mould has overtaken the structure in some areas, adding to the feel of decay. The sound of tiny creatures can be heard underfoot, scurrying for cover as we move into the dim space.

Despite the state of the building, there is a sense of curiosity that it invokes. Perhaps the cottage was somebody's home long ago, with stories and secrets still hidden inside the abandoned walls. It's plain to see that this little place that was once loved and cared for is now surpassed by the untamed wilderness. We pause, feeling a twinge of regret for the once vibrant respite that now stands desolate and forgotten amongst the rainforest's verdant beauty.

At first, the house clearing is uneventful, but the tension increases as we move deeper into the building. The creaking of floorboards, the whisper of footsteps, and the sound of heartbeats pounding in our ears feels amplified in the silence.

From inside a room on the lower floor, I catch a glimpse of movement out of the corner of my eye. I freeze instantly before indicating to Lucy that I have spotted something or someone, by pointing to my eyes with two fingers and then showing the direction I'd seen something with my left arm.

From the shadows of the corridor, Lucy covers me. At the same time, I move forward cautiously until I have wholly entered the room, where a single occupant about five feet seven inches tall with long black dreadlocks in blue shorts and a white t-shirt stands leaning against a wall.

The room is strewn with empty liquor bottles and assorted drug paraphernalia; the man inside appears unkempt and clearly under the influence of some illegal dope. After searching the room, without warning, the man springs to life, lunging towards the nearest weapon he could find – a broken bottle.

But not quick enough, as Lucy and I incapacitate the man before he could do any damage. We can't afford to have any witnesses, who might inform the cartel that we are in the area. Any shot might echo through the forest, even at a distance. The rain might dampen the sound, but I can't take the chances – only one thing for it.

While Lucy holds him, I remove my knife from my jacket and drive it deep into the side of his neck. Then, in one swift movement, pull rapidly forward, slicing through his throat. The body jerks as his life spurts out from him, blood squirting several feet onto the dusty floor. In one way, I've done him a favour and given him a quick death. The drugs would have killed him in time, anyway.

A scan of the rest of the room confirms no other threats – time to continue to the other rooms that need to be made safe. With the lower level clear, Lucy and I head for the upper part of the building. Stop at the bottom of the wooden staircase and look up. They appear sturdy, but we will soon find out. I go up first while Lucy covers me, her rifle pointing towards the top corridor.

One step at a time, I inch my way up, trying in vain to prevent any creaking as my weight is transferred to the battered-looking board. Seconds later, I'm on the landing and take up a covering position before indicating for Lucy to come up.

The upper storey consists of several rooms running off a central dust-filled corridor with rubbish scattered across the floor. The air is the same as downstairs, with the overpowering stench of mould and decay filling your nostrils. The only faint light is through the gaps where the doors used to be.

We come to the first room on our left, where I take a firing stance just to the right of the doorway, my pistol close to my body. With Lucy by my side, I nod, not wanting to whisper any commands in case it alerts anyone inside. With that, we both rush in, our weapons pointing anywhere someone might be hiding.

Carry out the same procedure in every room until we are 99 per cent sure the place is now void of any more people.

Outside, Simon and Derek ensure the exterior is clear of potential threats. As they round the back of the house, they are confronted by a vast open brown timber deck that wraps itself around three-quarters of the building. Off to the right is a door hanging off its hinges. Several neglected, battered old picnic tables are rotting away along the righthand edge of the house.

The space behind the door needs to be checked; following the usual procedure of house clearing, Simon stands to one side of the doorway while Derek takes up position on the other. On the count of two, they rush in with weapons held out, ready for action. The room is clear of people but full of old paint tins, with their colours dried solid down their sides, indicating their contents. The vegetation has broken through the ceiling, taking over most of the near-empty space.

The front veranda is about 10 feet wide, with a four-foot wooden railing running along the entire length. Green vines have made their way up from the rainforest, which stretches out into the distance and covers the decking with a natural, greenish-coloured carpet.

More tattered tables are scattered around, caked in years' worth of bird droppings, giving off an overwhelming stink of ammonia that hurts the eyes. On one sits a variety of syringes, water bombs, rolling tobacco papers and three half-filled cigars. As the objects appear new and don't match the other rusted and decaying items spread around the rest of the property, it would appear that locals high on drugs frequent the house on a regular basis.

The front side of the house, between the vast grime-covered windows, most of which have been broken over time, lumps of plaster that have detached from the house, exposing the wooden lattice beneath and now lay dotted about the deck.

They finish clearing the exterior a few minutes later and haven't heard any commotion inside. So, sit on one of the benches after scraping off most of the year's grime, overlooking the dense forest below and wait for the others to join them.

Lucy and I finished making the interior safe, so we walk onto the front veranda, where Derek and Simon are sitting on a bench.

"The house is secure for now. Better radio George and tell him to start packing up his equipment."

"While Lucy and I remain here, the rest of you can fetch everything from our last position," I say, turning to Simon.

After they leave, I begin forming a plan for the remainder of the night and early tomorrow morning. Once back, Simon finds a dark spot in the old kitchen. He ignites the gas stove and starts to brew up and, using a spare cooker from Derek, places an assortment of foodstuffs into a pan and begins to make scran for everyone.

I line up the map to the ground. Over in the distance is a clearing in the forest. Through the binoculars, I can make out a group of buildings surrounded by a high wire fence. It isn't long before the aroma of freshly made coffee and cooked food wafts outside to where the rest of us are sitting.

"That will be the camp we are heading for," pointing in the general direction.

"Yep, that must be the place, Steve," agrees Simon, handing me a steaming mug of hot caffeine.

"You're a lifesaver, mate."

"I know, and scran will be ready in a few minutes, so you messy bastards better wash your hands if you want to eat in my restaurant."

"Yes, sir, is it a black tie event?"

"If you come in just wearing a black tie and your birthday attire, George, you're going on a diet, you fat bastard," Simon laughs, heading back to the kitchen to grab the rest of the drinks.

"Dirty stinking combats it is, then," replies George.

The food doesn't take long, and with the daylight starting to fade, we can't afford to use any form of artificial light as we are so close to the target and can't risk anyone spotting a glow from inside the house. So, everybody ensures that all equipment is packed away.

Take the maps and photos of the drug cartel's makeshift prison camp and the local terrain from my kit and spread them out on the table. The team gather around it in intense concentration.

"First, onto tonight's plans. This being a vast area to cover would suggest that rather than one single location for the sentry post, we have a roving one where everyone takes turns roaming about the place.

"You're all professionals, so I will leave it to you how you complete this — starting when we finish this brief. Each of us takes one-hour stints. We should all get at least four hours of interrupted sleep."

"I'll grab the tail end one so I can get a brew going," announces Simon.

"Good idea, Simon, but I don't think we will have time as we must be in position by first light. But you can have the last one if you work out the roster working backwards from yourself.

"If there are no questions on the stag, I'll resume with the morning activities."

Wait for a few minutes before I continue. "Zulu time will be 03:00, so we all must be ready to depart by then. The plan is to leave here along this track and make our way in formation until we reach this spot," I point to the map.

"From here, we will move around the camp, leaving our two snipers in positions where they can cover the front and rear guard towers. Make sure you have the radios on. Derek will sort out the frequencies after the briefing."

"I've been thinking about the best one that works in this terrain," says Derek.

"Once the message comes across the airwaves that Lucy and George are in location via the radio, Simon, Derek and I will recce the area near the fences, trying to get close enough without compromising our locations to discover what is happening beyond the perimeter fence. With any luck, we will locate where they are holding Ana and James. Any questions or recommendations?"

"One suggestion. It might be better if Lucy and I stay together, covering the whole camp from this high vantage point, instead of splitting us up. That way, while one is peering through the scope, the other can jot down notes," George suggests, looking and pointing at the map and photos.

"If you think you can cover from there, I have no issues."

"What's the matter, fat boy, scared of being alone?"

"No, Simon, if there are two of us, we won't miss putting a bullet in your skinny arse," George says, pretending to hold his rifle and aiming at Simon.

"Moving on. Everyone collects as much info as possible when we are on target in case someone misses something vital. The more information we gather, the easier the rescue will be."

Before continuing, I take a drink of water. "The plan is to stay there for at least five hours. The extraction will be the reverse of the insertion. Us three," I point to Derek and Simon, "we will return to the sniper position and collect you two before returning here. Any questions?"

There is silence, "If anything should go wrong and we need to make a tactical withdrawal, then the first emergency RV is here," I place my finger on the map at the location where we will first stop on the way to the camp. "If, for any reason, we are under fire and everybody becomes separated, everyone makes their way back to Windover Cottage, where we will regroup."

Once I am optimistic each member knows their role and the complex backup plan in case of trouble, we all prepare mentally for the gun battle that may occur tomorrow and start preparing for our roles in the operation, just in case we need to extract James and Ana tomorrow morning.

Lucy, the group's trained interrogator, reviews the documents we obtained and familiarises herself with the prisoners' information, paying attention to what they look like from the photos. Plus, going through her interrogation plans if we capture one of Aron's men and need info. Derek, the radio operator, is testing frequencies and checking our communication equipment to ensure a clear signal when we were in the dense undergrowth area around the drug cartel's camp.

Over on one of the other tables, George has the two sniper rifles stripped down and, using an oily rag, is lubricating the metal parts. With a clean cloth, he ensures no smears on the telescopic lenses; while our transport guy, Simon, is reviewing potential extraction points close by where Butch can land his helicopter and extract us all in an emergency, if required.

With the plans in my head, I focus on a basic outline for extracting the hostages. A more detailed project can't be completed until I have more information from our recce in the morning.

By 22:00, everyone has finished what they were doing and go to grab some shuteye for a few hours, apart from me. The bastard Simon ensured that I not only have the first stag but the second to last one as well.

Chapter Eight – The Recce

After my stag is finished, I clamber into my maggot but can't sleep as today's activities are bumping around in my head; the thought that if the recce didn't go as planned, the hostages could face the consequences keep coming to the forefront.

I wouldn't normally give a toss about the group of people on a mission with me due to my lack of empathy. It all came as part of the job. They all know what they have let themselves in for. But we have become a close-knit team over the time we have done this line of work, so would hate for them to get killed. Plus, I can't comprehend what I would do if Lucy got killed.

As I lay in the pitch-blackness of the night, not far away, I detect the sound of someone trying to creep through the house, bits of broken glass snapping under their weight and heading in my direction. With one hand, I undo the sleeping bag while holding my 9mm in the other, pointing toward the disturbance.

Whoever is coming my way is now only a couple of feet away from me, when Simon appears out of the darkness. "Come on, you lazy bastard, it's time to drag your sorry arse out of bed. Here, have a brew."

"What happened to the no more naked flames?"

"Don't throw your teddy out of the pram, Steve. I made it last night and put it in my thermos. You want it or not?"

"Do bears shit in the woods?" I reply, taking the mug from him.

Moments later, I stroll onto the veranda, lugging my kit for the recce, and sit at the table. Ten minutes pass in silence as I stare across the rainforest. Even at this time of the morning, the forest below is alive with sounds and aromas that you will only find in such a place.

I'm awestruck by a sensory symphony that surrounds me. The gentle noise of the ruby-throated hummingbird darting around, its wings humming like a tiny helicopter as they make their way up into a small nest hanging from what is left of the rafters.

A chorus of insects rises from the damp earth, whirring, chirping, and buzzing as if each sound is part of a grand musical composition. The call of distant birds echoes through the trees, and as I listen, the rustling of leaves as a creature scurrying along the veranda comes from close by.

The moment of contentment is broken minutes later as Lucy joins me. "Strange how such a beautiful place can hold a vast amount of danger and misery," she says, sitting beside me.

"You're right there, Lucy, especially with Aron and his mates still walking around."

"Not for much longer, hey honey."

Soon, the rest join us on the veranda. "If we are all ready, better make a start," throwing my Bergen on my back.

Once everyone dons their gear, we set out, leaving Windover Cottage the way we came in yesterday, before turning onto a narrow track that winds through the forest—flanked by dense foliage that obscures the sky. I lead the way, my eyes scanning for signs of movement. Simon followed behind me, his rifle trained on the path ahead, with the rest of the team in patrol formation.

As we move deeper, the trees grow taller and the undergrowth thicker; the rainforest comes alive around us. The sound of chirping crickets in the background plays havoc on your senses, with their constant throbbing creating an electric atmosphere.

Like many things in nature, you're safe if you can still detect their presence. You have an issue when they stop, and the area goes quiet. Fortunately, they accompany us along the trail to the RV.

Finally, we reach a point near the ridge and pause to catch our breath. Beckon George and Lucy to my position.

When they are close enough for me to whisper, "This will be a good place for the sniper location. It overlooks the camp."

I follow Lucy as she and George crawl through the undergrowth until they can peer over the ridgeline without skylining themselves. While they set up, I take out my binoculars and scan the area. Grab a sheet of paper from my jacket, sketch the watchtowers' positions, and try to identify potential obstacles. From the look of it, there is only one person in each tower.

"Before us three leave, check your comms with Derek," I whisper, putting my hand to my mouth as though speaking into a mic.

"DR, Radio Check, Over," George transmits.

A second later, Derek comes over the airwaves, "GD, OK, Over."

When they are set up, I return to where the other two have concealed themselves, protecting the rear.

"When you're ready, folks, we better make a move," I whisper.

The plan is to make our way as close as possible to the perimeter, avoiding the entrance, to which armed guards will be stationed to protect who or what enters. Stopping at the forest's edge, I scan the area to my front, looking for anything that might give us cover. Off to my right is the dead ground and small ridge I saw from up where Lucy and George are positioned. This may give us some cover as we approach the fence.

A group of thick foliage runs parallel along the fence for about 30 metres. Directly opposite the bushes inside the camp is a bamboo structure away from the other three. This might be where the hostages are being kept.

In case we don't glimpse sight of Ana or James while observing from outside the perimeter, we may have to risk entry beyond the fence and try to find them by peering into all the buildings one at a time. But first, we have the small task of getting closer.

With that in mind, we crawl on our bellies through the remaining dense underbrush close to the forest's edge, stopping short of the open ground, and wait for the best opportunity to move for a better view.

We have two issues. First, tonight is a full moon, so the sky is clear, and the moonlight reflects off the surrounding foliage, casting shadows across the forest floor. Second, one of the front tower guards keeps shining a bright flashlight, scanning the area outside the perimeter at irregular intervals. Either he thinks he has seen someone moving through the undergrowth, or our guard is a coward jumping at every noise.

What is on our side is that the trees lining the forest's edge cast long, dark patches over the ground, stretching into the camp. We will maximise this natural concealment to move to our desired position.

For what appears like ages, we lay still in the cover of the forest, waiting for the idiot in the tower to stop shining his torch in our direction. While lying still, concealed in the bushes, my mind wanders off into a daydream-type state.

I never thought that in my wildest dreams, I would end up on a covert mission deep in the heart of the tropical rainforest, infiltrating a small drug cartel's prison camp in search of hostages. Still, here I am, alongside Simon and Derek, determined to bring Ana and James and any other hostages we may find to safety no matter what it takes.

The instance the beam of light goes out, I propel myself across the short distance to the dead ground. Dive down onto my belly and crawl a few feet. Keep as near the deck as possible, and try not to make a sound. Take up a firing position inside the foliage facing towards the potential entry point in the fence. Derek and Simon soon join me seconds later.

"Right, gents. Derek, if you stay on this edge of the camp, Simon and I will check the rest of the perimeter. We will meet back up with Lucy and George three hours from now. If you spot Ana or James, note which building they emerge from," tapping him on the shoulder.

"Roger that," comes the reply from Derek.

"You ready, Simon?" He nods before scrambling away from the ridge.

Moving back among the trees is the best way to reach the back undetected. Every step is calculated, each breath hushed as we progress, following the direction of the fence line towards the rear tower. Once there, we both creep through the dense undergrowth, our hearts racing with excitement and controlled fear. The darkness envelops us like a cloak. The only light in the forest comes from the full moon, casting eerie shadows through the thick foliage.

Beyond the barrier, the base is illuminated by several bright searchlights. Voices of men in the towers echo through the night, mingling with the drone of insects, rustling leaves, and animal sounds. All are overshadowed by the near-silent hum of generators providing electrical power.

Moving deeper, the dense underbrush muffles our footsteps. The first tall and foreboding watchtower loom above us, throwing a long shadow into the camp. The wire mesh fence that encircles the compound looms, menacing in the dim light of the predawn hours. Still using the cover of the forest, I stop and indicate for Simon to close up.

Keeping our heads down to avoid detection, I scrutinise what is happening to my front. At the same time, Simon takes up a defensive position, his rifle pointing back the way we came. The sound of laughter and chatter drifts towards us on the slight breeze blowing through the camp. Two guards sit behind a building, chatting and laughing in hushed voices, their shadows flickering against the wall. One is displaying a machete strapped to his hip, glinting in the light of the nearby fire. Through my binoculars, I detect two AK-47s resting on the bench seat.

I would guess, going on the time of day, these two are likely to be the sentries and, like most, are doing anything but patrol the area. It reminds me of some guard duties I completed in my army career, where if the rain started to piss it down, we found somewhere to hide, only going back when it stopped, or our shift was over.

Something is unsettling about the scene. Over to my right, beneath the far tower, three men are gathered around a rusty old 45-litre oil drum; inside is a fire. Their faces are illuminated by the bright orange dancing flames, with the scent of burning wood filling the air. They chatter and laugh so loud, a deaf cricket would have covered its ears to muffle the sound. With their carefree behaviour, they appear at ease, a jolting contrast to the seriousness of their duties, as though the guards lost sight of the deadly game they were playing.

Spot two vehicles standing in the shadows of a bamboo structure outside the perimeter through the gap between the buildings.

Still no sign of any of the hostages. The last thing we need is to shoot the shit out of one of the huts to find we attacked the only one we shouldn't have. I must confirm which of the four structures they are being held in. Plus, I want to check out the area near the office building to establish the number of guards operating the gate and where they stand inside or outside the fence.

Crawl back to Simon and whisper, "Come on, mate, we better push on to the other side while the darkness is still in our favour. With any luck from here, we might catch a glimpse of Ana."

Leaving the cover, we try not to make a sound as we move about 20 metres back into the protection of the forest and head for the far corner.

Freeze, motionless as the man in the tower sweeps the area with his flashlight, not daring to move a single muscle. The moment it passes by me, I dive to the deck close to where Simon has already taken shelter.

Using hand signals, I indicate we should go a little deeper into the rainforest and make a large arc around to a point where we can better monitor the buildings. The sounds surrounding us blend into the background as we go, our minds set on the task.

Ten minutes go past before we arrive at a spot on the left-hand edge, as you look at it from the gate, where we can monitor the front of the buildings without being seen.

Again, I peer through the binoculars while Simon keeps an eye out for any danger coming our way. From here, I witness a small group of people enter the facility closest to us. White smoke drifts into the air from an opening on the back wall. Minutes later, two men leave, carrying plates of food and walk into the building next to it. Taking a rough guess, this would be the cookhouse and an accommodation block.

We must have been here lying under dense undergrowth observing for some time, and my other senses have returned due to the lack of activity inside the camp. First light begins to break through the treetops as the sun rises over the horizon. The aroma of damp earth and verdant foliage starts to fill my lungs. The canopy above is a mosaic of greens and browns, with long tendrils of vines and creaking branches blending to form a lush tapestry.

The forest comes alive in unison with a symphony of sounds and colours.

I am about to head back into the rainforest for the journey back up to meet Derek and onto the sniper team, when Simon taps me on the shoulder and whispers,

"Isn't that Ana over on the veranda of the first building, holding a bucket of some type?"

"Think so. Let's see what she does and which one she returns to."

Watch as she strolls, bent over as though she is exhausted and beaten towards a square of matting, constructed from the local vegetation on the floor just inside the wire, not too far from our present location.

Behind her is a man with short, brown hair, tattered blue jeans, and a grey t-shirt. In his mitts, the favourite weapon of any thug is an AK-47. To reinforce that he is in charge and that she needs to do what he says, he urges her forward by poking the barrel in her back.

After putting the bucket down, Ana lifts the bamboo to uncover a hole in the ground. This must be their cesspit. Holding the container, she pours the contents a little at a time so as not to get a backsplash. The moment she starts pouring, there is a loud buzzing noise as thousands of flies break for freedom from the pit, accompanied by an unmistakable stench of human excrement.

After replacing the lid, she stands up and stares into the forest, her beautiful brown eyes set back in her gaunt face. Her long black hair flows across her shoulders, moving in the slight morning breeze.

Behind her, the man barks orders in a rough menacing voice, "Hurry up, bitch." She glances into the rainforest again, hoping her rescuers will come soon, before turning and returning to where she came from only minutes ago.

I want to jump out and rescue her, but I know better, as this would screw up the whole mission.

With my eyes fixed on her, Ana comes to a halt in front of the last hut from our location. She swings the door outwards, and the man shovers her hard in the back, forcing her to stumble through the door.

The good news for us is that we now know which building the hostages are housed in and that the door opens out, not in. This information, along with what Derek witnessed from his position, will come in handy when I put a plan together on how we liberate them at first light tomorrow.

There isn't much more we can do now until the rescue, which must be at daft o'clock tomorrow morning at dawn. Which, by the look of Ana can't come quick enough. Take out my map and look for an alternative route back to join Lucy and Simon that doesn't involve making our way back to the other side of the camp.

I find a trail about 100 metres to our rear that follows a river line. Turn to Simon.

"OK, mate, let's get the fuck out of here. A track behind us takes us back to the snipers."

"What about Derek? He is waiting for us to return."

"Good point, well made, Simon."

With that, I grab the radio mic. "DR, RV, GD, position, out."

From that, Derek will understand that we are taking a different route back and that he should go to Lucy and George's location.

Keep close to the ground, trying not to make a sound until we are 30 metres inside the woods, where it's safe to stand and increase the pace. Above me, the canopy hangs like a tapestry, woven with vines and creaking branches, a rainforest fortress shrouded in secrecy.

Moving back and trudging through the forest, the humid air clings to our skin like a second layer. Our boots squelch in the mud caused by the downpour several nights ago. The natural green ceiling prevents the sun from penetrating through the trees and drying out the ground beneath our feet as we follow the narrow path, with verdant foliage pressing in on all sides.

To our right, the river flows with unstoppable force, beating against rocks and cascading down in an unbridled frenzy. Its rhythm is uninterrupted, the sound a deafening, but soothing lullaby to the creatures that calls this rainforest home.

I scan the underbrush for any signs of danger, gripping my rifle tight, ready to fire if required. Suddenly, a rustling noise stands out from the chirping of insects, making us both freeze.

"Stay alert," I whisper, my eyes flicking back and forth. "Could be anything out here."

We creep forward until we detect a small group of green monkeys chattering and swinging among the treetops above us. I let out a breath I didn't realise I'm holding.

"False alarm," I mutter, easing my stance. "Let's keep going."

We push through the dense growth, weaving around vines and branches. The river's roar grows louder, and we catch brief glimpses of it between the trees.

"We have company," I whisper to Simon. "Someone is approaching."

"We need to move. Now," says Simon.

Pick up the pace, our senses sharp and tuned into our surroundings as we near the rendezvous spot. The thick vegetation hampers our movements, forcing us to slow down. Without warning, Simon's foot catches on a root, and he goes sprawling down the bank.

"Are you okay?" I yell, helping him up.

At that moment, two of Aron's men spring from nowhere, firing in our direction. Through instinct built up over the years, we both take cover behind several trees tight against the ground. The noise is deafening, the rounds whizzing past so close you could sense the glow of the metal round. I aim and return fire.

"We need to move from this location now," I shout, my voice tense.

Formulate an immediate plan, dodging and weaving through the rainforest, making our way towards the RV, now only 500 metres away, just beyond the tree line. But Aron's men are still hot on our heels, spraying bullets in our direction. The heat is intense, sweat pouring from us as we fight for our lives.

Our attackers have the advantage of local knowledge and know the ground and are soon upon us. I pivot to return fire, but one of them catches me by surprise and launches at me with a machete, held aloft in one hand. I raise my rifle into the firing position and squeeze the trigger. A nanosecond later, the man lies facedown among the dead foliage of the forest floor. Blood is running out from beneath him, staining the green and brown leaves a crimson red.

Turn to find out where the other attacker is. Simon's arm is wrapped around the man's throat, holding him in a headlock. In what would appear in slow motion, he rams his knife into the side of the neck. Soon, like his friend, his body is contributing to the life of the rainforest.

"With any luck, Simon, the roar of that river would have drowned out the noise of the shots being fired."

"Hope so, mate, for the sake of the hostages."

Back up in the sniper position, George is peering through the sight of the rifle, surveying the camp's layout. Once he identifies each potential target, he calls out the estimated ranges and positions to Lucy, who marks them down on a sketch of the entire area.

The last thing they want is for someone or something to creep up on them while they are too focused on the base. So they stop every few minutes, using all their senses to listen to the symphony of sounds coming through the forest. Birds and insects are chirping away, and distant green monkeys are swinging through the canopy. Allow the aroma of a moist rainforest to fill their nostrils, trying to detect the scent of any unnatural chemical such as body spray.

They are safe for now. So, continue observing the camp and marking down on Lucy's map the location of all the physical structures and areas of any person who appears to be static in one place, like the man strolling about near a 40-foot metal container and never walking for more than five feet in any direction.

As early morning rays of light break through the canopy illuminating the camp, they witness what could be a change of guards. One of the two men from the gate changes places with the man in the watchtower close to them. This man then walks to the rear of the camp and clambers up that tower.

Off to the left of what appears to be an office, a black helicopter stands idle in an open area cleared of all vegetation that would interfere with the engine operation and blades.

Through the binoculars, Lucy spots a person leaving the bamboo building closest to the perimeter fence where Derek is concealed. She taps George on the shoulder.

"Isn't that Ana?"

"Think you're right," George says, after focusing the rifle sights on the woman walking along the front of the buildings.

"With any luck, one of the boys will spot her and confirm," says Lucy, marking the details in her notebook.

Another 20 minutes pass before the snapping of dry twigs, and the crunch of dead leaves attracts their attention through the early morning chorus. Something is approaching their location.

Without making a sound, Lucy turns and aims toward the disturbance. The index finger takes up the first pressure while she peers through the sight.

Seconds later, the shape of a person can be seen weaving its way through the undergrowth. The chirping of the insects goes quiet.

Soon after, a low-pitched voice comes from the forest, "Don't shoot. It's me," as Derek emerges from behind a tree.

Lucy eases off the tension on the trigger, "OK, where are the other two? We listened to the message for you to return here."

"They must be coming back via another route. I thought I detected gunfire earlier, but I could be wrong, as the sound of a river made it hard to distinguish," Derek says, concealing himself next to Lucy.

The trio ensures all equipment is packed and ready to leave immediately once the other two reach them.

Twenty minutes later, Simon and I come within 50 metres of where the rest should be and stop and listen for any noise that might indicate Aron's men have overrun the position. Wait a few minutes before moving closer.

In a voice that isn't too loud or too quiet, I call out, "Green Jackets rule."

"Fuck off, you green numpty," comes George's reply.

"No point in stopping. This confirms the location is safe, so we move in. Might as well head off back to Windover Cottage," I say, pausing for a few seconds, then, continue walking down the track.

In case we somehow managed to leave tracks on the trail we came in on, we take a different route back to the house. A long way, but it will piss anyone off who might be planning an ambush.

Our new course takes us along a pathway that is hard to detect among the dead foliage that covers the ground. It mustn't have been used that often, if at all, for years. The good news is that the dense vegetation protects us from view from all directions. We are only about one click from the house, when a rustling under the debris littering the forest floor has me freezing motionless, daring not to twitch a single muscle.

Signal for the team to take cover as I wait for whatever is making the racket to emerge. I aim my rifle at the noise. Then, catch sight of a head appearing, its tongue tasting the air.

"Get a move on, idiot. Or is the hard man afraid of snakes?"

"Fuck off, Simon."

Thirty minutes later, we arrive back at Windover Cottage. Done this too many times to walk back inside where an attacker could be waiting, or even friends of our druggy friend.

Stop short and listen for sounds of movement. There aren't any, so we move closer and clear the house using the same method we entered yesterday.

Everybody drops their kit on the floor and takes out any notes they may have made during the recce.

"Tell you what, boys and girls, why don't we take 10 minutes to sort ourselves out? Fancy making a brew and some scran, Simon? While you do that, I will start formulating a basic plan for getting the hostages out."

"Right on it, boss," says Simon, taking Derek's and his gas cookers.

With everyone attending to personal admin, I walk out to the veranda collecting objects to help me make a model of the camp and the relevant parts of the surrounding forest.

Put the final touches to the map when Simon walks over and hands me a fresh mug of coffee, its aroma replacing the stench of damp and rotting wood.

"Cheers, mate. Want to add anything?"

"All looks good. If that's the sniper position, you better replace that small stone with a fatter one to represent George. Scran is ready," Simon says, walking back inside.

Once the food is out of the way and all kit is packed away ready for an emergency bug out if required, and the team is sat around the model on the table, I start the brief.

"Objectives: to extract hostages from the grips of the cartel's camp unharmed. Our primary objective of the mission is rescuing Ana and James, but if there are more innocent people, we will also bring them out.

"Factors to consider: time of day - The operation will occur at dawn when the target location is not fully awake and alert. And before one of them empties the shit bucket.

"Weather conditions - we must consider that this is a tropical rainforest with the possibility of heavy rainfall. From what I know, none is expected for tomorrow.

"Terrain - we already know what type of topography we are looking at. We might have to take an alternative way and be ready for some unpredictable landscapes, including steep hills, deep rivers, and thick foliage, especially on the route to our pick-up location, which will be around here." I indicate to the map.

"Simon, can you contact Butch after the briefing and let him know? Any questions?"

"Nope, all straightforward so far," says George.

"Potential obstacles and threats: we all know a wire mesh fence encircles the target area. Our best bet for cutting through this is where Derek will be."

Pointing to our entry point on the model of the base. "This is the closest place to where Ana and James are being held. Armed people are in and around the camp who aren't afraid to return fire, so kill anyone you see."

"What we need to be mindful of, there might be some sort of traps or explosives that might have been set up. So, stay alert.

"Personnel roles and responsibilities: each team member will have specific functions.

"Lucy and George, your role will be setting up your sniper position first. It's best you use the exact location as earlier. From here, take down all guards in the towers. Then, Lucy, move your attention to the building outside the fence and shoot anyone who comes out.

"Derek, besides ensuring all the radios work, you will confirm that all communication is effective. You will do this from the same place as before. You will be the person who cuts the wire mesh and ensures it stays safe, as this is the way we will come back out. You will also assist the snipers in the dispatch of any of Aron's men running around the camp.

"Simon and I will enter the target area via the hole and go to the first bamboo buildings, where we believe the hostages are being held. When we have them, we will return to Derek's location and join George and Lucy. Any questions so far?"

"Not yet, Steve, all sounds good," says Lucy.

"Everyone give me a comms check after this, to ensure all radios are working," says Derek, tapping his radio.

"OK, let's move on to equipment. The team must carry all the necessary kit to deal with any situation, including weapons, ammunition, communication devices, maps and medical equipment. Any stuff not needed for the rescue we will leave in a hide behind the sniper location, ready to be picked up after we have the hostages and on the way to the helicopter.

"Procedures: mission briefing – everybody familiarises themselves with the camp. I've taken information from you all and have incorporated it into the model in front of you. Take time to study it, as I will destroy it later.

"Preparation – it goes with saying that you should inspect your gear and ensure no rattles or other sounds that might give away our position before the retrieval gets underway. When I've finished, we will do an ammo check. As mentioned earlier, Simon will have the helicopter waiting at the FRV.

"Launch – when we are all in our designated start positions confirmed by radio, Derek will send the following message, 'rescue is a go' over the airways, stand-by. The signal for the attack is when George takes down the first of the people in the front left watchtower. Before this, try not to open fire. If you are compromised, despatch them with as little noise as possible.

"Infiltration – once the sound of the shot echoes across the target area, Simon, Derek and I will approach the perimeter, where Derek will cut a hole big enough for us to infiltrate the base.

"Any questions?" Everyone shakes their heads.

"OK, on to Rescue of People. Extraction team deployment: inside the enemy camp, we will rush towards this building. Dispose of any guards before entering the hut." Again, a point to the map.

"Hostage retrieval - Simon and I will retrieve the hostages and move them back to the fence. Then, return to the sniper location, collecting Derek on the way.

"Extraction- once we have them, we will bring them to where George and Lucy are. Then, we will patrol along this trail to our FRV and the waiting transport.

"Security.- in the event of any complications or emergencies, before the mission gets underway, we will RV back here and regroup.

"Contingency plans - this recovery must occur tomorrow, as our intelligence source confirmed this will be soon. With any luck, nobody will be injured. But if you are, remain in situ. You will be collected on the withdrawal. If we come under gunfire during the extraction, Lucy and George will give covering fire. The emergency rendezvous point will be back here at Windover Cottage. If by chance it all goes wrong, then everyone make your way back here."

"Steve, what happens if we enter the camp and Ana and the rest are not where they should be?" Simon asks.

"In that case, we will call Derek to join us and clear all the buildings.

"Communication Protocols - we will have our radios. Ensure proper comms and chatter are kept to a minimum until the rescue is underway. Simon, can you take the radio frequencies from Derek and give them to Butch? That way, we can harmonise with him on our withdrawal. Derek will coordinate the pick-up once Butch has them.

"That's the plan, folks. If anyone wants to contribute more, now is the time."

"Think you covered it all, mate, apart from what time is Zulu time?" asks Derek, standing up to obtain a better view of the model.

"Same as this morning, 03:00. Suggest you all go to night, night for some beauty sleep, and let's face facts: Derek needs some, the ugly bastard."

Chapter Nine – Rescue

As I'm on the last stag, I have the privilege of waking everyone up, plus it gives me time to mull over the rescue plan in my head.

It's now 02:30 - time for the operation: 'hands off privates, on with socks', which consists of me going around and booting each of the four maggots, which contain unsightly people trying to catch up on some beauty sleep.

Ten minutes later, everybody is up and packing away gear and giving their weapons a once over to ensure they function and won't misfire. Luckily, I had time on my hands earlier, so I did my checks while the rest were sleeping.

With the team doing their last-minute admin in silence, the only noise is the nocturnal creatures chirping and screeching in the rainforest below. A glance down at Mickey on my wrist tells me the time is 02:55 - time to get the rescue underway.

"If you lot are ready, let's go and kill some people and recover the hostages," I say, throwing my Bergen on my back.

"Ready when you are, Steve," comes the reply from Derek, picking up his pack and coming over to join me.

With so much at stake, including the lives of the people we are about to rescue, we all walk in silence. I lead off in our normal formation with Simon behind me, then Lucy, Derek and George bringing up the rear. From this point on, the tension on the team will be high, with each member running their part of the rescue through their minds.

At this time of the morning, the forest might be a vast, ominous expanse of darkness, but this is a minor problem as packing the kit and admin were completed in the dark, which gives us all the time for our night vision to take effect.

I'm working on the assumption that if the cartel had set up an ambush on the route, they would have gotten bored by now, not being professional soldiers, and returned to base. So, I'm using the same path we used to approach the camp yesterday to make things easier. Plus, I know where I'm going in the near darkness.

The further we travel along the trail, the more it becomes engrossed by the local vegetation, like a black cloak suffocating every breath. Frogs call out to one another, their shrill voices cutting through the stillness and echoing off the tree trunks. Insects skitter across leaves, their legs clicking like the sound of an approaching predator. The rainforest truly is a living, breathing mystery.

Soon, we are near where George and Lucy will peel off, so I stop and crouch down to the right of the track and place my hand on my head. The team come in close.

In a quiet, only just audible voice, "OK, we are 100 metres away from the sniper position. Once we arrive, I will continue with Simon and Derek to our start location. Lucy and George slip out of formation and make your way to your sniper position. We will see everyone on the other side. Don't get killed, or we are leaving your sorry arses here."

"Yep, see you on the other side," says Lucy, after confirming with George that he heard what I said.

After a few minutes, we reach the point where the sniper team departs. Turn around to see them peel off and head through the undergrowth. Once they disappear from my sight, I continue to the forest's edge. The cartel's base of operation looms in the darkness. Its four looming towers cast ominous shadows across the clearing, while the only signs of life come from the flickering lights in two of the buildings. The remainder of the place appears silent, except for the occasional rustling of leaves and the muffled groans of the guards.

***

After peeling off from the rest of the team, George and Lucy trek the short distance through the dense undergrowth to reach their start location. First, they must check and clear the area to see if the site has been compromised. It hasn't, so they are soon close to the same spot as yesterday. Without any verbal communication, Lucy covers George as he moves one metre at a time, stopping and listening for any noise standing out from the chorus of the forest. Within minutes, the position is cleared.

The early morning light hasn't broken through the thick canopy of trees, and the chirping of nocturnal creatures resonates through the damp air. As they lay prone among the dense foliage of the rainforest, their rifles aim at the men in the watchtowers, their first assignment is to eliminate the cartel's tower guards.

Lucy's senses are magnified as her breathing slows. She trained for this moment, and her mind focuses on the task. She peers through the vegetation and studies the camp's layout in her mind. The entrance to the base, with its double gates is on the front edge, and an office building with an empty helipad stands nearby. A wire mesh fence with a watchtower in each corner surrounds it.

With a glance towards George, Lucy prepares to take a shot. She raises her rifle, steadies her aim, takes a deep breath, exhales half and then holds her breath as she squeezes the trigger.

But as this is a dry run, she says, "You're dead," as her finger skims the trigger guard.

They peer out through the leaves,as they both prepare for the radio message to come across the airwaves, "Rescue is a go," from Derek.

As she waits, Lucy takes in her surroundings. The thick rainforest is alive with the sounds of exotic creatures, and a warm, humid breeze brushes against her skin. She understands this is no ordinary mission. The drug cartel is notorious for its ruthlessness. Any misstep could cost someone their life.

As per the plan, their primary role is to kill the guards in the watchtowers, and then they can begin killing any of Aron's men who come into their sight.

It isn't long before the message they have been waiting for comes across the radio.

"Are you ready, Lucy?" George asks, his eyes locked on the rear towers.

She nods, her fingers already tightening around the trigger of her sniper rifle. "Let's take them down."

Their mission has begun, and the success of my, Simon and Derek's part of the rescue depends on their actions. They have no room for error. The stakes are too high.

Lucy peers through the scope, her breathing slow and steady. She sees the first guard. His head is visible above the tower's railing. With a swift caressing-like movement, she squeezes the trigger, and the man drops to the floor. With the first one eliminated, Lucy moves on to the next target in the other front watchtower. She peers through the optics. The second falls from the tower within a few seconds, his lifeless body lying at the base.

George, being the better shot out of him and Lucy, concentrates on the people in the rear towers. Thirty seconds later, he kills them both.

With the watchtowers now dealt with, Lucy and George focus on the area inside the perimeter. It's time to kill the remainder of the cartel's men and clear the way for the team to infiltrate the camp. They need to move fast before any of Aron's people can react. Lucy turns to George. Her determination is evident in her expression.

***

After Lucy and George peel off, we continue along the small track, which runs through the dense forest away from the sniper position and make our way through the undergrowth, staying as silent as a mouse, until we reach the edge of the treeline, stop for a few minutes to listen and scrutinise the area ahead to ensure no guards are in sight.

While Simon and I sprint across the open ground, Derek trains his rifle at the camp, his heart hammering in his chest, prepared to take out anyone who poses a threat. His radio bursts into life, and he hears Lucy's voice in his ear, "We're in position, waiting for your call."

Derek nods to himself, "Copy over," he whispers into the mic.

Now joining us, Derek crouches in the thick foliage alongside the high wire mesh fence surrounding the cartel's base. His radio crackles with static as he waits, ready to send the signal to initiate the rescue. I glance at Mickey on my wrist. It is still early morning, and the first rays of sunlight will soon filter through the dense forest, casting shadows across the ground. We need the cover of darkness, for the element of surprise to be on our side.

We shift on the lumpy dirt, trying to make ourselves more comfortable, and peer through the foliage. It is the rainy season, and the air is thick with the scent of damp earth and lush vegetation. Mosquitoes buzz incessantly around our ears as we bat them away.

I take out my binoculars and observe the area to my front. I can feel my heart racing with adrenaline. The centre is a hive of activity, men moving from one building to the next, some carrying weapons. Their lack of comprehension of what is about to happen amazes and baffles me simultaneously. Armed guards are positioned in a watchtower in each corner. They will not be an issue soon, as I have complete confidence in the two snipers.

After a few minutes, I tap Derek on the shoulder. He moves forward to the fence, keeping as low as possible, before pulling out the wire cutters and cutting a hole. He peers through the gap, checking for any of Aron's men. When he satisfies himself that no one is around, he glances back and indicates for Simon and me to move and join him.

Once we reach his position, I whisper to Derek, "If we are all ready? Send the message to start the rescue."

Derek swallows hard. The weight of his responsibility is heavy on his shoulders. He is the communications expert, and the team's success depends on his ability to keep them informed and coordinated.

After taking a deep breath, he presses the transmit button, "Rescue is a go," he says, his voice crackling through the radio. Moments later, the distinctive crack and thump of a bullet hits home. The snipers kill the first guards in the watchtowers and get the retrieval underway.

While scanning for any movement or any threat, Derek detects a cartel member coming closer. He must have spotted that the fence appears to have been cut. He needs to act fast. With the blink of an eye, Derek raises his rifle, aims, his finger steady on the trigger, fires and kills the man with a single shot.

The man falls to the ground, a pool of blood spreading beneath him. Derek's heart pounds in his chest. His eyes remain peeled on the camp's movements. He will provide cover fire when needed, as the team advances through the base, But his primary role is to be a spotter for snipers.

Once Simon and I have made our way through the hole in the fence, we make our way to the first of the four bamboo buildings. We creep closer to the entrance, careful not to make a sound. Detecting the sounds of muffled voices coming from within, we exchange a silent nod and slowly draw our weapons, preparing for the worst.

Moments later, two armed cartel men emerge from the shadows with guns firing. I react, aiming my rifle and shooting the first man in the chest. At the same time, Simon is wrestling the second man to the ground, his knife flashing in the moonlight as he slits the man's throat.

With the cartel's people down, we rush towards the veranda, our hearts pounding with adrenaline. We need to act fast, as time is not on the side of the hostages. It's moments like this that all five of us live for.

We know the door opens outwards from the information we collected from our recce. Crouch down in the shadows.

I whisper into Simon's ear, "You take up a position to the left of the door. I'll take the other. I will deal with anything inside when I nod, grab the door and fling it open."

Simon gives me the thumbs up. Leading the way, I step onto the porch, trying to be as quiet as possible. Yes, they are aware we are here due to the battle around us, but I don't want any of the cartel's men who might be hiding within to have an advantage. I'm soon followed by Simon, who stands to the left of the door, as this is the way the door opens. I stand on the right, my rifle tight to my body, the barrel pointing straight up.

I have seen many films where the hero enters a room with his pistol held at arm's reach out, making it easier for the bad guy hiding behind the door to grab their arm. When I was a young Rifleman, I did the same until I did my close-quarter and hostage rescue training.

Wait for a few seconds, not moving a muscle in case some brave idiot who might have heard us approach puts a round through the centre of the door. Watch as Simon grasps the door handle before giving the signal. With this, the door is flung open, and I rush inside.

The scene is chaotic and terrifying. The room is in near darkness, with the only light coming from a slit in the bamboo. The air is thick with the stench of human shit and sweat. In the back corner of the room, two hostages are huddled together, glancing up at me with wide eyes.

"Stay where you are," I yell, my voice echoing through the building. "We're here to help you."

They both nod, their expressions a mix of relief and fear. A few seconds later, Simon enters, his eyes darting around the room, his vision becoming accustomed to the dim light.

"You OK?" Simon asks as he moves closer.

In the quiet voices of two people standing on the edge of defeat, with tears running down their faces, they both reply, "Yes, please get us out of here."

"We will. What's your names?" I ask.

"I'm Ralph, and this is Eliza," the man says in a quiet, trembling voice.

"Stay fast here until we have cleared the rest of camp. Once we've done this, we'll be back for you. You have my word," I say, throwing them a bar of chocolate which, for some strange reason, is in my jacket pocket.

"You ready, Simon? Let's find Ana and James."

"Yep," says Simon, as he heads for the doorway.

I join him. We sprint out the door and take cover behind a pile of wooden crates. A quick scan of the area confirms it's safe to move to the next building. I am about to make a run for it when my radio bursts into life, "Targets are moving around the second building." It is Derek, spotting for the two snipers.

I'm scanning the ground to my front when I spot two of the cartel's people appear, rushing in our direction from the rear of one of the bamboo huts. This must be the two Derek is radioing through. I am about to take aim when I detect two distinctive cracks high up in the tree line. A split-second later, I hear the thud as both men are struck in the side of their heads, their dead bodies slumping to the floor. Glad to see Lucy and George are doing their job.

We follow the same procedure as the first one to enter the following two buildings. But there is no sign of the other two hostages. It's frustrating, but we needed to locate Ana and James alive.

Only the last structure, the one I identified as the cookhouse on the recce, to check, apart from the building outside the gate, but this can wait until the inside of the camp is clear.

When we reach the building, the door is open. Without stopping, we storm in. The kitchen is at the far end, with food steaming on the stove. To our immediate front are a few wooden tables and chairs with half-eaten breakfasts on metal plates. It is as though people left in a hurry, with any luck, the ones we have already killed.

"Something strange is happening here. Where is everyone? Sure, there were more of Aron's men when we recced the place," I say, turning to Simon.

"Just thinking that myself," comes the reply from Simon, who is heading for the kitchen area.

As he gets closer, a woman in chef's whites stands up, her hands stretched out, pointing at the ceiling. "Don't kill me. I was forced to work here. They have my family," she says with a tremor.

With my rifle aimed at the middle of the woman's face, I move cautiously towards her, my eyes scanning the room in case of any more surprises. I glance down to my left as the barrel rests on the lady's forehead. Beneath the counter is a young man no more than 16 years old.

"Get out," I yell, swinging the weapon backwards and forwards between the chef and the person under the countertop.

Still shaking, the youth stands next to the woman whose arms have now dropped, hoping we won't shoot her. I pause momentarily, deciding if this will be their lucky day. And if I wll let them live or kill them where they stand.

"Can any of you tell us where Ana and James are being held?" asks Simon.

They both shake their heads while mumbling that they don't know, as they flinch at the dull thud of a person hitting the bamboo veranda, the man's body now lying across the open doorway. I allow a smile to cross my face, as I know the sniper pair have us covered.

Moments later, "One guard approaching the gate," comes over the airwaves. It is Derek. A single gunshot follows.

The big question still floating around in my head is what to do with the people standing before me. When Simon reminds me of what we did with the chefs on Sain Halb, a quick scan of the room uncovers a battered, old-looking chest freezer. Open the door and peer in. There is nothing inside apart from some wooden crates of vegetables. Order the chef and the boy to remove them before telling them to clamber in. They hesitate but are nudged by Simon's rifle barrel.

Once they are comfortable, I put a rolling pin on the rim before closing the lid and securing it to allow airflow. After all, if they are innocent people caught up in this mess, I wouldn't like them to suffocate. I'm not a complete bastard.

To scare the crap out of them, and to confirm the message that if they leave and I find them any place else, it will be the last thing they ever do, fire several shots across the freezer, with the rounds hitting the wall behind, showering the freezer with fragments of bits of bamboo. There is a scream from inside.

Turn to Simon, "Come on, mate, only two more places to check - the 40-foot container and the building near the gate."

"Right behind you," says Simon, heading for the exit.

When we reach the red-painted container, the right-hand door is ajar. Not taking any chances, in case someone is hiding within and wants to spray us full of holes the moment we prise open the door. Take a stance with my hand on the door while Simon takes a firing posture, his rifle in the aim, ready to fire. I pull on the hefty door, which creaks as it opens. Simon moves in, followed seconds later by me.

The container is lined with rows of steel shelving running down both sides. Scattered across the wooden floor is some white powder. At a rough guess, this would be the drug cartel's final product. Not wanting any more surprises like the kitchen, I bend down and peer under the bottom shelf, looking for anyone who might think this would be a good hiding place. There isn't anybody about to stand up, when I spot two packets leaning against the end wall in the right corner.

Hand Simon my weapon, crawl underneath and grab the packages. "What you got, Steve?" Simon asks, as I rise to my feet.

"It looks like our druggy friends have left us a little extra payday bonus." I hand Simon the two packs wrapped in clear plastic. Inside is the same white substance as what covers the floor.

"That's nice of them. But unless they sent out a shipment to their dealers within the last couple of days, we have a significant problem."

"Sure have. With only a slight resistance by a few men and the absent product, I would say if we don't locate our missing hostages in that building, we are too late," I say, pointing to the structure outside the unguarded gate.

With no more sightings of the cartel's people in or around the camp, we walk over to the gate, still ready to kill any of Aron's people we find. As we make our way, I grab my radio and transmit, "RV at the main, what I'm calling the office near the entrance."

Stop short and scan the area. It's clear, so continue.

We couldn't afford to slacken off now, so the entry to this building is the same as the rest. Inside is basic and consists of a sitting room with several old brown PVC sofas that look worse for wear, and a table. Off to the right is an improvised kitchen with dirty, used cups and plates. At the far end of the room is a pine table and chair.

While Simon searches this room, I find another room behind a solid wooden door. From the appearance, this must be Aron's office, as it completely contrasts the other room.

The appearance of the rest of the room gives the impression that it's kept immaculate. Three half-filled glasses appear out of place, perhaps indicating somebody departed in a hurry. Behind is a plush executive chair. To the left is a green and brass five-foot-high biometric safe. The door is open, and it's empty.

With the rifle close to my chest, I scan the room; I can't see anything or anyone. About to leave and rejoin Simon when from the back of the room, in the small gap between the wall and the sofa, I detect what sounds like boots being scraped along the floor, and the heavy breath of someone doing their best to conceal their breathing.

Through the open door, I beckon Simon to come and join me. As he enters via the doorway, I place my finger against my lips and then point to the sofa. At the same time, I manoeuvre myself to a position where I have a line of sight on whoever is behind the sofa, in case they try something stupid. Whether they live or die will depend on their actions once Simon moves the sofa.

The instance Simon pulls the couch out, I yell, "Fucking come out with your hands out where I can see them. One foolish move, and I'll put a hole in your head. Take him to the kitchen and tie him up, Simon. Our trained interrogator will be here soon."

Five minutes later, a voice outside calls out, "Are there any green numpties about?" Both George and Lucy have arrived, followed by Derek.

"No, only some stupid donkey walloper," I shout.

When Lucy enters the room, Simon and Derek are standing beside a skinny-looking man with short brown hair, tied to a chair behind a light-coloured wooden desk.

"Glad you could join us. This man refuses to give us any information. Sure you can have our friend telling us what we need to know," tapping the man on the head.

"This will be fun, Steve," says Lucy.

While Lucy fetches a chair, Simon bends and whispers in the man's ear, starting the process and pulling the fear of what's to come in the man.

"If I were you, I would start talking before that evil bitch starts to interrogate you. The last person she interrogated died in so much pain, it was hard for me to keep watch."

With the chair placed on the other side of the desk from the captive, Lucy sits down across from him, her eyes studying the captive whose fate now rested in her hands. She is a trained interrogator with years of experience under her belt. And there are only a few cases she couldn't break.

The man opposite her is a member of Aron's drug cartel. He is an individual who is unafraid of violence and loyal to his superiors, making him a problematic informant to crack. But she knows gaining his trust would be the key to breaking him. So she spends the next hour getting to understand him, talking about his hobbies, family, and life on the streets. Lucy tells him she understands his world and is there to help him.

"Derek, can you fetch him some food and drink?" Not that she cares about if he is hungry or not. It is a way of letting him believe he can trust her.

Two pieces of bread and a water bottle are placed on the table before him. The man shakes his head.

"Don't panic. It's from your kitchen. The last thing we want to do is hurt you," says Lucy, pushing the items towards him.

He keeps his answers short and to the point, giving up as little information as possible. But Lucy is determined to break him and is prepared to use any means necessary. Despite all her efforts, Lucy only finds out his name is Khalid as he remains suspicious of her.

Switching between various tactics, including shouting, threats, and physical intimidation, she makes good on one of her promises and gets George to punch him in the side of the head. However, she understands that violence will only take her so far. Instead, she uses a technique she perfected over the years - the art of deception. She pretends to be sympathetic to his cause, even offering to help him escape the cartel.

At first, he is suspicious of her, but he begins to open up over time. She keeps the pressure on him, asking him question after question, until she manages to convince Khalid to reveal the whereabouts of the last two hostages. Lucy takes a deep breath. At last she has beaten him, with a combination of empathy, cunning, and sheer force of will without resorting to tactics that would have compromised her ethics. She only has a few.

"I need some fresh air after that," says Lucy, before leaving the building.

I walk outdoors to join Lucy. "Well done, honey, at least we now have the whereabouts of James and Ana," I say, putting my arms around her.

"We do indeed, Steve. It appears we have more travelling to do."

Back inside, Khalid shouts, "I gave you the information you wanted—now let me free."

"Now, here is my problem. If I do that, you will run off to your druggy mates and tell them everything," Derek says, standing beside him.

"I won't. I'll go back to my village and say nothing," says Khalid, pleading for his life.

"Sorry, can't take the chance."

With that, Derek rests his pistol on the man's head and squeezes the trigger. Khalid falls forward onto the desk, blood seeping from the hole in his head, slowly painting the tabletop a dark shade of red.

On hearing the gunshot, I go back inside while Lucy heads off to collect Ralph and Eliza, who are probably wondering if I would keep my word and go back for them.

"Better contact Butch, either by radio if he is in range or by phone, Simon, and arrange to be picked up three hours from now," I say, glancing at the man with his head slumped on the table.

A few minutes later, Lucy enters the room with Eliza and Ralph, doing their best through weak and beaten bodies to be happy to be rescued. If I were in their shoes, I would be sceptical about being released by a group of people they had only recently met. For all they know, we could be a rival drug cartel hoping to collect money for their release.

To help them relax, I take them to a phone and say, "Call your parents and let them know you are OK. Don't take too long. We have some distance to reach our transport."

At that moment, Simon announces, "Good news, folks, as there is a helipad next to the building, Butch has agreed to meet us here. Sorry, you three, I know you become over-excited about tabbing everywhere."

"Good plan, Simon. We must leave here ASAP, before Aron's men come looking." I reply.

Chapter Ten – Journey to Darwin

While we wait for our transport to arrive, George and Derek man the front watchtower closest to the building in case any of Aron's men decide to crawl out of the forest and try to take us by surprise. I use the time to formulate a plan to rescue our main objective, Ana and James.

"Simon, can you contact someone to arrange flights? We need to fly today as we are running out of time."

"No problem," comes the reply.

"Cheers, Simon."

Moments later, Lucy walks over to the table where I'm sitting and hands me a bottle of cold beer she's liberated from one of the fridges in the kitchen.

"Here, this should help lubricate your brain cells," she says through an intoxicating smile.

"Good point, well made," I say, looking up from my notebook.

The next hour goes without any problems, with Lucy and Simon changing over stag with Derek and George in the tower.

At last, we receive the message over the radio we have been waiting for. It is Butch. He is only 10 minutes away. Not wanting to hang around, everyone grabs their kit and heads outside to wait for the transport to arrive.

For an extra level of safety and to give us cover, in case more people are aboard the chopper than expected due to Butch stitching us up, we take positions inside the rainforest's thick undergrowth at the edge of the tree line.

From here, the landscape appears lush and verdant, with tall trees reaching towards the clouds. Green vines hang from their branches, and the vibrant colours of tropical birds flit above the camp. The humidity makes everything appear alive.

The heat is oppressive, with the aroma of wet earth and decay wafting in from the dense underbrush surrounding the landing zone, intertwining with the floral fragrance of the flowering vegetation that grows along the floor.

The sun is blazing high in the sky, beating down on the thick foliage of the rainforest, when we detect the sound of the rotor blades as they slice through the viscous air, drowning out all other sounds around us as the helicopter approaches.

As the aircraft descends, the sound of metallic skids clanging echo through the trees, and the dusty surface of the helipad is just about visible through the tiny particles of sand being thrown skywards. As the chopper settles, the forest shakes and the leaves flutter down. Despite the beauty of the scenery, we don't have time to take it in. We have a mission to complete.

As the helicopter's blades slow and the engine becomes silent, and we are sure nobody is onboard apart from Butch, we emerge from the treeline. Our eyes squint against the sun's intense light and the swirling dust that fills the air.

"Glad you could make it. We have two more passengers. They were held hostage by the cartel," I say, shaking Butch's hand.

"Always keep my word, Steve. If you are ready, clamber onboard and let's head back to San Juan."

Minutes later, everybody is on board. The team takes a deep breath as they have come out of this part of the mission unharmed. Tears of relief roll down the faces of Eliza and Ralph, as they see the camp that kept them prisoner for so long disappear into the distance.

Butch easily navigates the helicopter, his weathered hands skilfully guiding them towards their destination. I peer down at the breaking waves below, as the sun's rays bounce off the crystal-clear waters as we fly over the ocean on our way to San Juan and freedom.

I make the most of the time and review the plan after landing in San Juan to the Sea Drop hotel with the team. "We will separate into two groups," my voice steady and authoritative. "Lucy, Derek, and I, along with Eliza, will take the direct route, while Simon, George, and Ralph will take a different path to provide backup. Remember, communication is key. Stay in contact and be aware of your surroundings at all times."

Derek nods, one hand already on his radio. "Copy that, boss. I'll keep everyone informed every step of the way."

In no time, we are landing on the same helipad we took off from less than a week ago. Once the blades stop spinning, the team disembark from the helicopter and head for the small wooden building.

After Butch disembarks, I walk over to him, "Thanks, Butch. If it's OK with you, I will save your number in case we require your services again. Here is the remainder of the money."

"No problem, it was fun and if you need my assistance again, please call," says Butch, grabbing the envelope from me.

Join the rest, "Simon, if you head off with your squad, I'll give you five minutes head start before we move from here, taking the same route we came here on."

Without saying a word, Simon, George, and Ralph head off, turning right as they leave the park. Peer down at Mickey to confirm the time before I signal the others to follow as I trek towards the hotel.

Lucy keeps Eliza close, whispering words of reassurance and comfort as we walk along the footpath parallel to the seafront.

Derek monitors the radio, hovering his finger over the button in case they need to call for backup.

As we walk, my eyes are scanning the area for any danger or anything that looks out of place or unusual. This part of the mission may be almost over, but we cannot relax until we are in the Sea Drop.

As we approach the hotel, I motion for everyone to stop. We must stand off at a safe distance to avoid falling into a trap. To this end, Lucy and Eliza continue for another 30 metres before Eliza sits on a brown cast iron bench overlooking the ocean. At the same time, Lucy takes up position on the wall, looking back across the road.

A few seconds later, Derek and I repeat the procedure, but to get more eyes on the target, we sit on the two-foot-high wall and face the building. Ten tense minutes elapse before I'm satisfied it is safe, from the outside, at least.

"Derek, can you radio the other team to proceed to the entrance," as I gesture for Lucy and Eliza to move in.

Still not taking any chances, we enter the hotel with caution. Check that the 9mm pistol is still tucked in my jacket. My eyes scan the lobby. It is eerily quiet, and I can't help but feel a sense of unease, like something is out of place.

"Hello again. How was your camping trip?" comes the voice from the direction of the reception desk. It's the same receptionist I gave the bags to before leaving for Saint Ann.

"Hi, it was fantastic. Can we book a couple of day rooms so everyone can freshen up before we head for the airport tonight?" I reply.

"Of course, sir," the young lady says, checking her computer.

The rest of the team enter the lobby and plonk their arses down at the long table to the right of the doorway.

"Here you go. You must vacate the room by 18:00," she hands me two room keys.

"Thank you. Can you fetch the bags we left at the hotel and the one from the safe, please?" I say.

A few minutes later, a man appears, dragging our suitcases and carrying the Faraday pouch containing our electronics.

Give the man a 10 dollar tip before grabbing our stuff and heading for the lifts to the second floor and our room for the day. The boys take one room, and Lucy, Eliza and I take the other.

"Once everybody has sorted themselves out, let's meet in my room in about an hour," I say, as the boys head for their room.

I make the mistake of letting Lucy and Eliza enter the room first, about to follow them when Lucy turns and stands in my way.

"See you in 30 minutes, honey. Go and do something else while we shower," says Lucy, closing the door in my face.

With little to do, I head for the restaurant and bar terrace. They are both closed, but the place is ideal for overlooking the street below, the harbour and the cruise ships docked at the piers across the road. As I observe and the brain takes a well-deserved rest, I witness the Norwegian Epic glide past.

Give it the right amount of time, as instructed by Lucy. I didn't fancy an earful for being early returning to the room. When I arrive, Lucy and Eliza are sitting on the balcony drinking cold beers.

"Did you get me one of them?" I ask, pointing at the beer.

"Sure did, honey. Took the liberty of ordering several for when the boys come in."

"Cheers, I'll grab a hose down before they turn up."

After the last couple of days, a shower is a blissful escape from the oppressive humidity and grime. The warm water cascades over my skin, peeling away the layers of sweat, dirt, and insect repellent. The steam surrounds me, clearing my head and easing the tension in my muscles.

The scent of the shampoo is intoxicating, a sharp contrast to the musty rainforest odour that clings to me like an unwanted rash. The water acts like pure magic, washing away the exhaustion and weariness of the past few days—a welcome respite, rejuvenating and energising me.

By the time I walk out of the shower, the rest of the team is standing on the balcony, each drinking from a dark green bottle. I take a beer from the fridge and join them.

"You look different, Steve, after your scrub… Sorry, my mistake, you're still a fat, ugly bastard," George says after gulping a mouthful of beer.

"He may be all of that, but he will be getting some later, unlike you," replies Lucy, defending me.

"Cheers, Lucy, and if I look like you, George, I wouldn't be pointing things like that out," comes my reply.

Twenty minutes pass until I stop all conversation, "OK, folks, before we relax too much, we better discuss the plans for the way forward from here. As we know, the remaining hostages, Ana and James, have been removed, and according to the information our friend Khalid provided, they have gone with Aron and Ryan. Did you manage to make our travel arrangements, Simon?"

"Yes, but from here, it will be several long flights. The best route is to fly back to London Heathrow, landing at 05:00. The next flight leaves at 18:00, and we will arrive in Darwin, Australia, at 11:50 the day after, local time. I've booked us all in business class."

"Thanks, Simon. Lucky for us, we found some of the products left behind by Aron and his numpties which will cover our extra costs. Simon, could you call Philip, sure he will know someone who will want to buy the stuff?"

"Good idea, as we can't take it with us on the flights," says Simon, taking out his mobile to make arrangements for the meeting.

"Once we finally get to Darwin, Simon will arrange two off-road vehicles to take us to Burrow Creek. If we drive straight there, this should only take no more than 12 hours.

"Once more, according to the information supplied by Khalid, his boss has given the families until the end of the month, seven days from now, to come up with the ransom money. Or he will execute James, followed by Ana shortly after. This means when we arrive, we will not have much time to rescue the hostages."

"Do we know where they have taken them in Burrow Creek?" Derek enquires.

"From the info provided to me, they have been moved to a remote roadhouse off the Stuart Highway," replies Lucy.

"What about our two friends here, Ralph and Eliza?" George asks.

I turn to face Eliza, who is sipping on a Coke, "Lucy has contacted your families. We will hand you over at our hotel in Darwin."

There isn't much time left before we have to go, so we all slow down with the drinking. The last thing we need is for any of us to be denied boarding due to intoxication. It's agreed to meet in the lobby in three hours, ready to catch a taxi to San Juan Luis Munoz Marin airport.

To be on the safe side, I book a seven-seater cab via reception on my way out to our meeting with Phillip, to sell him our drugs haul. We can't afford to miss the flight, as time is fast running out for Ana and James.

While I linger with anticipation, not knowing what will happen, George conceals himself nearby in case things don't go to plan. Time ticks by with no sense of speed as we wait for Phillip and the unnamed third party at the abandoned pier close to the Sea Drop hotel.

The stink of seaweed and saltwater fills my nostrils. It is the perfect clandestine location to offload the two kilos of recovered drugs. The palms of both hands are slick with sweat, wondering if I've fucked up. My eyes dart around, taking in every sound and movement, my trigger finger itching with anticipation.

The pungent stench of burning tyres fills my lungs as a black SUV pulls up in front of me. The tension in the air is thick as Phillip and the third party, a middle-aged man with a hardened expression, clamber out and approach with a swagger. His eyes flick over the two kilos of cocaine I'd placed on the small wooden fence that ran along the pier's edge.

It doesn't matter how often I've done this type of meeting in my army days, I'm overcome with an overpowering sense of something I can't make out, which makes me uneasy. We are playing with the unknown. Yet, the lure of the profit is too much to resist.

"Steve, this is the man I mentioned who is ready to buy. Of course, I want my cut," says Phillip, pointing to the man on his right.

The man pulls out a wad of cash from his pocket. "I'll give you 4,000 dollars for the two."

"They are worth 10,000." I haven't a fucking clue what they go for on the open market, not being a druggy, but we need a reasonable price. Let's face it: nobody will give you their best price immediately.

"OK, 6,000, my last offer," comes the reply.

The drug dealer produces a gun from his waistband and aims it at me.

"On second thoughts, I'll take it all and pay you fuck all," he says, walking over and picking up the drugs. His pistol is still aiming at my head.

"How did I know you might try something like this," I say, as George emerges and swings his arm around the dealer's neck before resting his 9mm on the side of his head.

With that, Phillip draws his weapon and points it at me, "Tell your man to release him, or you are a dead man."

We don't have time for this crap, so tap my shoulder, which is the prearranged signal for George to waste the man the moment he gets the shot.

"Drop it, Phillip, or he dies," George says, pushing the barrel hard against the man's head.

A second later, Phillip turns to face George. I take advantage of this and, in one swift movement, remove my pistol from my jacket and fire. There is the sound of a crack and thump as the round lands in the left side of Phillip's face, and he drops to the floor. At the same instance, the drug dealer receives a bullet to the side of his head.

"That's a result, Steve. We have the drugs and the money," says George, going through the dead man's pockets and picking up the wad of cash the druggy dropped.

"We have at least 40 grand here. The man must have been planning a busy night."

Not wanting the drugs, we tear open the packages and dispose of the contents into the sea before returning to the hotel.

The next few hours tick by as everyone repacks their equipment, ready for the flights. We all ensure we have nothing in our bags that might have us detained by some nosey customs officials. The weapons will be broken down into components and stashed in several locations. If some numpty finds one package, they will not find all the elements.

Once my kit is packed, I collect George, and we head along the harbour with the weapon parts, towards the park close to where Butch flies his helicopter from, and hide the first pack wrapped in plastic in the bushes behind the toilets.

I'm tempted to take a photo of the area so we can all locate them if required, but I decide this would be a stupid idea. If my phone and I get separated, some intelligent person might be able to follow the trail of photos. Instead, we leave a marker where we would recognise the location, but it is difficult for anyone else.

Carry out the same procedure in three more locations before returning to the hotel. When we arrive, the team are sitting in the reception with their kit ready for the off.

"Your stuff is here," Lucy points to mine and George's bags resting against the orange sofa.

"Cheers, Lucy. The cab should be here in the next couple of minutes."

Right on time, an Indian man in his late 20s walks through the door and heads for the young receptionist, only to come our way a few seconds later. "Taxi to the airport for Steve?" the man asks.

"Yep, that's us," I respond, picking up my bag and following him out the door.

Once we arrive at the airport and unload everyone's kit, pay the driver, including a 10-dollar tip. I can't be arsed to carry my bags, so I throw them on the baggage trolley with everyone else's. The wheels squeak and clack against the polished floors as we search for the business lounge.

We make our way through the buzzing departure hall. Its hum of chatter and footsteps fill our ears. As always, my eyes scan the area and everybody inside, on the lookout for any danger as we navigate through the surging crowds of people, each with their own stories to tell.

As we venture deeper into the terminal, the sweet aroma of freshly brewed coffee and the buttery smell of baked pastries waft through the air, luring us towards the nearest cafe. But why pay extortionate prices when we are flying business class, where we have access to free food and drinks?

Weaving through the throngs of people, I overhear snippets of conversations in different languages, adding to the excitement and mystery of our journey through the airport. Every now and again, the robotic voice in the ceiling booms above the noise hum, announcing gate changes and departures.

Amid it all, Lucy teases George about his choice of snack taken from the vending machine near the entrance, saying that he would have a sugar crash before we board the plane. Simon makes jokes about Derek's travel pillow, which is strapped to his waist like a well-worn bum bag, calling him a modern-day traveller.

Our camaraderie draws laughs from strangers and warm smiles from airport staff, oblivious to the fact that this team of people only hours earlier had been involved in a gun battle and killed several of the drug cartel's people.

A few minutes later, we spot the sign for the business lounge we'd been looking for and quicken the pace. As we walk through the door, we all take a deep breath, grateful for the respite from the hustle and bustle of the terminal.

Inside, the place is chaotic with sharply-dressed businesspeople and weary travellers. All are clamouring for drinks and food from the overstuffed counters before scrambling for a seat at the crowded tables.

After finding seats in the far corner and plonking our backsides down, the battering of the senses continues—the sweet aroma of coffee and fresh, warm quiches wafting through the air. The hum of chatter and the clink of cutlery invites us over to join the action at the buffet. Lucy opts for a latte with a sprinkling of cinnamon. I pour myself a strong black mug of caffeine. Derek grabs a brew and several croissants still warm from the oven, Simon snags a chocolate chip muffin, and George clutches a green tea.

We sit in silence at the table with our hoard, stuffing our faces and sipping on drinks. It didn't take long before a voice from the chillers start to shout my name, and who am I to argue?

"Anyone else want a beer while I'm up?"

This is, as always, a stupid question, as I receive six resounding "Yes!".

"Steve, grab us all two beers each. Will save you from getting back up again in a minute," Simon shouts.

"Right on it, Your Majesty, I'll get straight on it," I reply, opening the fridge.

After dropping the drinks on the table, I walk to the large screen displaying travel information. Our gate number is showing. We have 30 minutes before we have to move our arses for the flight to London.

The journey goes by fast, with all of us taking advantage of the lie-flat beds in business class, and catching up on well-needed sleep; only waiting for the hostess to come around with food.

Before we know it, we have landed at Heathrow, made our way through transit, missing customs, and are heading for the transit gate and back into departures, ready for the long wait until our next flight. When we arrive, Lucy is already showing signs of weariness.

By the time the long 13-hour wait for the next flight is over, we are all bored of walking around the duty free shops, eating too much with the occasional drinks. For once, I'm over the moon to be walking back to board another aircraft.

At the boarding gate, Simon and I are busy making small talk with the check-in staff, Derek is double-checking his passport, and George is looking up information on the amenities onboard.

Getting on the aircraft is a smooth and orderly affair, and we again settle into our seats. Thirty minutes later, we take off with a roar of the mighty aircraft engines. The passengers next to the windows are treated to a panoramic view of London.

Once in the air, each of us settles into the comfort of our business class suite, complete with a plush seat that reclines fully, a personal 24-inch TV and a spacious work area. Being a gadget freak, I'm impressed with the suite's high-tech controls. Lucy enjoys the luxury of snoozing in a comfortable bed after sleeping on the ground over the last week.

Throughout the flight, the hard-working crew treat us to various amenities and services. Simon indulges, like he always does, on an aircraft and downs several glasses of champagne. Derek reads a book on his screen called *Covert-Ops: The Golden Camel*. George samples the movie selection in the seat next to me while Lucy purchases a magazine. When not in the land of nod, I take the time to refine the plan for rescuing the remaining two hostages.

Being such a long flight, meals are served at regular intervals, ranging from tempting appetisers to desserts, which would make anybody's mouth water. The aroma of the food wafts through the air as all the passengers eat their fill.

After what appears like an eternity, the plane touches down on the runway at Darwin International Airport. Our minds switch back to the crucial task, risking our lives to rescue Ana and James from Aron's drug cartel. The journey from San Juan has been lengthy, but now it is time to refocus on the mission.

The instance the seatbelt sign comes off, we join the pushing and shoving in the aisle full of people trying to get their bags from the overhead lockers; everyone panicking, fearing someone wants to steal their carryon luggage. Soon, the line of people in front of us thins out, and we make our way out of the plane.

Now it's time to pass through the dreaded passport control and customs. Plus if you've watched too many airport programmes on television, you're feeling guilty and expecting to be taken away and strip searched at any moment, me included, even though you're innocent of any crime; well most people are!

Today of all days, there is added security at the airport as some idiot tried smuggling a pistol through the terminal a few days back.

We should all fly through any checks. Besides, we left anything that appeared to be part of a weapon hidden in stashes around San Juan. Unless we have some switched-on official who can put the items in my bag together, we should be OK. Plus, the news of any killings on Saint Ann shouldn't have reached here!

As we approach passport control, the sound of metal detectors and the stench of disinfectant fills the air. It's a tense situation, and I can feel my nerves on edge as we all monitor the customs officials as they scrutinise every traveller's documents with a keen eye.

This is no time to relax, we must head for the baggage reclaim and navigate through the crowds of people. Time to use the extensive skills of working undercover to avoid detection. The team stands off and observes as their bags go around the conveyor. Only when it's completed several circuits, and nobody has paid any attention to our stuff, do we grab them.

Once we have everything, we make our way outside. Rows of waiting taxis are lined up along the edge of the highway. But I've been here before and know the Mercure Darwin Airport Resort, where we will stay for the night, is only a 10-minute walk.

"Come on, folks, follow me. It's not far," I say, leading off and following the footpath to the right.

We pass the massive car hire parking lot full of busy holidaymakers eager to pick up their vehicles and be on their way. Then, cross the road, passing in front of the Novotel Hotel. Five minutes later, we arrive at our hotel, exhausted and relieved.

The reception area is extensive and open to the elements at both ends, letting the natural light flood in. Ceiling fans slice through the air with a near-silent hum above us. The chirping sounds come from several small birds flying up into the rafters. You can see the swimming pool surrounded by lush green vegetation through the far end. Over to our left, two young ladies stand behind a dark wooden desk, speaking to an older couple.

Five more minutes elapse before we are booking in for the night. One of the young ladies behind the reception desk smiles and greets us.

"Good afternoon, welcome to the Mercure Hotel."

"Hi, we have three rooms booked," says Lucy.

"Give me a minute while I find your reservation," comes the reply from Jane, the receptionist.

As she does this, I turn to face the others sitting on the edge of a raised flowerbed in the centre of the room. "Once we have dumped our luggage in the room, we will meet up in the bar. Which is around to the left."

"Trust you to know where the boozer is, fucking pisshead," Simon chuckles to himself.

"Takes one to know one," I reply.

"Here you go, rooms 506, 507 and 508. If you follow the path to your right, you will find them in the first block you come to," says Jane, handing Lucy the keys.

After throwing my bag in the corner, I grab a beer from the fridge and walk out onto the terrace overlooking the airfield, the occasional planes' engines roar and thunder, punctuating the stillness with a constant hum.

Moments later, Lucy joins me, leaning on the metal and glass railing that surrounds the balcony. We both stare at the airport, savouring the rare moment of calm, each of us enjoying a cold one. The coldness in our hands is refreshing, the icy condensation dripping down the sides of our bottles and pooling on the tiled floor beneath our feet.

Several minutes pass in silence as we finish our drinks. "OK, we better head down and meet the others," I say, walking back into the room and picking up a green folder.

As we enter through the enormous glass doors, a sense of warmth and relaxation encases us. The spacious room is bathed in sunshine, which pours in through the windows, casting a golden glow over everything. The square-shaped bar stands in the centre of the room, its polished wooded surface gleaming in the light. Adorned with sleek stools, patrons sit sipping drinks while chatting and laughing.

To the left and right are more high tables and chairs. Atmospheric jazz music and gentle chatter blend in the background, creating a soothing and convivial atmosphere. I breathe in the aromatic scent of freshly brewed coffee and wood polish, mingled with the aroma of delicious cakes and pastries baking in the restaurant nearby.

As I gaze about the room, taking in the greenery scattered around the area, it's like I am in an upscaled tropical paradise. The large patio doors on two sides of the bar allow you to take in the views of the surrounding palm trees, which sway in the breeze, creating a tranquil mood that soothes the senses.

Outside, the sun beats down on the decking, reflecting on the polished floors and slick surfaces, producing a shimmering and laid-back environment.

My worries simply melt away as I take in the sumptuous, relaxed ambience. But I can't help but think of this as an oasis of tranquillity amid the hustle and bustle of a mission.

"Fancy another beer, Lucy?" I say, standing up from the table.

"Yes, please."

Moments later, as I'm joining Lucy at one of the tables on the outside deck, the rest enter the bar, spot us and come over.

"Before we start, Eliza and Ralph, it's best you know nothing about our plans. Safer for you both. Besides, your families will be here within the hour to take you home," I say.

After leaving us, they walk back inside and take up a couple of seats along the far wall.

Once they are out of earshot, "OK, it's time to discuss the plan I came up with on the plane for rescuing the hostages. Studying the maps and satellite images of the area around Burrow Creek where they have been taken onboard, I evaluated and analysed every possible outcome and plotted a course of action to result in a successful rescue."

Now, as a team, we try to predict Aron's cartel's movements and figure out the best approach for the mission, refining the plan I came up with. We speak in low voices, so no nosey bastard can hear us as we review strategies and assess different scenarios.

The conversation is intense, each member bringing their unique expertise. The stakes are high. Anything less than a flawless execution could have catastrophic consequences. Time is running out, and we have to act fast.

After 30 minutes, we have a sort of plan. We need to get eyes on the target for the finer details.

"Simon, have you booked the vehicles?"

"Yep, we pick them up at 08:00 tomorrow from the car hire place we passed on the way to the hotel."

"In that case, we will pick up the vehicles and proceed to some shopping area, then head to Burrow Creek," I say.

We spend the next couple of hours enjoying the sun and the beers, until we all take some private time before the mission gets underway again.

Chapter Eleven – Trip to Burrow Creek

The alarm on my phone blurts Reveille at 05:00, bursting me out of the deep slumber I've been in since I last checked the time four hours ago. With my body now alert and ready for action, I head for the bathroom for my usual routine of shit, shave and shampoo.

When I re-enter the room, I'm greeted with, "Hope you haven't stunk the place out," from Lucy, heading for the shower.

"Morning, honey, nope, it's stink-free. You want a drink?"

"Yes, please."

I head over to the wardrobe and pull out the brew-making kit. Hotels have started doing this for some reason, probably to make the room appear uncluttered.

With coffee in hand, I head onto the balcony and sit on one of the cream-coloured chairs on either side of a small glass-topped table. As I sip on the hot mug of caffeine, I start going through today's plans.

After we pick up the vehicles and buy supplies, we will make a straight dash for Burrow Creek, swapping drivers every two hours. I will run it over once more with the team at breakfast. I aim to reach a point close to the roadhouse just before last light and set up camp. From here, we will complete an early morning recce before rescuing the hostages the same or the next day, depending on time.

Behind me, I detect the sound of the kettle being turned on—Lucy must be out of the shower. To be sure, I swivel in my seat and peer back toward the noise. A minute later, she comes out and sits on the other chair.

"What time did we say we are all meeting up for breakfast? I'm starving," I ask.

"Don't worry, fat boy. You don't have long to wait. We said 07:00, but we can go down earlier."

I glance down at the timepiece on my wrist. The time is now 06:00.

"Perfect plan," I reply, getting up to make a fresh brew.

As we enter the restaurant, its high ceilings and two sides of floor-to-ceiling windows allow natural light to flood the space. The air is thick with the scent of freshly brewed coffee, sizzling bacon, and a hint of citrus, coming from the buffet-style breakfast, which is set up against the restaurant's back wall. It's a cornucopia of delicious aromas and flavours. Stacks of golden pancakes drizzled with syrup, scrambled eggs, and bacon crispy enough to tempt almost anyone. The whole atmosphere hits you like a wave.

It must be too early for most people, as only a few occupy four tables. We find ourselves at a seat by the window and gaze at the stunning view while waiting for the waitress to come over.

"Morning. Can I have your room number, please? You can help yourselves to breakfast from the buffet," comes the voice of a young lady standing next to Lucy.

"Of course, it's 506, and thank you," I reply, before she walks away.

Dump my loaded plate on the table, then return to the counter to grab freshly squeezed orange juice and more coffee.

As we tuck in, the place becomes alive with the hustle and bustle of people looking to fuel up for the day. With the hum of conversation coming from all around us as more people pile in for breakfast, the sound of cutlery clinking against the china plates and the occasional laughter breaking through the chatter, the distant chirping of birds outside drifts inside to join the ambience.

Ten minutes later, Simon, Derek and George appear in the doorway, talking to the same woman who took our room number earlier. On spotting us, Derek comes over.

"Morning, folks. I'll grab some nosh and be over," he says, before heading to the buffet, where George is piling up his plates.

Once we are all sat at the table, I run through the plans again, from checking out to arriving at our campsite for the night, making sure I don't use the words drug cartel or hostages, so it doesn't attract the attention of any nosey bastard.

After everyone is finished and loaded with a few extra food items for the trip, we are about to leave when Eliza arrives, accompanied by an older man and a woman we haven't seen before. This surprises me, as she should have departed with Ralf and his parents last night.

Intrigued, I walk over to greet them, "Moring Eliza, I thought you were leaving yesterday with Ralph?"

"I was going to, until I received a call informing me they were flying here and would arrive at 21:00. By the way, this is Bob and Margret, my mum and dad."

"Nice to meet you," shaking the man's hand.

"We wanted to come and collect our daughter in person. Plus, thank you for rescuing her from the hands of those terrorists," he replies.

"Not just me, but the whole team," I gesture towards the table where the rest have sat back down.

"Can we join you for a few minutes? We want to discuss something with you before you leave," asks Bob, pointing at the group.

"Yeah, no problem. Can I get you a drink?"

"Yes, Please. Two coffees will be nice," says Bob, before heading to where the team are sitting.

While I'm getting the brews, Bob, Margret, and Eliza sit beside Lucy.

Once I return to the table, I place the drinks down. Picking up the mug, Bob sips the steaming coffee.

"Sorry to be a pain and rush you. But we still have some work to do."

"Of course, Steve, this will not take long. To show our gratitude to you all for rescuing Eliza and bringing her to Darwin, we want to thank you all personally and give you a small bonus in person," Bob says, while removing an envelope from the briefcase he'd been carrying.

"That's appreciated but unnecessary," I reply, taking the package.

"It's not a problem. Just go and rescue Ana and James. One more thing before you go, take this," Margret pushes a business card in my direction.

"What is it for?"

"When you are ready to return to the UK, call this number and ask for Nigel. He will arrange your transport home."

"Thank you. We will have to leave you here, as we need to go and find someone," raising to my feet and offering them my hand.

After shaking their hands, we depart and head out of the restaurant, arranging to collect our bags from our room and meet in 10 minutes outside reception before walking to the car hire pickup point.

When we arrive at the grey portacabin, the time is 08:30. A young man in his early 20s, dressed in the company's uniform, is standing behind the counter.

"Hi, we have two vehicles booked with you under the name of Simon."

"Morning, Simon, give me a minute, and I'll have them brought from the parking lot once we finish the paperwork and take payment," explains the man, whose badge displays the name Ethan.

A few minutes later, another employee enters the office and places two keys on the desk. After a couple of signatures on the hire form, we follow Ethan into the huge car park, with hire vehicles as far as you can see. Two white, beefy-looking Toyota Land Cruisers stand in front of us in a separate area. One has a roof rack, while the other has a flat panel spread across the top.

"What's on the top?" I point to the left of the two Land Cruisers.

"As you are going off-road, we have supplied you with a solar panel to charge all your batteries and communication equipment," the salesman says, handing me the keys.

"Thanks, see you in two weeks," I say.

Once the man returns inside, we check both vehicles for any damage and take photos of all around the vehicle. I learned the hard way when I handed a hire car back a few years ago; when I arrived home, I received an email wanting money for the large scratch, which already existed when I picked up the damn thing.

Everyone knows what they are doing from the planning. So Simon, Derek and George clamber into one of the Land Cruisers and Lucy and I in the other. As we pull out of the parking area, Derek sends a radio check over the airwaves.

"LK, Radio Check, Over."

"DR, OK, Over," Lucy answers to confirm her radio is working.

We have been driving for about 15 minutes before we come across a shopping centre with a Woolworths supermarket. We must purchase some stuff for the next few days, so go in and park up. They are different from the stores that used to be in the UK many years ago. The ones in Australia sell food, not clothes.

Once inside, we stock up on supplies and the all-important beer, plus I find the remainder of the gear I may require for defences and to make things go bang. Collect three mobile pay-as-you-go phones and a soldering iron. I will convert these into remote detonators if I have the time tonight.

The other equipment we need for the mission will be picked up at Daly Waters, six hours from our current location, courtesy of our friendly arms dealers, Katie and Cody. They have arranged for a man called Tyler to meet us there. Because they have never let us down in the past, the man, the weapons and the explosives will be there. But in case they aren't, I formulate a plan to deal with the situation if it arises.

With the stuff loaded, Simon, as our recce troop, will lead the way with Lucy and me following in our vehicle about 100 metres behind. To be sure we don't miss them turning while in town, Derek will communicate every turn by radio until we reach Stuart Highway, where it will be a straight run to the next RV near Davenport.

After two hours of driving through the wild landscape of Lichfield National Park, with its overwhelming scent of eucalyptus from the plants and trees that line the roadside, we come across the small townlet of Adelaide River, a cluster of houses and caravan parks on either side of the road.

Outside the town, Simon pulls over as this is the two-hour mark, and we need to change drivers. The stop is only short as we can't afford to waste any time. So once Lucy and George take over the driving, we depart, heading for the weapon collection at Daly Waters. Of course, Simon and I can drive the whole way, but the idea is to arrive with every person being 100 per cent ready to take any action that might present itself.

Not long after leaving the changeover point, Lucy needs to swerve as several kangaroos dart out of the rainforest in front of her.

Two more hours go by before George turns off the highway, followed by Lucy, and drives down a street to nowhere. At the bottom is Daly Waters. As you pass the two welcoming signs, on your right is a field. The green grass is divided by three reddish dirt tracks running in straight lines leading away from the road, rows of electrical power hookup points along the middle of each patch of grass. Two vehicles are parked near a row of toilet blocks at the far end. Beside them are four brown swag tents.

Off to our left are several large grey buildings with a collection of transport bits, including the cockpit of a light aircraft. One section is cordoned off by a wire mesh fence. Next to it a large sign saying 'Snappy lives here', with a picture of a crocodile.

Further along the street is Daly Waters pub, where we will meet Tyler in about 40 minutes. A small museum and two fuel dispensers are in front of the building on the opposite side. Checking out the area for apparent dangers, George continues to the end before turning around and heading to my vehicle, which Lucy's parked near the pumps.

With everyone out of the vehicles, "OK, folks, this is where we are to make contact with Tyler, the person with the equipment we need, at 15:00, which gives us plenty of time. Nobody will have any idea of why we are here, so, there's no point in being too tactical. But keep alert as always. We might as well top up the cars with petrol and grab something to eat."

"Steve. I'll go over and tell them we are refuelling. The sign says to fill up and pay in the boozer. I'll take George with me in case of any issues," says Lucy, heading towards the pub.

With the fuel paid for, we move the vehicles over to the other side of the road outside the main building, facing the way we came in. We may need to move from here in a hurry.

The bar is in front of you, plastered with photos and stickers as you walk through the door. Off to the left is a small souvenir shop selling local items and stuff relating to Daly Waters. To the right are several wooden tables and chairs, and a television hangs on the far wall. All the walls and ceiling are adorned with photographs, placards and t-shirts of every description. Another door leads to a covered outdoor sitting area with more timber tables and bench seats.

What is strange is that the place is quiet apart from the TV blasting out a sports channel. On a couple of the tables are menus. I grab one.

After scanning the list of items, "Derek, come over here; something on the menu you might like."

"What is it, numpty? Bound to be something stupid," Derek says, taking it from me.

"Bum nuts," I say, trying my best not to laugh out loud like a deranged moron.

The young lady behind the counter announces that Australians call eggs bum nuts.

The fit of laughter over, everyone orders food and a few beers and we make our way outside, where our conversation can't be overheard.

While we eat, "Once we have finished eating, we must take precautions for when Tyler arrives. I would hate for us to be taken by surprise. So Simon and I will be the ones who make contact. If Derek covers us from somewhere over there," I point to the far end where a stage has been erected.

"If Lucy waits in our vehicle at the front of the pub, George, take your vehicle, drive around the back, and park on the grass close to the exit," I gesture towards the exit leading to the camping field.

"Roger, we will keep the engines running in case we need to bug out at speed," replies Lucy.

"Anyone seen where the bogs are?" asks Simon, getting up from the table.

"They are over in the corner. If you're confused, you are the one without the sign saying Sheila," comes the helpful remark from George.

A glance down at Mickey confirms the time is now 14:45, so everyone downs their drinks and heads to the positions for the weapons collection.

Another check of the time. The next 15 minutes tick away, hurrying for nobody. The time is 15:05, so he's late. My mind starts to review the plans I'd formulated earlier about starting the rescue minus the firepower. Then, I detect two people chatting from inside the bar. Kick Simon under the table and point towards the doorway.

Positive we have covered all possibilities, I lean against the wall, hoping the man whose voice I've heard is Tyler.

Didn't have to wait long when a man in his mid-40s dressed in blue jeans, a green shirt, and a dark brown rimmed hat walks through the door. Simon and I scrutinise his every move as he ambles over to the stage before turning right and heading for the exit.

"Shit, this isn't him," I say under my breath. Seconds later, he comes back and approaches us.

"Hello, you must be Steve, one of the people I'm here to meet," the man says, as he sits beside Simon.

"Hi, how do you know I'm the person you are meeting?" I didn't want to share too much.

"Simple, you're the only ones here apart from the staff, and I met all of them on many occasions. Sorry about the little detour. Wanted to check that I am not walking into some trap."

"Fair enough. I'm Steve, and that's Simon. Do you have the stuff we requested through our mutual friend?" still not wanting to give anything away.

"Yes, Katie and Cody are friends of mine, informed me of what you need. It's all outside in my truck. They also told me, you are here to take down some drug cartel. So I will provide you with some extra kit to dispose of these arseholes. On a personal note, a close family member was killed in a gunfight between rival drug gangs in Sydney a year back."

"Thanks, will do. We already despatched a few on Saint Ann. Can we grab the stuff now? We must get a move on as time is short for the people they are holding hostage."

"Of course, Steve, come with me," Tyler says, getting up, walking back inside the pub, and exiting through the front door.

Tyler heads for a small truck with a canvas cover over the cargo compartment, parked around the corner from the fuel pumps. As I go past Lucy sitting in the Toyota, I tap on the glass and gesture for her to follow us down the road.

We have just met this man, and as I don't trust anyone, Simon walks down the right-hand side, surveying the building down both sides of the street, peering into all the positions that might be hiding an accomplice of Tyler's.

My hand grips the hunting knife purchased from the shopping centre. I walk 20 feet behind our contact, expecting him to turn and fire at any point. Moments later, Tyler reaches his vehicle and places one hand on the canvas. He lifts it a few inches. Then, he inserts his arm. I freeze, observing his every move before turning to see where Simon is. He's also stopped and is looking in the direction of the truck.

A clanging of metal echoes in the confines of the street, scattering a flock of birds situated in a tree at the end of the road, as Tyler drops the tailgate. He turns and beckons me over, while pulling back the sheet even further.

Standoff for a minute, still not trusting him. Once I reach his location, I peer into the back. It's loaded with green wooden boxes. Tyler lifts the lid of one of them to reveal an M4 carbine with an effective range of 400 metres and four magazines.

"I have five of them for you, with 2,000 5.56 nato rounds," says Tyler, opening another longer box.

"Great job, just what we need," I reply, taking the carbine out of the crate and handing it to Simon, who's joined us.

"Only have two of these L115A3 sniper rifles and only 300 rounds. But let's face it, snipers don't require many," Tyler hands me the weapon.

"This will keep my sniper team happy as they have used this rifle numerous times. Got anything else?" I ask.

"Yeah, Katie said you like explosives," Tyler opens another metal container. Inside is packed with bundles of C4.

My eyes light up. I have some play equipment, "Got any detonators and detonator cords?"

"Of course, explosives aren't much cop without it, apart from lighting fires. They are in the cab. Didn't want to put them together," Tyler walks to the front of the truck and collects another metal box.

"That's everything we need. What about payment?" taking out several envelopes, each holding 10,000 dollars.

"Remember when I said a family member got shot by fucking druggies? If you kill them all and send me a photo as proof, I have an amazing price for you. You can have the lot for 20,000 to cover my costs. Deal?"

"Can't argue with that," I hand over two bundles containing the money.

"One more thing before you head off. I offered you something extra," Tyler reaches to the back of the truck and pulls out a LAW 66 anti-tank weapon.

"That's a gift from me," Tyler smiles as he hands it to me.

Lucy backs up to the tailgate, and we transfer everything. We say our goodbyes and drive around to meet George, still parked on the camping ground with Derek, before driving off.

I don't want to remove the weapons at Daly Waters, in case someone spots them. We push on for another hour down the road. I take the lead until we encounter a sideroad and a sign indicating a disused World War II Australian army base. Several old concrete slabs are 300 metres along the red dirt trail. They probably supported wooden buildings when the camp was in use.

Pull up on the side of the track and clamber out, first checking my surroundings for anything that might be slithering in the grass. Let's face it, some of the world's deadliest snakes live in the Australian Outback. If you are bitten out here, you're fucked.

"Give us a hand to unload this stuff," I say, opening the back of the vehicle. In no time, we have the boxes laid out on the ground.

"So, what did you buy me, Steve?" says George, stepping over several crates and heading for the longest box.

"Something you and Lucy are familiar with. For the rest of us, we all have M4 Carbines and plenty of ammo."

Spend the next 20 minutes unpacking everything, sharing the ammunition and separating the detonator, cord and explosives, with the C4 going in one vehicle and the detonators in the other.

We can't afford to leave the wooden boxes with our grubby fingerprints all over them, so stack them up in the centre of the concrete pad and set them alight. With a bit of help from some fuel, they soon burn down into a pile of black ash.

Time appears to skip a few minutes as I glance at my timepiece. We only have a few hours left before it gets dark, and we must be in our RV.

I take out the splash map from my jacket pocket. Luckily, I purchased it for my last trip here and always take it with me as it's got multiple uses, including using it to cover my mouth in dusty situations.

"Come on, boys and girls, better make a move. Simon, you retake the lead and drive nonstop for three hours or until we reach this spot," I place my finger on the map. Once Simon is clear on the location, we head for the rendezvous point.

Back on the Stuart Highway, we make reasonable time and soon arrive at the turning for the Devil's Marbles Hotel, only one hour from Burrow Creek Roadhouse, where Ana and James are being held. Simon turns off and stops across the road next to a four-trailer road train.

With me now leading, we head off further down the highway until I find an area of bare ground in the middle of some trees. As the light is starting to fade, I pull in.

I lean forward in the driver's seat, squinting in the setting sun as I drive into the isolated clearing. Both cars drive at five kilometres an hour, to not kick clouds of red dirt into the sky, giving away our position. Before doing anything else, I take out my Splashmap and mentally note our location.

Through the open window, "Simon, after we unload the equipment, we better conceal the two vehicles in that hole tonight."

"No problem, mate," comes the reply.

Once everyone disembarks and unloads the gear we need for tonight, we stand under the shade of a clump of trees with the sun beating down mercilessly, the air still simmering with heat. It may be March in the Australian Outback, but the unforgiving climate punishes us at every turn.

As soon as the vehicles are hidden, I call the team for a briefing. "OK, folks, here is tonight's plan. Once we are set up here, the rifles need to be checked and zeroed. We are at least a 30-minute drive from the roadhouse, and with the trees and terrain, the sound from the weapons shouldn't be an issue. Just separate each check fire a few minutes apart. The ground dips over between those trees we can use."

I point towards the far end of the clearing, about 200 metres away.

I unfold my Splashmap of the area and spread it on the floor. I kept it as we came this way on my last trip to the Outback. I am glad I brought the set of three with me. Pick up a small twig on the floor next to my feet and utilise it to point at the map.

"We are here and going to recce the roadhouse here." Place a stone on the roadhouse so everyone has a reference point.

"Like always, Derek, you're in charge of comms and responsible for keeping us all in radio communication. You will be with me when we try to find out where Ana and James are located. From the terrain, we will need two different sniper positions. George and Lucy, you two are our snipers. I'll leave it up to you to scope out the area, one at the front across the road and one on this ridge line to the rear of the buildings."

"Roger that. I'll take the front, George, if that's OK with you?" says Lucy.

"No problem. Sure I can find some cover around here that overlooks the rear," George points to the area behind the roadhouse on the map.

"Once we have the hostages, we might have to make a fast withdrawal. Simon, you will locate yourself in the dead ground to the right of the property, after you have dropped us all off close to our start positions. The map shows that a dirt track leads off in that direction."

"Sounds reasonable to me. We will need both vehicles even for the recce in case we are compromised," said Simon.

"Good point, mate. I'll drive the other vehicle, and Derek and I can make our way from your location. We'll try to make our way closer to the roadhouse for a better look. Remember, stay sharp and alert. We don't know what we're up against. It could be just Aron, Ryan, a few of his men, or a group. One thing is for sure: they will be armed. Any questions?"

Everyone shakes their heads, "In that case, two more points. First, we are in the Australian Outback. You will have wildlife slithering past, so no screaming like little girls and running through the undergrowth. If you are bitten, radio straight through. We will take you to the hospital as fast as we can. Our lives are far more important than the hostages."

"That's you fucked then, George. You will be racing around like a sissy on heat," says Simon, laughing out loud.

"If I were you, Simon, I would check your swag before you clamber in tonight. And what you chuckling about, Derek? I'm opening the flaps to let all the mosquitoes in," replies George.

"My second point: make sure you take extra water with you. Plus, make time for some rest. We will move out at 04:00."

After the briefing, everyone disperses and checks their weapons and their kit. Lucy and George head off to zero the sniper rifles before the rest of us take turns doing the same.

Chapter Twelve –Burrow Creek Recce

I had been awake most of the night with the plans running through my mind, so I get up and pack my gear. The rest, apart from George, who is on stag, are asleep. So I take time to prepare the phones into remote detonators, using the equipment purchased earlier.

With extreme care, remove several bricks of C4 from the metal storage box in the back of the vehicle. Put them in two small hessian sacks, two in each bag, connect two electrical detonators into two separate blocks of C4. One would do the job but want a backup in case the first doesn't work.

Attach one wire from the detonator to one of the wires protruding from the mobile. The other cables won't be connected until Derek and I disembark from the vehicles and get closer to the roadhouse. Place them in the holdall.

By the time I finish, I can hear George banging on the swags to wake the rest of the team. A few moments later, with everyone crawling out of their tents and quietly packing their equipment into the back of the Land Cruisers, George wanders over to join me. He had packed his stuff away before going on sentry.

"What you been up to, madman? Saw you doing something from over there," George declares, pointing back towards the road.

"Not much. Couldn't sleep, so made these explosive devices," lifting one for him to see better.

"Where are you going to place them?"

"Not sure, probably beneath the cartel's vehicles if there are any. Failing that, close to accommodation blocks where Aron's men should be hanging out."

"There might be innocent people sleeping there as well," says George, half expecting the answer.

"Don't know them, so not my problem. And since when did you give a crap," I say, putting the explosive in the back of the Land Cruiser.

Dead on Zulu time, both vehicles manoeuvre through the trees and back onto the dirt road under cover of darkness provided by the trees, and head for the roadhouse. There is a clear night, so there is no need to turn the lights on. Besides, it's only a short trip to the drop-off point.

Twenty minutes later, the roadhouse appears out of the shadows. A few beams of light flicker from the tops of the refuelling pumps. Beyond them is the central entrance – an open area with what looks like a corrugated roof spanning the two buildings. Two massive four-trailer road trains are parked along the edge of the dirt patch between the highway and the roadhouse.

As we drive past, we ease to a crawl, keeping the speed below 10 kilometres per hour; therefore not creating a cloud of dust behind us, which might blow into the motel part of the complex.

Through the dim light, make out three vehicles standing motionless outside, facing the small veranda which runs across the doorways to the rooms.

To conceal our actions, in case Ryan has placed round-the-clock guards around the roadhouse, continue 200 metres beyond the roadhouse before turning off the road and into the trees lining the dirt highway.

In front of me, I can make out the shapes of several old cars left here to rust away. Suppose you break down here, being in the middle of nowhere; you're fucked. There is little chance of any breakdown service coming to assist. Once off the Stuart Highway,

I halt next to what looks like a pile of rusty battered beer cans covering most of the area around us.

After everyone clambers out of the vehicles, I crouch behind a rusty old pickup truck intertwined with the local vegetation.

"OK, folks, this is where we split up and head for our assigned recce locations. Now we have a better understanding of the ground, it would be best if you take one of the Land Cruisers, George. There is no way you can get into position in time if you walk."

"Makes sense, Steve," comes the reply from George.

"Remember, if all goes to plan, meet back here in six hours from now; apart from you, George, you head back to the RV location," I glimpse down at the time.

"Roger," says Derek, checking the radio.

While Lucy and George head off to their respective sniper positions, Simon reverses the vehicle between a group of trees before pulling up to some buses and concealing the front. Places a couple of pieces of used cardboard over the headlights, stopping any glare from attracting anybody's attention, if they happen to glance over in this direction, before heading for a concealed position by the road, to monitor any vehicles which might turn into the grounds of the roadhouse.

"You ready, Derek?" I whisper.

"Yep, let's go and find out what's happening on the target."

The night is draped in an eerie stillness as we trudge along the red, sandy, dusty track, keeping to the available cover as much as possible. As we get closer to the roadhouse, make a command decision to head for the buildings at the rear. This is probably where James and Ana are likely being held.

Our boots kick up small clouds of sand particles which shimmer silver in the pale illumination of the full moon. The air hangs thick and heavy, seemingly void of all life, as if nature is holding its breath in anticipation of what will come.

As we pass another rusting wreck to my front, I spot something that makes my heart skip a beat. In the short, dense foliage, I clasp sight of something emerging with sinuous grace, its red eyes piercing through the darkness. Slithering out from under a clump of vegetation about 10 feet ahead, a five-foot red-bellied black snake appears. Its glossy ebony scales glisten in the moonlight like polished obsidian, contrasting against the devious pathway it traverses.

We both freeze motionless, our senses heighten to a primal intensity. I feel time stretching out before me, each heartbeat thundering in my chest like the hypnotic banging of war drums. The fragrance of the damp earth mingles with the sharp tang of pine, infusing the ambience with an intoxicating aroma hinting at the deadly secrets hidden in the bush.

Scrutinise the area in trepidation and wonder as the snake moves with an elegant fluidity, seemingly oblivious to the stunned intruders frozen to the spot. Its forked tongue flickers out, tasting the air, gathering the scent of unexpected visitors and prey lying in its path. Moments later, its ruby-red eyes lock onto mine. Those eyes hold a quiet intelligence, ancient wisdom that whispers of untold mysteries and untamed worlds.

Fear, curiosity, and awe fight for dominance within me. I turn to face Derek for a second to see him motionless, eyes also fixed on the creature to our front. I move my head in slow motion, my eyes searching for the deadly serpent.

My breath hitches a raspy intake of air. Sweat collects on my brow, the salty tang mingling with the scent of the forest. The beating of my heart reverberates in my ears, creating a symphony of fear and fascination threatening to overwhelm my senses.

Time resumes its normal rhythm, and the world springs back to life. The wind whispers secrets as it rustles the leaves. Nocturnal creatures resume their journeys, and the snake, as if satisfied with its silent assessment, continues on its undulating path into the unknown.

Once more, turn to Derek, exhaling a breath he didn't realise he is holding, shoulders slumping in a mixture of relief and concern. The encounter leaves us both shaken.

I whisper, "Fucking hate snakes."

"Me, too. Especially out here," Derek replies, gaining composure.

"We better get closer to our objective after a short detour from the snake's hiding place, to err on the side of caution."

"With you on that one, Steve."

At our two o'clock, a lone tree stands proud of a lump of green and brown bushes about 50 metres from the end building. The only issue is a patch of dead open ground between us and the potential OP. Without saying a word, tap Derek on the shoulder and raise my rifle to the aim, pointing at the row of buildings before indicating the direction with my right arm. Derek takes up a kneeling position, his weapon ready and covers me.

We still have one advantage on our side. The first rays of light still haven't broken through the darkness. Make the most of this as I sprint towards the cover, zig-zagging as I cross in case someone tries to lock their sights on me.

Remembering Hissing Sid from moments ago, I stop short of the long grass-like plants growing by the edge of the clearing leading up to my next location. I heard from a friend who lives in Australia that if you bang the ground, snakes bugger off. The last thing I need is to encounter a pissed-off deadly serpent who's got the hump because I'm invading its territory. So slam the butt of the rifle several times on the deck.

Listen for a few seconds for any sound of the undergrowth being disturbed. There isn't any, so carefully manoeuvre in, pushing the bush branches apart gently, trying to make any movement appear natural to any onlookers. A few minutes later, I have constructed a small observation post, ensuring I leave some foliage in front to help disguise any barrel flash if we come under contact.

On seeing me disappear from his line of sight, Derek springs to his feet and sprints across to join me in the hide. Once we are both set up, Derek presses the button on the side of the mic and whispers,

"DR and S3, confirm."

This is followed by Lucy and Simon confirming they are also in position. This only leaves George, as he has further to go than the rest of us.

The air hangs heavy with anticipation as the first timid rays of dawn tug at the darkness, as we lay within the sanctuary of a cluster of bushes. Our eyes fix on the row of motel accommodation 50 metres away, each succumbing to the flickering embrace of awakening lights, painting a fragmented mosaic of life behind the hotel room window.

The wooden veranda, stretching along the front of all the rooms except for the final one, becomes enshrouded in an ethereal glow, casting eerie shadows dancing harmoniously with the mounting tension.

As the golden tendrils of moonlight continue their journey across the sky, the first flicker of a room door opening, the creaking hinges echoing in the morning air. A cacophony of sound erupts, piercing the silence that clings to the Outback. Through my binoculars, I detect several figures leaving the sanctuary of their rooms and entering the light, stopping for a few seconds.

The muted laughter of early risers and the clinking of coffee cups fill the air before they turn in unison and head for the building. As they walk, every creak of the wooden boards beneath their feet reverberates through the stillness, amplifying the suspense.

My attention turns to the isolated room void of any warm light. It appears inconspicuous, like an unassuming pawn in a much larger game. My mind races with the countless possibilities of what lies within those walls, heightening the weight of the mission.

Outside, a lone armed figure leans against the wall. Through the dim light, a red glow becomes brighter before falling back to a reddish flicker. Nice of the person to confirm where I need to aim.

There is no movement at the motel as we monitor the target. The bush, usually teeming with life, is silent in these early morning hours. The throaty hum of insects and the restless calls of nocturnal creatures are all muffled beneath the blanket of anticipation as though nature expects daylight to burst into life with a concoction of explosions.

A gentle breeze whispers through the trees, carrying with it the sharp and earthy aroma of local vegetation socialising with the distant fragrance of damp earth, heightening the mind and sharpening our focus on the task.

As the darkness slowly recedes, swallowed by the bold intrusion of light and the heat rises, sweat trickles down my forehead. My senses are heightened by the uncertainty of what could happen next. I can taste the saltiness on my lips, mingling with the scent of eucalyptus and dust hanging in the air.

The radio crackles into life, "GD, Confirm." It's George—he's reached his sniper position.

Thirty minutes pass before a figure materialises on the veranda, walking towards the room with the guard outside, still leaning against the wall, carrying a tray and stopping for a short conversation before pushing the door open and entering. Through the binoculars, I can just about make out what appears like water bottles located close to something covered by a cloth.

Seconds later, he re-emerges, minus the tray, followed by two others. I refocus my field glasses. It's Ana and James.

A sense of relief pulsates through my body, as I now have confirmation that the two people we come all this way for are here, and this whole part of the mission hadn't been a complete waste of time. I turn to Derek and hand him the binoculars.

"Look at the veranda. It's James and Ana."

"Think you're right. Wonder where they are escorting them?"

"Don't know, but taking an educated guess, Aron, if he is here, wants to check his assets are intact," I say, grabbing the binos back from Derek.

The place appears deserted for the next 10 minutes, with no sign of any movement from either the motel or the roadhouse.

While I keep observing the area, Derek picks up the radio mic, "All call signs, this is DR Sit Rep, Over."

First to reply is George, "All Clear, Over."

Five seconds later, Simon's voice comes across the airwaves, "All OK. No, scratch that; white vehicle approaching your location at speed, Over."

"Seen, it's turning into the roadhouse," comes Lucy's message, from her sniper position on the other side of the highway, looking through and under the small, old, rusting road train parked on the strip of grass between the dirt parking area and the complex. The local vegetation nearly hides its wheels.

While I focus on the vehicle and who is about to clamber out, Derek concentrates on the zone around us in case some idiot plans to take us by surprise.

A cloud of fine sand billows up in the distance, obscuring my view. I squint through the haze, my curiosity piqued. As the dust settles, a figure emerges, a youngish man wearing a faded blue t-shirt clinging to his sinewy frame and brown shorts, dusty with grime from the journey. A bush hat, battered by countless trips, shields the man's face from the unforgiving sun. He slams the door and spends a few minutes looking around. From my experience, all his actions are not that of a typical local or tourist. This must be one of Ryan's men.

Turning on the sandy ground before trudging methodically towards the motel, his gait exudes a quiet confidence, a purpose as yet unknown. Footsteps leave behind a hushed echo on the scorched earth, the only sound breaking the heavy, eerie silence in the air.

As the figure nears the motel, I am drawn to another man standing on the veranda like a lookout. The stranger on the porch shifts his weight, a glimmer of recognition in his eyes, before ambling toward the arriving man, they meet at the halfway point.

We can't hear much from mine and Derek's location, as their conversation takes place in quiet tones. Their voices blend with the rustling of the parched leaves and the intermittent creaking of the roadhouse sign, creating a symphony of secrecy. The tension that hangs between them is palpable and thick.

A few moments pass, as fleeting as the desert wind, and the following handshake speaks volumes. Whispers of clandestine alliances, hidden agendas, and dangerous paths merge under the disguise of the motel's rustic facade. Both turn as one, resolute in their shared purpose, and begin their walk back, swallowed by the distant walls of the building.

Once they are out of view, I turn to Derek, "That's someone I don't recognise from any photos or our operation so far."

"Me neither. Must be a local contact," comes the hushed voice of Derek.

With my eyes back on the target, I witness two people flanked by two armed men, being led back down in front of the motel towards the end room. It is, of course, Ana and James, their heads bent forward, staring at the deck as if trying to block out everything going on around them. They are more than likely hanging onto the last slivers of hope that someone will rescue them soon before they get on the Grim Reaper's to-do list.

On reaching the darkened room, their prison in this hellhole, the door is flung open, and they are shoved with such force through the doorway that Ana falls to her knees. The bigger of the guards grabs Ana's upper arm and half-lifts her from the floor before him, launching her into the room.

If they only knew the torment would be over shortly, and the hellish nightmare would end. I only wish I could give them something to grasp hold of.

My rare bout of empathy ends when Derek taps me on the shoulder, "Glance over near the fuel pumps. Isn't Aron with the man who arrived a short time ago?"

About to reply when Lucy's voice comes over the radio, "S3, have you seen who is standing at the entrance? Want me to waste him?"

"LK, this is S3, stay on mission, observe only."

A few minutes pass before the new arrival, still supporting the bush hat, ambles over to the vehicle he came in, then drives close to the main door leading into the roadhouse. Through the cloud of dust being kicked out by the Land Cruiser, I can about make out the figure of Aron clambering into the rear seat.

There is someone besides the driver with him. Due to the angle and this fucking dust, I can't make out who. With any luck, Ryan will be the person with him. In my experience, hired thugs from the local area don't put up much of a fight. Why should they? The drugs aren't theirs, or the millions of dollars. All they are fighting for is the money they are being paid.

While Derek gets a sitrep from the rest, I monitor the Land Cruiser as it turns left onto Stuart Highway, disappearing in the plume of dirt kicked into the air.

From Simon's vantage point, he and George couldn't have seen the previous activities at the front of the complex. This is one of the reasons I try to place people covering all aspects of a target whenever possible.

So, no surprise, a minute later, my radio crackles in my ear, "S3, this is TS, one vehicle, three occupants, believe one of them is Aron."

Moments later, Derek sends confirmation via the radio, "TS, confirmed, DR, out."

A banging sound of clanging metal echoing through the air from the principal building grabs my attention. incoherent shouting follows before a man can be seen being ejected from the property.

Perfect, it looks like there is discord among the troops. All the better for us, should make the rescue easier once the retrieval gets underway. Nothing makes a job go without problems than the enemy fighting amongst themselves. This means their hearts are not in the fight.

While I'm watching, the man stands up and slaps both legs several times, futilely attempting to bang off the dust clinging to his jeans. He composes himself for a few seconds before walking back inside. As he does so, I turn to Derek.

"We better check the interior and locate a spot to place these explosives. Plus, find an emergency escape route in case this way is compromised." I pat the holdall containing the remote bombs I made earlier.

"Totaly agree. I'll radio the others and ensure they are covering their arcs of fire and not dancing with the local wildlife," Derek picks up the mic.

"Have Simon relocate back to the vehicle and prepare to depart. We may need to withdraw at a fast pace."

With any luck, the person we couldn't make out getting into the Land Cruiser with Aron was Ryan, leaving us free to move about and not raise any alarms.

Mind you, I'm working on the assumption that we didn't leave anyone alive in the rainforest camp who could recognise us and relay the information to Ryan. This means the people here will have no idea what we look like and, therefore, think we are tourists taking a break. I'm basing this on the fact that our photos are unlikely to be distributed to the troops in this type of organisation.

Moments later, Derek sends out via the radio, "All call signs, sitrep, S3, and this call sign to infiltrate target location, TS have assets ready, Over."

"LK, have eyes on the target's interior," Lucy replies.

"GD, Roger, all clear at the rear, Over," comes the message from George.

"Moving now, access route, clear, Over," says Simon, returning to the vehicle.

To confirm that everyone understands and ends comms, Derek transmits, "All call signs understood, out."

Watch the area for a few minutes to ensure nobody is in a position where they can see us emerge from the OP. We will leave the rifles here, ready to grab once we bug out. We will only take our 9mm pistols and the holdall inside.

The midday sun beats down mercilessly as we exit from our OP beneath a cluster of gnarled trees. The dusty Australian Outback stretches beyond the roadhouse — a vast and desolate landscape that appears to go on forever.

Without saying a word, we exchange glances to acknowledge the danger of what we are about to do. But we have both done this many times and accept we could come under fire and need to fight our way out.

Our first objective lay ahead: a dust-covered four-trailer road train parked outside a roadhouse. The goal is to make our movements appear to any observers that we have come from the cab. At the same time, our actions must be concealed from Aron's men established in the motel attached to the roadhouse.

From every waypoint, we outline our way to the next one until we reach the truck. From here, we will amble as though we are two people after a rest from a long journey. Making a tactical approach would be stupid and stick out like a spare prick at a wedding.

As we enter the building, the ambience shifts from the desolate Outback of the car park and surroundings to a bustling environment filled with clinking glasses and laughter coming from inside.

The roadhouse is a simple structure covered by a corrugated canopy, offering a respite from the scorching sun. The open door of the bar greets us, revealing several tables on the right. Two green plastic tables with four battered-looking chairs are outside beneath the tin roof.

I peer in to see two old gents sitting on stools against the long wooden counter, adorned with photos and an assortment of vehicle number plates. Behind the wooden counter, a man in his mid-50s with a fading hairline is topping up empty glasses. Beyond him are rows of spirit bottles lined up on a shelf. From what I can see, the walls are decorated similarly.

From how the two men are dressed in shorts, trucker boots and t-shirts, they are more than likely the drivers of the rigs parked close to the building. They appear relaxed and enjoying their drinks. Background music pulsates through the air, its rhythm weaving into the fabric of the scene.

The contrast between the two sides of the roadhouse is striking. On the right, the bar buzzes with activity, a haven for weary travellers seeking solace from the barren landscape. On the opposite side, a separate room that functions as a restaurant, its tables empty, waiting for hungry travellers eager to feast on hearty Outback fare.

At the rear, a sign hangs from the ceiling, weathered by time and dust, indicating the way to the toilets, showers, and the motel; somewhere I need to access without arousing suspicion, because of the appearance of the layout, possibly an excellent location to place one of the IEDs.

Luck remains on our side as we venture deeper, unnoticed by any of Arons's armed thugs who are hidden among the usual roadhouse patrons. From here, every movement must be calculated. We can't afford to drop our guard, not even for a moment.

The only person we encounter is the owner, a weathered man whose face tells of a life spent battling the harsh elements of the bush.

"Hello, gents, what can I get you," says the old man a broad Australian accent.

Pause my scanning of the place and turn to face him, "Hi, any chance of a few beers, not bothered what type and busting for a shit, where are the bogs?"

In a hushed tone, "Coming right up. Take a seat, and the dunny is down the back."

Then, he provides us with directions and a code to access the toilets, his words accompanied by a warning that sends a shiver down my spine.

"Mind the snakes and spiders, mate," the man's voice is laced with a mix of caution and resignation. "They're seeking refuge from the scorcher outside. Best not to disturb 'em. And check before plonking your arse down."

We nod to confirm we understand before positioning ourselves at one of the tables. Waiting for the owner to return, my eyes start scanning the area again for any sign of trouble. Still keeping our cover story, we blend seamlessly with the two gentlemen from inside who are now sitting at the other table.

While we wait for the drinks, the scorching sun beats down without mercy, reflecting off the tin roof. The faint scent of truck fuel intermingles with the mouthwatering aroma of food from the restaurant, teasing our senses with conflicting signals.

Within a couple of minutes, the beers arrive. "There you go, gents, enjoy," the man from the bar states, putting them down in front of us.

"Thanks," Derek replies.

When the bartender is out of earshot, I lean closer to Derek, "OK, you stay here while I recce a good position for the explosive. With any luck, it will kill a few of Aron's men or at least block the rear route once we have Ana and James. Press the transmitter on your mic if you spot anything." I bend down and grab the holdall before standing up.

Turn and head for the bogs at the back of the open space we are sitting in, down a small alleyway.

I reach for the hefty-looking handle. The coldness of the metal against my palm feels like a welcome relief from the sweltering heat. Opening the door leading to the ablutions cautiously, I brace myself for whatever lies beyond.

The air is thick with an earthy, tangy scent flaring my nostrils. The smell of damp moss mingles with dusty wood, epitomising the Outback's spirit. The ceiling fans twirl above, futilely attempting to provide some respite from the relentless heat.

Venturing further into the dimly lit space, my ears are bombarded by a cacophony of sounds. The incessant buzzing of flies echoes in my head, their aggressive persistence cutting through the air like tiny, annoying helicopters.

The occasional cry of a harsh and deadly bird pierces the silence as a stark reminder of the bush's untouched and wild nature. This brings back the gravity of the words the owner imparted about the local wildlife, crossing my mind as I approach the toilets and showers.

A shiver runs down my spine at the thought of encountering deadly creatures in such close quarters. I would rather face a hail of bullets than a snake, any day.

The floor is coarsely tiled, the tiles uneven and worn, confirming that this joint is unaffected by luxury or modernity. I step into the dimly lit cavern of the toilet block, my sense of sight offset by the lack of light. Shadows dance along the floor, seemingly alive with the secrets of the Outback. Every corner holds the potential for an unexpected encounter, the thought sending a chill down my spine.

A quick scan confirms there is no place to conceal the explosives, so I make my way towards the showers. A few shafts of sunlight pierce through the small cracks in the tin walls. Dust particles float in the air, catching the light. The warmth on my skin provides a soothing contrast to the tension that clenches my muscles.

Perfect, a half-filled container leans against a wall close to another door. By the look of it, the bin isn't emptied very often, so with any luck, it will still be there when we return later tonight. My attention now turns to the door. With my right hand, I press down on the cool metal handle, push the door ajar and peer outside. There is a dirt path leading towards the motel.

Decide that this is where I will place the first IED. With any luck, no innocent people like the two truckers will be in here when the explosives go off. But if they are, hey, war is war.

Remove some rubbish from the bin, then lower one of the packages inside before placing the waste back on top. Time to head back to where Derek's sat—drinking beer, lucky git.

When I arrive, Derek is blending in and talking to the two gents. Plonk my arse down in the seat next to him.

"I would wait a few minutes if you need the dunny—I might have stunk the place out, " I say with a false laugh, to keep up the pretence.

Our new trucker friends join in with the laughter; Derek adds, "Smelly bastard," even though he knows what I've been up to.

At that moment, the sound of three men appearing from the back grabs my attention. The taller ones walk over to the table, stops, and looks at Derek and me as though the man recognises us from somewhere but can't pinpoint where.

My training has me scrutinising him, looking for weak areas to benefit me if things kick off. The unmistakable bulge of a concealed weapon from under a loose hanging green T-shirt directly above his waist attracts my gaze. It goes to prove that we are not dealing with a professional. We would have hidden any small firearm in the natural curve in the spine. This is where my pistol is located, which I confirm discreetly.

After a few awkward seconds, "Can I help you, mate?"

The man shakes his head and enters the bar; our cue to leave, head back to the OP and collect our rifles. On the way across the car park, Derek radios the team.

"All call signs, End Ex, DR Out."

This is the signal for everyone to either relocate to the vehicle hide or, in the case of George, head back to last night's RV.

By the time we arrive back, Simon has uncovered the Land Cruiser and is sitting in the driver's seat with the engine running.

As I open the door, Simon asks, "Everything go OK inside?"

"Yes, mate, we will tell you more when we return to our RV."

A couple of minutes later, Lucy arrives and clambers into the back. "Hello, boys, take it we all had a good time?"

"All went well, Lucy. When you're ready, Simon, head for the RV."

Chapter Thirteen – Outback Rescue Plan

By the time we reach the RV, the sweltering midday sun beats down upon the team as we set up the RV, making it feel as if we were caught in an unforgiving fire. The rustling leaves bring a gentle breeze, offering a slight relief. But the scorching temperature appears to steal it away just as fast as it arrives.

Without anyone saying a word, everyone clambers out of the vehicles and goes about their business. Each person concentrates on their area of expertise.

Sweat trickles down my forehead and stings my eyes, as I work alongside the crackling heat, despite the inhospitable environment. We all have a job to do. As the planner, my first task is to construct a model of our target area on the deck.

Every detail has to be executed with precision, reflecting the tactical thinking that needs to go into the plan. A mistake here can cost someone their life. Everyone must understand where they need to be and when. Plus, the routes in and out.

With my mind running through the possible scenarios, I crouch down amidst the gnarled roots of a eucalyptus tree, arranging twigs and rocks on the floor, and construct a miniature model of the roadhouse and surroundings around the target area.

Use sticks and clumps of leaves to represent the trees and vegetation; at the same time, stones symbolise buildings and structures, creating an accurate representation of the target area and the rescue mission's objective. The last step is to trace intricate shapes in the soft sandy terrain using a slender branch, mapping out routes and entry points with artistic attention to detail.

While I'm doing this, Simon prepares the two Land Cruisers for the forthcoming mission. Sweat glistens on his forehead.

His fingers and hands are gnarled from countless repairs and diagnostics, and covered in oil from checking the engine levels as he inspects the two Land Cruisers. I watch as he ensures every nook and cranny of the two vehicles are checked before inspecting the tyres and tyre pressure for any signs of wear. All bolts on the exterior and interior are checked and retightened if required. Simon leaves no room for mechanical surprises that would jeopardise our mission.

The engines are given the once over and run for a few minutes, ensuring they are in pristine condition. With unwavering focus, he ensures our only means of transportation are up to the job. Simon's experience and expertise shine through, as he performs each task with unmatched accuracy.

Over to my right, sitting on the floor, leaning against a huge tree, Derek sits unfazed by the heat, his focus on the small collection of team radios before him, with a keen eye and nimble fingers. He systematically moves from one device to another, testing their functionalities and ensuring seamless communication. He adjusts frequencies and dials with sharp precision; his trained ear attuned to any crackling or interference that would compromise their mission's vital comms links, his calm demeanour belies the fact that his role is crucial; any misstep can cost us our lives.

George and Lucy, the team's skilled snipers, crouch low to the floor in another corner of the tree cluster. They are inspecting their rifles with the same meticulous attention to detail that defines every team member. With unwavering concentration, they disassemble and reassemble their weapons, checking components with pure precision. Fingers that have become an extension of their sniper rifle move rhythmically, gripping barrels, scopes, and triggers with a familiarity that comes from hours of practised muscle memory.

They distribute the sniper rifle ammunition between them; each round loaded with accuracy, leaving no room for error, their movements fluid and efficient. Once George and Lucy complete the inspections of their rifles, they confirm the whole team's weapons. They check and ensure all are working before moving on to ammo distribution.

As everyone works on their assigned tasks, the atmosphere in the bush crackles with intensity. The air carries the sharp aroma of dry earth, mingling with the scent of eucalyptus leaves and a faraway whiff of smoke from the tireless Australian sun.

A symphony of sounds fills our ears; the distant hum of traffic on the highway,the chirping of unseen birds amidst the treetops and the occasional rustle of wind blowing through the desolate landscape. The hot sand beneath our fingertips shifts and slides, a tactile reminder of the challenging terrain that awaits.

As the sun dips lower in the sky, casting long shadows over the topography, I survey the scene before me. The model of our target area lies crafted on the sandy floor. Simon finished preparing the Land Cruisers and is now firing up the stove for a brew and some nosh.

Derek's steady voice crackles through the radio. By this time, Lucy and George have completed all the weapons checks. They walk over to join me near the model of the target area.

Twenty minutes later, Simon announces, "Scrans ready."

Pick up my black mug and wander over to his location. "Cheers, mate, could do with a drink and some food—my stomach thinks my throat has been cut."

We are soon joined by the rest of the team, who plonk their arses down on the floor around the hole Simon dug to place the stove.

"All the weapons are checked, and oiled, and prepared for the mission. George and I also inspected everyone's weapons and shared the ammo," says Lucy, grabbing a plate of grub from Simon.

Simon glances up. "Both vehicles are purring like the big cat we saw in Puerto Rico, and shouldn't let us down."

"What about the radios, Derek? All good to go?" I say, turning to my right to look at Derek.

"Yep, all good. Once you've gone through the plan, I'll brief us on the frequencies and codes," declares Derek.

"When we have all finished stuffing our fat faces, we can go to the model, and I will take you through everything I came up with."

"No problem. I did the cooking, so who's washing up?" says Simon, putting away the stove.

Without saying a word, George picks up the mugs and mess tins, walks over to the Land Cruiser, opens the back door, pulls out a plastic jerry can of water and cleans the kit.

Five minutes later, everyone is standing around the model on the deck.

"Before we begin, any questions or burning issues we ought to deal with? No, in that case, I will start with the brief. As always, if anybody has any suggestions, please shout out."

"Will do, Steve," Lucy calls out.

"Objectives: our mission is to rescue Ana and James, held by Aron's drug cartel at the Burrow Creek Roadhouse. Our objective is Ana and James, but if we find more hostages, we will also bring them out. We need to execute this with precision to ensure the safety and successful extraction.

"Factors to consider: time of day - the start of operation is just after last light, which should be around 19:00, when the guards at the target location will be winding down with any luck and probably drinking themselves stupid, therefore, not too alert.

"Weather conditions - going on the conditions earlier when we carried out the recce, the climate will be about the same: hot and sticky. We must factor in the potential of any sand blowing across the target area, either caused by nature or by trucks or cars driving through the site.

I've checked the forecast for this evening, and it shouldn't rain, but be prepared, just in case. In the unlikely event of any downpours, the vehicles for the withdrawal will be concealed on solid ground as much as possible.

Terrain – from the observations gathered this morning, we are already aware of what type of terrain we are looking at. From the information we collected, the rear is impassable and protected by dense foliage. So, we will not require cover from the back of the roadhouse for the rescue. Instead, George will be with Simon here." I point to the model on the floor.

"The route will be down the Stuart Highway. We will stop here, among the rampant undergrowth to the left of the road." Again, I put my pointer on the map on the deck. "From here, we move on foot to our start locations, which I will go through later.

"If we are forced to take an alternative route, be ready for some unpredictable landscapes, including open ground and thick foliage, especially on the way to our pick-up location after collecting Ana and James, which will be around here." I indicate the same place on the model where the vehicles will be.

"Potential obstacles and threats: from the info gathered, our problems are the open ground between the roadhouse and the highway." I draw my pointer across the sandy floor in front of the fuel pumps. "It looks like we might face some issues getting through the local vegetation back to the pickup. With that in mind, Simon will ensure a clear route from George's location to the Land Cruisers." So everyone understands the route, I trace a line in the soft sand.

"The main threat will come from any of the cartel's people close to the room where Ana and James are held captive. Some of them may be drunk. But we need to consider that they might try to put up some sort of resistance. To this end, while carrying out the recce of the interior, I placed an IED in the shower block. Simon will detonate this once the rescue gets underway. The signal will be Derek sending 'go' over the radio.

"If anyone tries to flank us via the front of the roadhouse, Lucy will be in her sniper position." I point to where she was positioned earlier. "They will more than likely be armed and firing in all directions. Lucy will despatch them.

"Any questions on anything so far?"

Everyone shakes their heads.

"Personal roles and responsibilities: each team member will have specific functions. Simon and George will be located here," pointing to the clump of vegetation along the left of the roadhouse. "Your role is to draw the attention away from the motel. Put down plenty of fire. The aim is to divide and conquer. We want to make them believe an attack is coming from your direction. As mentioned, once you receive the message 'go', set off the first two IEDs inside the edifice…"

"Where is the second one, Steve?" George interrupts.

"I will place this somewhere, if we need it to protect our withdrawal."

I continue with the brief, "Lucy, from your position, kill any of the cartel's people who come out of the building. Ensure you have a direct line of sight to the edge of the motel, paying attention to the far-right room. An armed guard will be outside the door, if it is anything like this morning. Once you receive the message 'go', you are to take down the sentry. Remember, innocent people might stay the night, so verify the target before dropping them.

"Derek, besides ensuring all the radios work, you will confirm that all communication is effective. You will send the comms to start the mission underway. As you recced the place with me earlier, we will penetrate the motel complex to retrieve the hostages.

"I will enter the motel with Derek when Lucy kills the guard and grab anyone inside. When we have them, Derek will transmit the message, 'targets acquired'. We'll then make our way out into the cover of the trees to the right. From there, we make our way behind Lucy and onto the pickup point. Any questions so far?"

"Not yet, Steve, all sounds good," says Derek.

"OK, let's move on. Equipment: the team must carry all the necessary gear to deal with any situation. This includes weapons, ammunition, communication devices, maps and medical kits. Any kit not needed for the rescue we will leave inside the vehicles.

"Procedures:

1. Mission briefing – familiarise yourselves with the roadhouse, the target area and the motel. I've taken information from you all and have incorporated it into the model in front of you. Take time to study it before I destroy it.

2. Preparation – after this brief, check your gear and ensure no rattles or other sounds might give away our position.

3. Launch – once we are all in our designated start positions confirmed by radio, Derek will send the following message, 'go'. On hearing this, everybody stand by. The signal for the attack is when Simon sets off the first IED. Prior to this, try not to open fire. If you are compromised, kill them with as little noise as possible.

4. Infiltration – after I see the guard drop to the deck, Derek and I will enter the motel.

5. Extraction team deployment – once inside the motel complex, we will rush towards this room. Dispose of any guards that might head to secure their prisoners, prior to entering the hut." Again, a point to the map. "Any questions before we move on to the extraction?" Everyone shakes their heads. "OK, on to rescue the hostages.

6. Hostage retrieval - the extraction team will retrieve the hostages and disappear into the cover of darkness and trees before bringing them to the RV.

7. Security: in case of any complications or emergencies, before the rescue gets underway, we will RV back here and regroup.

Contingency plans:

1. This rescue must take place tonight as, according to Tennille, they are to be relocated soon.

2. If anyone is shot during the operation, remain where you are. You will be retrieved on the withdrawal.

3. If we come under attack, Lucy and George will give covering fire while Simon heads back to the vehicles and waits for us to join him.

4. The emergency RV will be back here. If it all goes wrong, then everyone, make your way back here.

"Steve, what happens if we enter the motel and the hostages are not where they should be?" Simon asks.

"If that happens, we will clear all the buildings one by one until we find them. If we can't locate the people we are looking for, we can set our tame interrogator loose on any of Aron and Ryan's men still alive. "

"Roger that, Steve. George and I will watch the rear as much as possible, in case they are moved that way," replies Simon.

"Emergencies: if anyone becomes a casualty during the rescue, you need to return to the RV," I point to the location on the map. "If you can't move, stay where you are, and you will be picked up during the withdrawal phase.

"Next, due to the fact we are in the Australian Outback, if any snake bites you, remain calm and do the following:

1. Apply a pressure bandage
    - Wrap a bandage from below, upwards and over the bite site.
    - Extend it as high as possible (e.g., to the groin).
    - Keep the limb still.
    - Use the same tightness as for a sprained ankle.
    - Mark the area of the bite on the dressing.
2. Immobilise the bitten area
    - Use a splint if possible.
    - Joints to both sides of the bite should be immobilised.

"Again, stay where you are; we will fetch you ASAP and move you to medical help. As I've said before, your lives are more important than the hostages. Saying that, if you're killed, I'll meet you at the Final Rendezvous Point.

"Communication protocols: Derek, as you are our communications expert, your overall responsibility is establishing and maintaining seamless coordination among the team during the operation. Bear the following in mind:

- Set up a secure communication network for real-time updates with all squad members.

- Ensure each member is equipped with reliable communication devices.

"That's the plan, folks. If anyone wants to contribute more, now is the time."

"Think you covered it all, apart from what time is Zulu time," asks Lucy, standing up for a better view of the model.

"19:00 should give us time for a brew, check equipment and get any required rest. Over to you, Derek, for the radio brief."

"To keep this short, I've changed the frequency on the radios so they work in this terrain. From your reports, we had some issues during the recce. Once you are in position, send 'in situ' over the radio. Then, after I'm given the go-ahead from Steve, I will send the message 'go' — no need to respond. If you have an emergency, the code is 'bite'. Like always, folks, keep the chatter down. Straight after the briefing, I'll carry out a comms check."

"Cheers, Derek. I suggest we all rest as the time is 15:00, and we go in four hours."

I leave the model of the area up for the next 20 minutes, so the team can familiarise themselves with the site and their primary locations during every stage of the operation. While I wait, I pick up my radio, "DR, this is S3, Radio Check, Over."

A few seconds later, "DR, OK, Over."

With the comms check out of the way, I pack my own kit, ensuring I have no rattles on any of the equipment I will use on the rescue, before turning my attention to my rifle and pistol. I know the two weapons experts checked it, but like all professionals, I want to confirm that it will work when I need it to. The last thing I want during a gunfight is a silent click, where there should be a loud bang as the round inside the chamber explodes, sending a bullet flying into the assailant's body.

Kit sorted, time to dismantle the model. Given the timescale we are working on, it is unlikely that some clued-up person may stumble across it before the mission gets underway. They will have a map of our start locations, but it's good practice to break up your map; something drummed into me while on my first NCO cadre.

The interior of the RV hums with the familiar fragrance of dry heat and stale sweat, mingling with the scent of earth and eucalyptus wafting through the trees. The air feels thick and heavy, making it difficult to breathe as I sit near the door of my swag.

My eyes scan the horizon of the vast Australian Outback, as the sun begins its slow descent to a position lower in the sky, casting long shadows across the dust-filled landscape.

With the plan running through my mind, as it always does before any operation, give up on any idea of sleep. As I look around, the team are silent; each lost in their thoughts, savouring the fleeting moments of respite before the next phase of our mission will begin.

While observing, my reflections turn to my mortality, and I may not come out of the whole operation alive. But I know the risk as much as the other unit members. But if I should receive a fatal blow and die, it would be among a group of professionals and part of the small circle of what I like to call friends.

For added pressure, I sense a kicking sensation on one side of my head, as if my brain is reminding me that if any of them die, it will be down to me. After all, I'm the one who planned the assault and rescue. I try to shake the sentiment off, as we all understood the risks.

My eyes scan every inch of the RV, as I look at each member under my leadership and think about their demeanour and exceptional skills that brought us together. I've known George and Simon from Combat Stress a while back. As for Derek, he fell into place after missions on St Halb. Lucy started, on the other side; after recovering the weapons. We became close, and she now lives with me on the Isle of Wight. I think life wouldn't be bearable if she got killed.

Turn to my right and see Simon, not far away, sitting on the tailgate of one of the vehicles with his unruly mop of sandy hair and perpetual stubble; fiddling with a map, his thumb tracing a winding route with precision. Knowing him, he will be one step ahead and planning our way back to Darwin. His transport expertise is unrivalled, and his quiet confidence radiates through the cramped space.

Beyond him is Derek, our communications expert, tapping away on a laptop, his fingers dancing across the keys like a skilled pianist. He is a wizard when it comes to navigating the complex web of frequencies and encrypted transmissions, keeping us in touch.

George is sitting at the back of the RV, his rugged frame coiled like a spring, ready to be released. His piercing gaze never wavers from the scope of his rifle, his trigger finger twitching in anticipation. I sense his focus, his instincts honed from years of precision and stealth. His presence provides me with a feeling of security in this unforgiving land.

Sitting cross-legged on her folded swag, Lucy seems lost in her own world. Her beautiful eyes stare into the distance as if trying to decipher the secrets of the desert. Our interrogator, Lucy, possesses a unique ability to pry information from the most hardened individuals.

Her calm demeanour and unwavering determination conceals a subtle menace. I have seen her work magic in the past and in Puerto Rico; therefore, I'm fully aware that her skills will be invaluable if we don't find Ana and James.

I take a swig from my canteen, the warm water bringing a brief respite from the relentless heat. My gaze falls on the watch on my arm, ticking away every second. Only one hour until Zulu time.

As the sun descends, painting the sky with vivid shades of red and orange, I sense a familiar knot of tension building in my chest. The silence between us crackles with an unspoken urgency, the weight of the impending task heavy upon us. This is the calm before the proverbial storm. And I couldn't help but wonder what unseen dangers lurk in the shadows of the Outback.

After packing my unused swag in the vehicle, a noise different from the surrounding us attracts my attention. I turn rapidly to my right and remove my 9mm from its holster in one movement as the sudden sound of distant barking in the distance echoes through the stillness, the recognisable sound of wild dogs searching for their next prey. My hand tightens around the grip of my pistol. I exchange a glance with George, who nods. He knows that even during downtime, we can never let our guard down.

The pack barks, becoming louder as they close in on our location. Spin around to see that the rest have now taken up firing positions. With any luck, this will be just wild dogs and not someone herding them our way. We can't afford to take no action.

"Come on, George, let's take a gander and find out why them bloody dogs are barking," I say, leading off into the undergrowth. I take a deep breath, letting the scent of the Outback seep into my lungs. It is a mixture of earth, sweat, and fear, a potent concoction permeating the air. The tension is palpable, making my skin prickle with anticipation.

"Right behind you. The noise came from over in that direction," George points off to his 10 o'clock.

We move tactically through the undergrowth, doing our best to prevent the dry twigs from snapping underfoot, which might warn any potential attackers of our whereabouts. Stop at the edge of a small clearing in the bush and signal George to close in on my position.

I stand, frozen. My eyes are transfixed on the scene unfolding before me, as a pack of wild dogs emerge from the scrub. The sheer power and determination emanating from their feral countenances sends shivers tracing down my spine. Each step they take seems calculated.

A wild pig bursts through the undergrowth as fast as a round leaving a rifle. Its grizzled body cuts through the light, like a harbinger of chaos, fear etched in every crease of its bristly hide. It huffs and grunts with desperate urgency.

The pack unleashes a chorus of fearsome barks, sharp and piercing, tearing through the stillness of the air. The sensation is electrifying and chilling, like a primal call to arms echoing across the vastness of ancient, untamed land.

The dingos, with eyes sharp and in in focus, move in perfect unison. They strategise, silently forming a plan of attack. Their movements are precise, as they alternate their positions around the wild pig. One dingo runs ahead, darting to the left, causing the pig to instinctively shift its course slightly to the right. Another quick as lightning, pounces from the right, forcing the pig to swiftly change direction. The pack is relentless, adapting to each move the pig makes, their teamwork unwavering. Can't help but relate the way they work together is like our own team of five. Maybe there is a simularity between nature and a team of highly trained group of people.

Dust kicked up by their movements creates a chaotic whirlwind, adding to the primal scene. The clattering of paws on the rough terrain echoes like a thunderous drumroll. The pig's laboured breaths reverberate, intertwined with the pack's low, guttural growls, creating a haunting melody of life and death.

I watch, spellbound, as the pig fights valiantly, its muscular bulk futile against the relentless pursuit. Its grunts and snorts intermingle with the dogs' barks.

The chase reaches a crescendo, the atmosphere pulsating with raw energy. The pack closes in, their fangs bared, and eyes gleaming with untamed ferocity. The lead dog sinks its teeth into the pig's flesh in one final, desperate lunge. The others follow suit, rending and tearing at the vulnerable flesh until victory is achieved.

The wild dogs stand triumphant, their eyes lock onto mine. The surge of animalistic energy recedes. The Outback returns to its predicted silence, only faint echoes of their barks linger.

"At least we don't have any idiots with guns to deal with, George. Better make our way back to rejoin the others," I say, moving back with care; I didn't fancy becoming the dogs' dessert.

George raises the thumb of his right hand and follows me back to the RV. When we arrive, Simon sits in the front Land Cruiser, and Derek and Lucy stand by the rear doors.

"Anything out in the bush to worry about, Steve?"

"Nothing much, Lucy, just some pooches grabbing a bite to eat."

"It will be last light soon, so might as well clamber in the vehicles and head for the rescue RV," says Lucy.

"Might as well make the most of the fading daylight and head down the highway. There is no reason why Aron's men will know we are in the location with any luck. But to be safe, we will pull off the road short of the RV and wait for nightfall before we move." I say.

"George and I will follow you three," says Simon, firing up the engine as Lucy, Derek and I head for the first Land Cruiser.

Simon and I drive both of the vehicles at a slow speed so as not to kick up any dust storm, leaving the RV via a different route than the one we came in on, joining the Stuart Highway further back up the road.

Many people would drive out the same way they came in, creating several lines of tracks in and out. Even if you go out using the same tyre marks as the ones you came in on, a person with half a brain would be able to tell the direction the last vehicle was moving in.

We drive for about 20 minutes at a constant speed towards the RV close to the roadhouse, before I turn and head off into the bush before stopping. Simon drives his Land Cruiser a few feet away and parks behind a clump of trees.

There are still 10 minutes to wait before last light. Nothing to do now but wait in the Outback that knows no mercy; and neither did the mission that lay ahead. We all sit in silence, each making sure we understand our part in the recovery of Ana and James.

Chapter Fourteen – Extraction

The moon ascended as the sun dipped below the horizon, its piercing light illuminating the desolate Outback, casting an eerie glow over the vast expanse before us—time to go. Signal for Simon to follow me.

The ground is rough and uneven as we drive without the vehicle lights illuminating the way over an unknown landscape. Navigating the treacherous topography with precision, I tighten my grip on the steering wheel as the cruisers bump along the rugged terrain towards the RV. The team have been briefed on the mission, and our objective is clear - rescue two hostages held captive by a ruthless drug cartel at a remote roadhouse.

The air grows dense, carrying the scent of dust and dry earth, mingling with a touch of eucalyptus. While a chorus of cicadas fills the night sky, their relentless humming adding a layer of unease to the already tense atmosphere.

My eyes sweep across the surroundings, scanning for any signs of movement. The Outback is a hostile terrain, and the shadows play tricks on the mind. My ears strain to pick up any hint of danger; the crackle of branches, the soft rustling of leaves. Derek is sitting by my side, steady hand on the microphone, ready to relay information to the rear vehicle.

The two Land Cruisers rumble as we approach our start position, 500 metres from the roadhouse. I could sense the team's heartbeats quicken as their senses heighten, each pulse in sync with the hum of the engines.

In front of Simon's Land Cruiser, he and George sit, scanning the horizon with his rifle, his trained eye seeking out a potential threat. Lucy, the other sniper, crouches on the back seat behind me, finger poised on the trigger of her weapon.

Swallow the lump that has formed in the back of my throat, my mind racing through endless scenarios. Every team member is professional and comprehends their role in the plan. And how to react and act alone if the rescue takes a different course than the one planned. But they also understand the importance of an organised approach. One of the reasons Derek is with me with his radio is that the team will rely on my ability to make split-second decisions that could mean life or death. With my experience, I am like a conductor orchestrating this deadly symphony of precision and skill.

After 20 minutes of slow driving, we reach the RV. Reverse the vehicle close to a clump of undergrowth. The aim is to make it easy for Simon to conceal the two Land Cruisers before rejoining George in their start positions.

Uncertainty hangs in the air, mingling with the scent of danger as I open the driver's door, giving a subtle nod to the team to emerge from the vehicles. The silence is magnified in the vastness of the Outback; the only sound, that of the nocturnal nightlife signalling its presence with a chorus of sounds.

The darkness would be overpowering if not for the moon's glow delivering enough light to see our way forward and, at the same time, providing a sufficient amount of dark shadows to conceal our movements.

We know what we are up against with the retrieval. We did a similar sort of rescue back in the rainforest of Puerto Rico a week back. With everyone spread out, covering all arcs of fire, we wait 10 minutes, watching and listening for any sounds that aren't natural. This procedure will be repeated several times before we are all in our start locations. It's imperative to keep the element of surprise.

I glance down at my wristwatch; it's time to make a move and get the rescue underway. Raise my right arm straight up, pause for a moment, then bring it down in one swift movement in front of me. This is the signal for us all to depart the RV. Leave Simon and George to make their way to the left of the roadhouse to set up their firebase.

***

Once Derek, Lucy and I have left to make our way to our respective starting positions, Simon and George move through the thick undergrowth that fills the area where their firebase will be set up.

'It's only a short distance compared to the others, but it is imperative we make it without being detected if the rescue is going to happen as planned', George thinks to himself, leading off with Simon close behind. With only 60 metres to go, George stops and goes to ground, taking up a kneeling firing position.

In a quiet whisper, "Simon, our location is over in that direction," George points to a small mound of earth close to the open ground. "I'll set up the position and wait for you to return, after you make the route back to the RV clear and ready for a fast retreat."

"No problem, give me 10 minutes," Simon replies.

"No problem, see you soon."

This is where George's sniper training comes in, as he moves through the bush as quiet as a big-eared rodent going to church. The sounds of any noise are cancelled out by the night chorus of insects and strange animals calling out in the night. Soon, he is within metres of the dirt bank, stopping at the bottom to check the area for any unwanted creatures that might cause a problem. Once clear, he inches his way to the top, scraping away a section of dirt just big enough to poke his sniper rifle through.

Through the scope of the rifle, he can see across the road where the roadhouse stands as a beacon of opportunity and danger. Its walls are vibrant with garish advertisements for cold brews and blazing sunsets. Inside, the two hostages we came to rescue are trapped, prisoners to the ruthless grip of a notorious drug cartel, but not for long.

While peering through the darkness, a rustling sound comes from the rear of the location as someone or something does their best to move through the bush without making a sound. Some think most people wouldn't detect it, but due to George's training, it sticks out like a vegetable in a mixed grill.

Moments later, Simon arrives and lies on the bank next to George, "Could have wasted you, mate," Simon proclaims.

"I knew it was you, Simon. Call yourself a recce specialist. You make more noise than a pig in a slaughterhouse."

Simon's fingers dance across the glossy surface of the digital phone, half concealed under a cloth to prevent the glare from giving away their position. The phone number he needs to call to detonate the IED flashes in stark red numbers, each second a heartbeat in its own right. Sweat trickles down Simon's temple, misting his eyes, but he refuses to blink, his focus unwavering.

Deep breaths, in and out, fill Simon's lungs and steady his nerves. He knows that once he calls the number on the phone, any innocent people in the roadhouse could be killed — a classic case of being in the wrong place. As for the cartel people: you live by the gun, you die by the gun.

"You ready to get this shit fest underway, George?" Simon asks.

"Yep, send the message," comes the reply.

Pressing the transmit button of the radio, George sends the message to the team to confirm they are in position, "All Call Signs, this is GD, In situ, Out."

With one last breath, Simon closes his eyes for a moment, the weight of the world and the lives of the innocent resting on his shoulders. Thoughts of his family, of loved ones left behind in a world far from this desolate landscape. But he dismisses them, for to falter now would mean the hostage's imprisonment would continue, and probably their demise.

Now, all there is to do is wait for Derek to confirm the go. Time appears to stand still as Simon and George lie against the sandy bank, listening to the cacophony of cicadas filling the air. Their deafening shrieks are a symphony of chaos. They ignore their song, attuned only to the silence between each note. Simon's finger hovers above the detonator, ready to unleash the fury hidden at the rear of the roadhouse. His mind is a warzone, thoughts battling for supremacy as doubt and fear knock at the door, desperate for entry.

***

After leaving the RV, Derek and I make our way to the other side of the complex, to our position near where Ana and James are being held. So, I lead off with Lucy and Derek, following with a 30-metre gap between us.

Close to the highway, I detect a rumbling sound as a vehicle bounces over the underlying tarmac road, getting closer by the second, its dim headlights piercing the blackness. Dive to the floor and take up a prone firing posture. Moments later, a white Jeep comes into view, almost coming to a standstill at the entrance to the roadhouse. My heart pounds in my chest, my muscles coiled as tight as a wound spring; the sweat trickling down my forehead, joining the dust already residing on my face.

Shit, the last thing we need right now is more people to deal with. Motionless, I monitor the situation as they drive in front of the fuel pumps. The silhouette of a person clambers out of the driver's seat. Seconds later, the driver wanders inside, returning after a few minutes, climbing back in his vehicle and driving off.

I wait for the Jeep to disappear into the distance before I stand up, doing my best not to make any rapid movement that might catch someone's eye if they happen to be looking in this direction. No need to turn around, Derek and Lucy will be watching and move when I do.

At the edge of the roadway, I pause for a moment, then sprint across. Once over, I take up a prone firing stance, covering back up the road, ready to protect Derek as he races across. Thirty seconds later, his silhouette springs from the bush, sprints the short distance to join me and faces the roadhouse. Lucy follows close behind him.

Using the protection of the extensive bank of green grass that runs along this side of the highway, we move as one towards our first objective, about 50 metres from Lucy's sniper position. The ground is soft underfoot. Due to this, the rain from the highway soaks away. Perfect for us, as terrain swallows any sounds our footsteps make.

Signal for Lucy to close up. Once more, we remain motionless, listening and watching for any movement in the roadhouse. The anticipation is palpable, each breath mingling with the cool breeze that sweeps through the Outback. The tension is so thick it feels like a living entity, pulsating with the rhythm of our hearts.

"OK, Lucy. We will cover you while you sprint across the road and scramble into your sniper hide before we move."

"See you back at the RV, Steve."

The moment she is in position, I lead off, keeping to the cover of the bank. A hundred metres away beyond the other entrance, I stop until Derek is by my side. After a glance down the highway in both directions, I dash over the street. Take a kneeling stance next to a large tree and wait for Derek to come over.

As I kneel motionless in the blackness, my eyes on the target, my heart skips a beat as I sense something long and smooth brush past my boot. A tiny hint from nature to say you're not alone out here in the silence. Turn to see Derek, his rifle aimed at the deck.

In a whisper, Derek says, "Did you feel something graze your leg?"

"Sure did, mate. Haven't a clue what it was," I say in a low, barely audible voice.

"I do, it's your lucky day. That was a fucking snake."

"Shit, let's go."

Derek nods, so we return to where we were hidden earlier today, our start location. With each step towards the roadhouse, the darkness looms, a curtain willing to unveil the unknown. But we are prepared. Ready to face whatever lies ahead. The fate of the hostages rests in the team's capable hands. Failure is not an option.

The team takes a collective breath in the Australian Outback's dark, silent heart. The mission is about to unfold. The cartel's men have no way of knowing the hell that is about to be unleashed on them.

With my start location only 100 metres away, I pause and take a deep lung full of air while scanning the area to my front. All appears quiet. So, keeping as close to the floor as possible, I make my way forward and crouch in the dense treeline hidden among the ancient gum trees that provide a slim veil of concealment.

Moments later, the rustling of the bushes behind me alerts me to Derek's presence as he slides in beside me. His hand is already holding the mic, ready to send any messages. The roadhouse stands on the other side of the short patch of open ground, an innocent façade against the desolate landscape.

We wait in the stillness of the night for everyone to confirm they are in position. We'd received Lucy's confirmation not long after we went our separate ways. George will be waiting for Simon to return, after ensuring the vehicles are concealed in a fashion that will allow a rapid withdrawal and stay hidden from view. Plus, clearing the route from their location back to the Land Cruisers ensures we have a path back to the RV, unhindered by any local vegetation.

In a whisper, I turn to Derek, "Send our confirmation."

Without replying, Derek sends, "All call signs, this is DR, In Situ, Out."

As we wait, I tap Derek on the shoulder and point towards the veranda of the motel. Two men are making their way along in front of the rooms, bouncing off the walls and railings that line the front of the motel. No doubt in my mind they are pissed. With any luck, the rest of them will be half-cut, making the rescue much easier. Drunken people are not going to put up much of a fight.

Light beams through the windows of the motel rooms, with the occasional burst of brighter lights as doors swing open and people come and go. The guard stands by the entrance of Ana and James' makeshift prison, shuffles and glances down at his wrist.

Minutes later, another person appears, strolling towards him in no hurry as though he's pissed off at being taken away from having a good time in the bar. Watch as the man spends a short time chatting with the man outside the room before swapping places. A smile spreads across my face at the thought Lucy will have the crosshairs of the scope of her sniper rifle trained on the gap between his eyes.

Time ticks by, waiting for the transmission that will get the rescue underway with sweat beads on my forehead mingling with the dirt streaking my face. The air is still, heavy with anticipation, as we await our moment to strike Once Simon detonates the first IED, the stillness is palpable, broken only by the distant hum of annoying insects and the occasional rustle of leaves.

The time for waiting ends at last, as George confirms they are in position, "All call signs, this is GD, In Situ, Out."

I turn to Derek and give him a raised thumb, "You ready?"

"Sure am. Let's go and fetch Ana and James."

With that, he places the microphone to his lips and sends the message, "All call signs, we have a go. I repeat, all call signs. We have a go."

***

Back in the firebase, the shrill call of a distant raven breaks through the symphony of insects, its haunting melody carrying a message of impending doom. Simon's grip tightens on the mobile, knuckles white and resolute. The time is now.

With a tap of his finger, the world explodes in a blinding cascade of fire and noise. The IED at the rear of the roadhouse erupts, tearing apart steel and concrete in its devastating wake. Flames lick the sky, casting a macabre dance of shadows upon the barren expanse before him. The cartel has been awakened from its slumber, caught in the whirlwind of chaos we have unleashed. The moment the IED goes off, George lays down a hail of fire in the direction of the roadhouse.

Joining George, laying down diversional fire, Simon grips his weapon, his dance partner, in this deadly waltz that emerges from the shadows between buildings, crumbling under the impact of the explosion. Men come running out of the roadhouse, some half on fire, others with blank impressions on their faces, their eyes staring into the abyss of the diversion.

Bullets fly like angry hornets, their stinging kiss a reminder of the fragility of life, double tapping rounds into the burning men in an attempt to stop their suffering. The world becomes a blur of movement, sound, and pain. George's senses sharpen, each fibre of his being alert, as he unleashes a storm of fire and lead upon those who dare stand in his path.

Some try to put up a fight as they rush towards our diversion, firing blindly into the darkness. A jolt of adrenaline courses through Simons and George's veins, electrifying their senses and clouding any thoughts. Bodies move with a precision honed through years of training, each step a calculated dance of life and death. Fear is a flickering flame, hardly noticeable amidst the chaos.

Seconds stretch into eternity as the firefight rages on. Gunpowder marries with the acrid stench of sweat, the sweet tang of copper, and the pervasive scent of fear. And through it all, death dances on the periphery, a silent spectre with his skeletal fingers outstretched.

***

Thirty seconds after sending the go message, Derek and I watch as a booming explosion shatters the silence like a thunderclap. The tranquil desert air tears through the rear of the roadhouse with an ear-splitting boom. The ground trembles beneath me, reverberating through the earth as if it's about to split open. The sound resonates through my skull like a ferocious earthquake, rattling my core as if the planet itself has been brutally shaken awake.

The force of the blast tosses dust and debris scatters through the night sky like jagged, malevolent confetti, while chunks of concrete and metal crash to the deck with a resounding thud. Fragments of glass cascade through the air, twinkling like malicious shards of stars, creating a deadly whirlwind. Splintered pieces of wood splatter across the road, a cadaverous hailstorm; one large chunk landing to my right, missing our location by several metres.

Flames surge high into the sky. A vibrant orange inferno devours the air with its insatiable hunger, engulfing the area in a wild inferno as it mingles and crackles with the metallic tang of fear, forming an intoxicating yet repulsive mixture that suffocates the air around me. The thick, acrid smoke coils into the air, intertwining with the smouldering scent of burning wood and flesh. The stench fills my nostrils, invading my senses with its sickening presence.

And then a burst of fury erupts from the opposite side of the roadhouse. The sound of rifle fire reverberates through the darkness, fierce and unwavering, a symphony of gunfire from the cover on the left of the roadhouse as George and Simon open up with short, sharp bursts of fire snapping through the air, their echoes ricocheting off the nearby trees.

Tracer rounds cut through the darkness, vibrant streaks of light illuminating the darkness like twisted, malevolent fireflies streaking across the night sky and igniting a hunger for destruction. With each piercing flash, we trace the trajectory of the covering fire coming from the other side of the roadhouse. I can almost sense the vibration of every bullet being discharged, a savage percussion reverberating through my bones. The stench of gunpowder hangs heavy in the air, mingling with the acrid smoke of the explosion.

As the chaotic scene unfolds, I'm overwhelmed by a dizzying blend of emotions. My hands tremble, aching with adrenaline. The hairs on my skin stand on end as if they anticipate danger lurking beyond the treeline. The heat of the flames sears my face, making me squint against the searing brightness. My breath becomes shallow and ragged, as if I'm almost participating in this heart-stopping drama, rather than just observing it from the sidelines.

Amidst the cacophony of explosions, gunfire, and the primal cries of men locked in a mortal dance, it appears as if time itself slows down to a crawl at that precise moment, stretching every second into an agonising eternity. My heart pounds in my chest, each beat reverberating with a mix of fear and determination.

The dry Australian Outback air clings to my sweat-soaked skin, intensifying the anxiety that grips us all. Beads of anticipation roll down my forehead, mingling with the sand and grime that coats my face. I strain to listen through the disorienting symphony of chaos. Gunfire echoes in my ears, incessant and unforgiving. The crack of bullets splitting the air sends shivers down my spine, a chilling reminder of the fragility of life. But as each shot ricochets, the line between life and death, so often obscured, becomes razor-sharp and impossible to ignore.

A haunting melody reverberates in the darkest corners of my mind, yet amidst the turmoil, there is a crude harmony to their shots, precise and synchronised confusion serving as our fleeting sanctuary. Fear courses through my veins, mingling with a sense of duty and determination, like a spectator watching a horrific play unfold – the raw intensity of this firefight, the fury of the burning roadhouse. The vulnerability of those trapped inside all elicits a knot in my stomach, as if I'm holding my own thunderstorm hurricanes inside.

An odd sensation of relief washes over me, socialising with the disarray and devastation surrounding us. The tide of battle shifts and salvation can be found within the storm. Steeling myself against the cacophony, I embrace the violent clarity of the moment.

The moment Lucy fires her first shot, the guard outside the room slumps down the wall, leaving a streak of blood painting the wall a vibrant red. Derek and I sprint towards the target room. Each gritty step feels both audacious and necessary, a high-stakes ballet between stealth and urgency.

On the way, we pass two vehicles I recognise from this morning. They belong to the cartel. Good news, the rear door of one of them is open.

Not long before bullets whizz past me, crackling like angry wasps. The echoing thuds of their impact punctuate the air, a symphony of danger. Bile rises in my throat, leaving a bad taste, an unwelcome companion in this dangerous dance. Sharp and undeniable, fear prickles my skin like a thousand tiny needles.

There is no time to dive for cover, so I return fire, the round hitting him in the chest, dropping him like a stone. In front of me,

Derek has reached the veranda and is crouched down, his eyes scanning the area.

Seconds later, I squat beside him and take a steadying breath. From the other side of the roadhouse I can hear the intermittent sounds of gunfire as George and Simon lay down deadly fire. Each burst of fire is separated by a 20 to 30 second gap to reserve ammo, killing anyone who rushes their position.

Above us, footsteps pound the wooden boards as people scuttle about, not knowing which way to run. I am about to move when a single shot echoes from the front of the building. Lucy is doing her job.

Time to rescue our hostages. Make our way via the five steps leading up to the veranda's end as I approach the room on the right. From inside, I detect voices shouting orders. There must be guards inside the room. I turn to Derek. Using a combination of hand signals, tell him to take the right of the door and when we enter, I'll take the right of the room while he takes the other. This is something we have trained for often in the time between missions.

My heart pounds in my chest, the adrenaline surging through my veins. The sound of my breath fills my ears as I press my back against the timber wall, coil my muscles, and count down in my head. One, two....

Shit, at that moment, one guard flings the door open and comes outside.

"Go now," I yell, after a well-aimed shot from Lucy eliminates the guard at the door, his lifeless body crumpling to the ground.

We burst into the room, and a scene unfolds before my eyes: a macabre exhibition of violence and desperation. The flickering lightbulb casts eerie shadows on the cowering figures within, its feeble glow barely illuminating the chaos around us. The metallic scent of blood hangs heavy in the air, mingling with the musty odour of fear.

A single shot echoes in the room, as Derek despatches a man emerging from the shadows of the bathroom to the rear of the room.

My eyes scan the room for any other attackers still lurking in the dim light. With my rifle still in the aim, I check the entire room, paying attention to the dark areas and under the two beds stripped of any bedding, when Ana screams from the opposite side of the room.

"One of the guards is over in the corner, behind the door."

Spinning on my feet, I scream, "Fucking drop that weapon and stand up."

The man slides the weapon across the floor, like a naughty schoolboy hiding in the corner after his parents gave him a bollocking, fear etched on his young face.

Without warning, Ana, a woman known for her timidity, seizes an opportunity to change the tides and get revenge on the people holding her captive for so long, threatening her with death on many occasions. Her nerves snap.

She lunges towards the trembling guard, her eyes wild with a newfound strength. From the corner of my eye, I see her hand grab the knife from his trembling grasp, and in one swift movement, she buries it deep into his flesh.

The scene unfolds in slow motion, as if time has been suspended, each detail etching itself forever in my memory. The knife pierces the guard's flesh, slicing through muscle and sinew with a sickening squelch. Ana's eyes watch as thick red blood spurts from his neck, painting the floor a crimson red. In that moment, she embodies the human spirit's fragility and untamed strength.

I hear Derek send the radio message through my earpiece, "All Call Signs, Target Acquired, Out."

"The bastard probably deserved that, Ana, but we need to go," I say, taking the knife from her trembling, blood-stained hands.

"Make sure when we leave, you stay between Steve and me," says Derek, heading for the doorway.

He has been on too many missions to make a rookie mistake and poke his head around the doorframe at head or kneeling height. So he lies down on the floor, pushing his rifle out first. As he glances around the corner, a cartel member sprints along the veranda. He only makes it a few feet before Derek double-taps two rounds into his chest, dropping the man to the floor like a discarded rag doll.

"Coast clear, Steve," shouts Derek.

***

Meanwhile, at the sniper position, Lucy lay in the long grass beneath the battered old road train, across the sandy-covered parking area.

The sun descends, casting long shadows across the blistering Australian Outback. She crouches in the sand-covered parking area, concealed from prying eyes. The abandoned roadhouse smoulders in front of her; its charred remains a testament to the explosive chaos we unleashed only moments earlier.

Lucy's heart pounds in her chest, adrenaline coursing through her veins, amplifying every sensation. The acrid aroma of smoke lingers in the air, blending with the scent of burning timber and the faint whiff of charred flesh. It is a deadly cocktail that dances upon her senses, igniting excitement and fear.

Laying still in her hide, Lucy's gaze remains fixed on the roadhouse. Its flickering flames are a cruel reflection of the violence that has taken place. The crackling of fire and the distant hum of destruction can be heard from the roadhouse. But her focus remains sharp, honing in on any movement that dares to breach the crumbling walls of the cartel's stronghold.

This is not the first time she's been in the line of fire, nor will it be the last. But in these pivotal seconds, life and death hangs in perfect balance. Her internal conflict wages a fierce battle within. The weight of the lives she has already taken presses upon her conscience, but the importance of those I am about to save pushes her forward.

The index finger of her right hand hovers delicately over the trigger, a testament to the precision and control years of training instilled within her. The anticipation gnaws at her soul, an unyielding hunger that threatens to consume her. She's become the predator, lurking in the shadows, waiting for the prey to expose themselves.

Suddenly, a silhouette emerges from the smoke, its form wavering in the distorted reality of heat and flames. Her heart quickens, and time snaps back into motion. Lucy closes her eyes, driving the doubt away. She's trained for this moment. She's focused her entire existence on honing these skills, becoming a lethal force, someone to be reckoned with. It is not just her duty; it is her calling. And now, it all comes down to this.

She inhales deeply to steady her breathing, the cool night air filling her lungs, while her trained eye assesses the potential threat.

Fingers tighten around the cold metal of the rifle, her connection to the world. Lucy is the hunter, the protector. Fear has no place in Lucy's heart. She banished it a long time ago. But a flicker of doubt, of raw humanity, dances at the edges of her mind. Muscle memory takes over, her finger applying just enough pressure to release the deadly projectile.

A single shot rings out, shattering the serenity of the bush. The silhouette crumples, falling to the earth like a puppet with severed strings. The adrenaline surges through Lucy's veins, mingling with the satisfaction of a well-executed task. But deep within, a part of her soul recoiles, haunted by the echoing silence that follows.

Now, two enemy targets lay motionless within 10 minutes, their lifeless bodies blending into the sandy terrain. The silence is deafening, broken only by the crackling of flames. She sees the face of every victim in her mind, etching their pleading gazes into her memory. The internal conflict rages on, each breath a delicate balance between her chosen life and the lives she has taken.

A burst of reality breaks her thoughts, as Simon and George lay down more fire once they hear the same message, "Target Acquired" come over the radio.

All she needs to do now is wait 10 more minutes, to allow the others to make their way to the RV without any of the remaining cartel's men chasing them.

A final glance through the scope makes her heart skip a beat, so she picks up her radio and sends, "All call signs, this is LK, Ryan spotted. He re-entered the building before I could get a shot off, over."

"LK this DR, roger that, out," comes the reply from Derek.

***

Over in what is left of the roadhouse, Derek and I make our way down through the thick curtain of smoke, my heart pounding in my chest. The acrid stench of burning timbers fills my nostrils, the crackle of the flames echoing in my ears. I can feel the heat on my skin, so intense it feels like a physical weight pressing down on me.

At the end of the veranda, I stop and take cover behind a pile of broken and charred beams. Scan the area for any of Ryan's men still not playing by my rules and heading for the firebase. It looks clear. Spin to check on Ana and James. They cling to each other, their faces twisted in fear, eyes wide with desperation. My grip tightens around my assault rifle, my fingers slick with sweat. As I turn, Derek opens fire on a man racing towards us, splattering the contents of his skull across the wooden boards.

The rear exit of the motel, our intended route is blocked by burning, broken timber beams still glowing, sending flames and thick black smoke into the darkness. Mangled, contorted metal sheets block our way to the RV. Make a snap decision: we will need to go via the front.

I pivot on the spot to face Derek, who has now taken up a firing position to my right, behind a pile of bricks that used to be part of the wall separating the bar from the passageway.

"Let the rest know we are on our way via the front door, or what remains of it. Don't fancy getting a bullet in the head from the three idiots outside."

A split-second later, Derek sends over the radio, "All Call Signs, coming your way, main entrance, DR Out."

Start to lead everyone through the wreckage, clambering over what's left of the bar area, shards of glass crunching under the weight of my boots. A burst of gunfire erupts from the far end.

We dive for cover, ducking behind a crumbling wooden counter. I peek out, searching for the source of the onslaught, as bullets whizz past my head as if in slow motion. We return fire, our weapons spitting death back at our pursuers. My fingers move over the trigger, each shot precise, every bullet finding its mark. The thunderous crack of the assault rifles fills the air, mixing with the harsh screams of agony as men take their last breaths. Adrenaline courses through my veins, quickening my breath and sharpening my focus.

Minutes later, as fast as it came, the shots from the armed cartel members standing their ground recede, leaving only the roaring blaze of the burning roadhouse and the intermittent gunfire from outside from the team.

Time to make a move. We crawl through the debris, each movement deliberate and measured. The smoke thickens as a gust of wind blows through the roadhouse, choking my lungs and clouding my vision. Every sense is heightened, every sound amplified, as if the universe is holding its breath.

The way out is now only a few feet away. Again, I stop and check the place; it appears clear. Stand up, ready to sprint from the entrance to the first bit of cover outside a bullet-ridden vehicle, all its windows shattered, and the tyres shredded, when I notice a familiar face across the once-covered area in the doorway of the remains of the restaurant; it is Ryan, standing close to another man. Both have weapons pointing in our direction.

I'm about to open fire, sending a hail of bullets over the expanse, when Ryan turns and shoots the man next to him. I stand motionless, dazed and bewildered. What the fuck just happened? Are my eyes playing tricks on me? Keep my rifle in the aim. Ryan drops his pistol and raises his arms in the air.

The noise of the battle appears to hush, as Ryan says, "No need to shoot. I wanted out of the shit for some time, since Aron had one of my family members killed. You're my way out. Take me with you."

Still confused, I reply angrily, "OK, but make any stupid moves, and I will put a bullet in the front of your ugly mug."

We still require Derek to cover back the way we came, in case any more of Ryan's people get a shot of bravery and try to sneak up from the rear. Give James my 9mm pistol.

"If he tries something, blow the bastard away."

With that, Ryan runs over the remains of the furniture that once stood outside the bar and kneels behind me, in the knowledge that several of his men have been killed by the sniper concealed in the darkness, as they ran out from the entrance. Turn to Derek, "Before we move, let the others know we are coming out now."

Derek sends the message. I take a deep breath and spring to my feet, bring the rifle to the aim, then, sprint to the vehicle. I'm halfway across when Ryan makes a fatal mistake. He follows me out, without waiting for me to reach my objective.

While running, I detect the crack of a single bullet leaving a rifle from the direction of the road. A second later is the inevitable thump as the round flies through the air at high speed, hitting its target. Lucy is doing her job.

She had no way of knowing he had just surrendered. I turn around to see Ryan lying face down in the sand, blood oozing from a massive hole in the side of his head. He wanted out, and that is what he has now. Better for us as we now don't have to haul his arse to Darwin.

I make it to the protection of the vehicle, take up a position facing towards the bar, and indicate for Ana and James to sprint over to join me. Let's hope Lucy is identifying her targets. They both reach me. I can see the fear still etched in their faces. Moments later, we are joined by Derek, who takes up a similar stance to me.

Wait for Simon and George to stop firing, then race across the 30 metres of open ground between our present location and them. The occasional rounds hit the sandy deck near my feet. Once we all have reached George, pick up Simon, who leads us all along the route he prepared earlier, with George bringing up the rear. As we run, Derek transmits a message to Lucy, telling her to go to the RV.

At the RV, we all spread out, every person covering a separate arc of fire, with Ana and James crouched by the nearest Land Cruiser. For the moment, the gunfire falls silent. The air is thick with tension, so palpable that it electrifies the very molecules around us. Every flicker of movement, each shift in the wind sends adrenaline coursing through our veins.

As I crouch near the front of the RV, facing the direction of the road, my heart thuds mercilessly on my ribs. My ears strain against the backdrop of silence, listening for any sign of Lucy's arrival or any of Ryan's men still willing to put up a fight. The vegetation rustles subtly as if whispering secrets to the night itself. The earthy scent of the Outback fills my nostrils again, replacing the odour of burning buildings, mixing with the acrid aroma of gunpowder hanging in the air.

Ana and James, the hostages we have managed to rescue huddle close to one of the Land Cruisers, their eyes staring out into the darkness with fear and gratitude. Their breath comes in short, shallow bursts, echoing the rapid pace of our hearts. We know we're not out of danger yet, but we find solace in our unity for now.

The moonlight drenches the surrounding landscape, casting long shadows stretching hungrily in every direction. Lucy, our skilled sniper, is the last piece of the puzzle in our escape plan. In the distance, a screech tears through the silence. A lone bird takes flight, its wings flapping with urgency and echoing through the night. I grip my weapon tighter, my fingers feeling the cool metal against my skin. As we wait, the seconds prolong into eternity, our senses are primed to detect the faintest hint of danger.

And then, like a spectre emerging from the darkness, Lucy appears on the horizon. The moon ignites her outline, turning her into a ghostly silhouette. With her arrival, the tension dissipates, replaced by a renewed determination. Our mission is not yet complete. We now need to retreat to Darwin.

Chapter Fifteen – Retreat to Darwin

I look down at Mickey. The time is 22:30. The full moon hangs low in the expansive Australian Outback sky, casting an eerie glow on the sandy, dust-laden road. The luminance paints the landscape with a spectral hue, illuminating the vast, barren plains that stretch out in every direction. No doubt the drug cartel would be on our tail in no time if there were any of them left.

Time to leave this place. I clamber into the driver's seat of my Land Cruiser. Beside me, Lucy clings to the passenger seat, eyes wide with a mix of trepidation and exhilaration. Derek and Ana are huddled in the back, their faces etched with resolve. Wait for Simon, George and James to board the other vehicle before turning the ignition key.

The motor roars into life, shattering the stillness of the night. The deafening growl echoes through the emptiness, a symphony of determination and fear. This isn't the time for caution, so I drive at a rapid pace, weaving through the bushes and trees and making my way to the Stuart Highway.

I grip the steering wheel so tight that my knuckles turn white in the dim light of the dashboard. The engine growls beneath me, hungry for speed. We race along the sandy and dusty highway in the rugged Australian Outback, kicking up clouds of golden dust that follow us like a beacon. The full moon casts an eerie glow on the barren landscape, illuminating the way ahead. Tyres screech against the sand, searching for traction within the loose sand.

The breeze is blowing across from right to left, sending billowing dust clouds erupting in my wake, obliterating any trace of our presence. The thick haze becomes a shroud of disguise, obscuring us from anyone who might be following. With Simon driving behind me, I move over to the opposite side of the road to get a clear rearward view of the track. In the distance, three sets of headlights come out of the darkness.

Half turn my head, "Derek, contact Simon and George and ensure they have spotted them. They could be innocent people travelling along the route, but let's not take any chances."

With the mic in one hand, "GD, this is DR. Have you seen the vehicles approaching you from the rear? Over."

A few moments later, "DR, yes, and whoever they are, they're gaining on us!" George's voice crackles through the speakers of the radio, the tone of his voice cutting through the roar of the engines.

I don't care who they are. We need to get away from them. So, I press my foot down on the accelerator. The car surges forward, the engine roaring with newfound vigour. The vehicle strains against its limits, muscles of metal and machinery pushed to their breaking point as we navigate the treacherous route. The tyres grip the sandy road, propelling us with raw power.

The vehicle leans into the sharp curves, defying gravity as we race through the perilous terrain. Each glance in the rear-view mirror reveals the three cars closing in, menacingly flashing their headlights as if bearing a predator's fangs ready to strike.

The hot wind blows sand through the open windows, stinging my face and filling my mouth, gritting between my teeth. I can sense every bump, jolting the car and testing our resilience.

Then, like a warning out of a whodunit game, the unmistakable sound of rifle fire echoing over the noise of the engine. At least we now know who is behind us - it's the cartel. The question is, where did they come from? We wiped out everyone we came across during the rescue. The bastards must have radioed for help.

The chase has become a high-speed ballet, a frenzy of metal and adrenaline. In the oppressive heat of the Outback, the vehicles weave through twisting bends, engines groaning under the relentless pursuit. A symphony of screeching tyres echo through the night, harmonising with the rhythmic thud of pounding hearts.

With every twist and turn, my heart leaps into my throat. The cartel cars inch closer, their headlights growing larger in the rearview mirror. I can almost taste their vengeance, a sour mix of desperation and grim determination. They will stop at nothing to see us crushed beneath their wheels.

A sudden explosion of gunshots lash the air, jerking me back to reality, the sound deafening in the confined space of the car. Shots whizz past us, leaving trails of burning air in their wake. The bullets tear through the Land Cruisers, the windows shattering under the assault, showering us with shards of glass; leaving behind shattered glass and shredded metal. Lucy shields her face, a stray cut trickling streams of crimson blood down her arm.

My focus narrows, tunnelling in on the road ahead. The sand, the dust, and the moonlit shadows that dance on the edges of my vision blur into one as my senses become heightened. The moon looks down in silence, casting its pale light upon a road filled with desperation and conflict. Each twist and turn, every confrontation with the harsh desert terrain, intensifies the stakes. With every passing second, the pursuit begins to boil over, the atmosphere crackling with electric energy.

George's voice rings out again over the radio, resonating with determination. "Keep going, Steve!" His words are only just audible above the cacophony of the engines and the gunfire.

I grit my teeth, my grip on the steering wheel intensifying. The car swerves, missing a boulder that appears to materialise out of nowhere. Sand kicks up in our wake, a golden swirl of chaos and freedom. The chase stretches on, each heartbeat pounding away like an eternity in the face of danger. The desert night seems to hold its breath as we hurtle forward, our fates uncertain. But we will not go down without a fight.

"Derek, tell Simon to come alongside us," I yell.

Seconds later, Simon is driving to my right, creating a massive sand cloud which covers the entire road, blocking the view of our vehicles to the chasing cartel behind, and giving me time to think. I have it. I reach inside my jacket pocket and grab my telephone. Pass it to Derek.

"Call the number on the screen."

As though he is in tune with my brainwaves, "I was wondering what you did with the second IED," comes the instant reply.

Derek clenches the mobile phone in his hand, its plastic casing slippery with sweat, and dials the number, waiting for the connecting click.

To follow the events of what is about to happen, Derek turns in his seat and stares out the shattered rear window. The cartel's vehicles are closing in fast, their headlights piercing through the darkness like predatory eyes. The air electrifies as he presses the call button. A shiver races down his spine, a premonition of the impending chaos about to be unleashed.

A surge of electricity ripples through the mobile phone, a spark of life transferring from Derek's hand to the dormant explosive device connected to the other mobile. It's an electrical current, alive and malevolent, charged with the imminent destruction of their nemesis.

A mix of satisfaction and triumph wells up inside him. His breath catches in his throat as the current travels down the wires, daringly bridging the gap between technology and devastation. Time seems to slow, each second expanding into eternity as the invisible energy courses through the detonator, mere inches away from death incarnate.

A bead of sweat trickles down Derek's temple, tasting salt on his dry lips. His eyes dart from the phone to the vehicle behind, a wolf in pursuit. The moment becomes crystallised, suspended in a macabre dance between life and death. He knows that once the electrical circuit is completed, chaos will be unleashed upon the sandy road that became our battleground.

After what seems like a time without an end, a deafening roar rips through the night. Flames erupt from the cartel's vehicle, transforming it into a fiery inferno that dances hungrily in the moonlight. A vengeance engulfs the pursuing vehicles in a tempest of chaos—metal twists and warps like a monstrous creature, splintering in its violent dance of destruction. The blast reverberates through the ground, its thunderous howl ripping through the ruptured silence.

In a blinding burst of light, the explosion transfigures the sandy road into a canvas of fire. Derek's eyes widen, fixed upon the grotesque spectacle—skeletal remains of the vehicle spinning through the air like fiery spectres.

The scent of smouldering rubber and acrid smoke fills the air, overpowering any trace of the Outback's natural fragrance. Derek scrutinises the area as the twisted metal carcass crumbles, crumbling beneath the weight of the inferno. Flames dance, licking the night sky hungrily, a living entity spawned from vengeance. But there is no time to reflect on what happened, as there are still two vehicles to take out.

Ahead of us, the road narrows and turns 90 degrees to the right. Not knowing what is around the corner, Simon tucks back in behind me as another burst of fire comes our way. I zig-zag the vehicle, making it harder for our pursuers to get a fix on any of us.

We need to deal with the remaining cartel people soon, before we get to a settlement not too far down the road, which, even at night, could have innocent people walking the streets. I may be a heartless bastard, but if I can avoid these people's lives coming to an abrupt end, I will.

Around the corner, and I'm pushing the Land Cruiser to its limits, but somehow, they are catching up with us. I glance to my left to see Lucy starting to stand up through the sunroof she just opened.

With Simon back driving side by side with me, Lucy grips the edge of the roof, fingers digging into the metal. Below, I swerve to dodge a rock jutting from the sandy, dusty road, shaking the vehicle with such force, she bounces off the sides.

Lucy's heart races like a thundering stampede of wild horses. The weight of the sniper rifle presses against her shoulder, its cold metal a stark contrast to the burning determination in her eyes. Beads of sweat mingle with the sandy dust that clings to Lucy's skin.

Unwavering, Lucy peers through the scope, senses heightened as she surveys the relentlessly pursuing vehicles of the drug cartel units closing in with nefarious intent, racing towards us, weaving through the desert landscape like desperate serpents, their tyres kicking up clouds of sand behind them. This is a dance of life and death, and Lucy has been chosen as the executioner of the second vehicle.

The sniper rifle trembles a little in Lucy's grasp, anticipation surging through her veins with each heartbeat. She closes both eyes for a nanosecond, tuning out all the chaos. This is the moment where time seems to slow, each breath measured, each heartbeat echoing like a drum in Lucy's ears. She's done this countless times, but no matter how many many scenarios she's visualised or targets she has practised on, the intensity of the situation never wanes. This is what she lives for.

Homing in on the first vehicle, its headlights illuminating its silhouette against the vast darkness, Lucy hunches over the roof and steadies the grip on the weapon, the stock cool on the palm of her hand.

The index finger carefully finds the trigger, and she takes up the first pressure with unparalleled precision. As she applies the second pressure, the world seems to hold its breath. The resulting recoil jolts through her body, but Lucy remains resolute, her focus unyielding. At the same time as an ethereal apparition, the bullet exits the barrel, a stunning defiance against the chaos that appears to defy the very laws of time.

Slow-motion-like, it etches an otherworldly trajectory through the air, a graceful dance as it merges with the moon's dim glow. Each nanosecond stretches out into infinity, intensifying the suspense as the round travels on its designated path toward the driver of the first pursuing vehicle. Lucy observes in awe as the projectile cuts through the air, a streak of silver slicing through the night.

Time speeds up again as the round finds its mark with a primal roar, shattering the windshield like an explosive shower of diamonds, the resounding symphony of fragments mingling with the cool night breeze. In that fleeting moment, the driver's eyes widen in horrified realisation. The target jerks violently a second later, his torso convulsing as pain courses through him. His foot slips off the pedal, and the vehicle veers off the road, careening into a ditch.

The impact is cataclysmic, the twisted metal and tortured tyres creating a cacophony of chaos. The driver's body and his passengers are beaten within the confines of the doomed vehicle, surrendering to the inevitability of their untimely demise.

As the dust settles, Lucy exhales, her muscles relax, and her heartbeat returns to normal. She withdraws from the sunroof, her senses still heightened. The tension lingers, coiling like a wound serpent, as we press further into the unforgiving Australian Outback.

George's eyes widen as he observes Lucy taking out the second vehicle, his mind shifting into overdrive. One car is still chasing them, and it needs to be stopped. At that moment, George remembers the extra gift Tyler had given the team in Daly Waters. So, reaches under the passenger seat, his fingertips brushing against the cold fibreglass of the LAW 66 rocket launcher. It feels weighty and powerful in his grip, a weapon capable of turning the tide in their favour.

An adrenaline-induced tremor courses through George's veins, as he stands up precariously through the sunroof, ignoring the bone-rattling bumps and jostles, focusing on nothing but his target - the remaining cartel vehicle, its driver bearing down on them with steely determination, the menacing glare of its headlights piercing the storm of dust and sand kicked up by its tyres.

He pulls the two halves of the LAW 66 apart, exposing the front and rear sights, its cold body in his hand. The faint aroma of gunpowder dances in the air, mixing with the dry scent of the Outback.

Time once more seems to slow as George lifts the anti-tank launcher to his shoulder, the weight familiar and reassuring in his hands, his finger hovering over the rubber trigger. The anticipation hangs heavy, every second stretching out like the hands of a clock ticking around its face.

Locking the sights on the enemy vehicle in one fluid motion, he pushes down on the trigger. Then, in one explosive burst of power, the LAW 66 unleashes its fury. The missile leaps from the tube — a silver streak slicing through the moonlit sky. A fiery vengeance tears through the air with unforgiving velocity, leaving behind a trailing curtain of smoke and fire. Moonlight shimmers off its sleek surface, dancing among the shadows cast by its deadly purpose. It seemed to defy gravity, defying both time and space itself.

The vehicle's engine roars in George's ears, drowning out all other sounds. His eyes focus on the rocket, tracking its trajectory with unwavering precision.

Seconds stretch out, elongating into an eternity before a thunderous explosion; the missile strikes its target. A brilliant blast erupts, illuminating the night like a thousand suns in a blinding wave of fire, and engulfing the cartel's vehicle in a fiery maelstrom. The earth beneath them shakes as if startled by the sheer force of the explosion.

The power of the explosive sends the drug cartel vehicle careening into the air, defying gravity's grasp. Time seems to freeze in that impossible suspended moment, the car soaring several feet high, an emblem of destruction and ruin, before crashing down onto the scorched terrain in a pile of twisted and mangled pieces.

The deafening sound echoes across the vast expanse, drowning out the sound of the chase and the roar of the engines; smoke billows in thick, suffocating clouds, engulfing the remnants of the obliterated vehicle. Fragments of metal and shattered glass rain like deadly confetti, littering the barren landscape with evidence of the confrontation.

In the front vehicle, I look in my rearview mirror at the chaos behind us, before easing off on the speed so the team can catch their breaths. From her face in the reflection, I can see the events have taken a toll on Ana.

"Relax, Ana, we will be at Darwin airport in no time, and this nightmare will be over," I say, in an attempt to get her to calm down and forget about what just happened.

In the back, Derek confirms over the radio that everyone is OK, and we have no injuries or bullet holes to deal with in the team or James. Thank God, so far, we have all come through the last couple of weeks with no significant injuries. All we need to do now is sprint to Darwin to catch a flight out of Australia. Meet up with

Bear, our contact, and grab the rest of our money, then some well-deserved R&R. I've been on too many missions to switch off now, but it appears like a straight run from here.

The following 30 minutes go by with no further incidents or sightings of Aron's people. With any luck, Aron will be among the dead scattered across the Outback.

By the left side of the road, a green sign states we have 51 kilometres until we reach the next roadhouse. The vehicles are running low on fuel, which we are going to need if we are going to make it to Darwin. Plus we could all do with some refreshments at the same time.

"Derek, let George know we are stopping at the roadhouse for a piss stop and to get some diesel."

"No problem. DG, this is DR, we are taking a break at the next roadhouse. It should be in about 30 minutes."

"DR, roger that. I've got a mouth like a camel's flip-flop," comes the reply from George.

Not long before the lights of the roadhouse come into view, a situation is developing in front of us. Across the road are two Australian police cars blocking the way and forcing all vehicles to drive off and into the roadhouse.

As we approach the checkpoint, the moonlit night stretches ahead of us like an inky expanse. The air is heavy with anticipation, and a sense of unease settles in my chest. I can feel the collective tension among the group, as Simon drives his vehicle close behind us. The engine's hum is the only sound that breaks through the silence.

A blinding beam of light sears our eyes as the police officers halt us in our tracks. The torch slices through the darkness, casting harsh shadows on our anxious faces. I squint, trying to shield my eyes, gripping the wheel tighter in my clammy hands.

"Keep your hands on the steering wheel, sir," a stern voice commands, as a uniformed officer approaches my window, his presence looming ominously. The tension in the air is suffocating. I comply, my heart pounding in my ears. Surley the mission can't fail at this late stage.

"Good evening, officer," I respond, my voice trembling a little, even though my training always said to play it cool but always show a little apprehension to make it believable. "Is there a problem?"

The officer's gaze is sharp and penetrating, his eyes narrow beneath a brimmed hat, inspecting every inch of me.

"We're looking for five individuals involved in an explosion at a nearby roadhouse," states the officer, his voice brimming with urgency. "Have you witnessed anything suspicious?"

While my mind process the information, I steal a glance at Lucy and Derek, their faces showing no emotion, unlike Ana, whose face is etched with worry. I shake my head, attempting to find the right words. "No, officer. We've been driving from Katherine and haven't seen anything unusual."

The officer studies me for another agonising moment before breaking his gaze. The man nods, his jaw clenched, finding my response satisfactory.

"Alright, proceed to the next checkpoint," he instructs sternly. "Stay safe and report any suspicious activity immediately."

Relief washes over me for a few seconds as the officer steps away, but it quickly dissipates as another officer approaches the vehicles, flashlight in hand. My heart resumes its frantic beat as the flashlight illuminates the interior of our car, casting eerie shadows on Lucy, Derek, and Ana's faces. I sense a trickle of sweat making its way down my spine.

The officer moves methodically, inspecting every nook and cranny in search of evidence and threats. The beam of light dances across the surfaces, lingering on each of our faces. The gravity of the situation bears down on us, the fear of being caught palpable as we sit stone-still, waiting for the verdict.

Minutes stretch into an eternity, as the officer examines every inch of our vehicle. I clench my jaw, trying to suppress the rising adrenaline flooding my veins. The seconds tick by agonisingly.

After what seems like forever, the officer steps back, his inspection complete. I don't think the officer's heart was in the inspection. He was likely pulled away from a night out on his day off, otherwise, he would have questioned the broken back window and several bullet holes.

A rush of relief surges through my body, and I let out a deep breath. Simon's vehicle is also deemed clear, and the police officers motion us forward.

As we accelerate away from the checkpoint, the shadows of the night swallowing us whole, my heart returns to its average pace. The overload on my senses begins to fade, replaced by an overwhelming sense of gratitude and relief.

The fuel pumps are outside the entrance, similar to the now derelict roadhouse we left burning. While Simon and I refuel the two Land Cruisers, the rest go inside to pay for the diesel and grab some drinks and snacks.

Deep down, I know that as we leave the checkpoint behind, we're entering a dangerous game with unknown players who could lurk in the shadows, waiting for the perfect moment to strike.

We've only driven a few kilometres down the road when Lucy turns to me.

"If there was a roadblock at the roadhouse, we are more than probably facing the same thing at the airport. Suggest we call the number given to us by Eliza's parents to see if they can pick us up away from Darwin?"

"Makes sense to me, Lucy, who's got the number?" comes my reply.

"Me, I have it," replies Derek, pulling a sheet of paper from his jacket.

"Give it here; I'll contact the number. My female voice may help. You never know."

"It's the top number," says Derek, handing her the bit of paper.

Using the vehicle interior light to read the numbers, Lucy enters them into the phone. There is a slight pause before she hears a ringing tone on the other end. Thirty seconds later, someone answers.

"Hi, I'm Lucy. Margret and Bob, Eliza's parents gave us your number — she said you could help us with flights?"

After a short conversation Lucy, hangs up, "We are in luck. I spoke to Eddie, a friend of Eliza's dad. They have a plane in the area. We are to make our way to Daly Waters Aerodrome. The aircraft will get there as soon as it can."

"Cheers, Lucy, good job we called then, as we are not far from there," I say.

It's not long before we pull into the aerodrome, the corrugated hanger looming around us, a menacing backdrop to our high-stakes operation. The moonlight casts elongated shadows across the cracked concrete, mirroring the ones that swirl within my mind. Being in the heart of the Australian Outback, it's a desolate place at the best of times, but tonight, at 01:00 a.m., it seems even more eerie. The full moon throws an ethereal glow over the surroundings, painting the landscape in shades of silver and black.

The moment comes to a halt, the team's training kicks in, and they spring from the vehicles and take up defensive positions in the dense vegetation surrounding the site. At the same time, Simon and I conceal the two cars.

I turn to Ana, "Stay in the vehicle until we have secured the area," before moving to Simon's vehicle and telling James to do the same.

We remain concealed for the next 10 minutes, listening and observing our surroundings for any traces of the cartel that might still be chasing us. Immersing ourselves in the eerie glow of the moonlight, the flickering shadows dance across our faces. The bush surrounds us, an abyss of black stretching as far as I can see. Only the distant hum of insects fills the silence, underscoring the tension in the air.

When I'm convinced it is safe to move, we take up positions and wait in and around an abandoned World War II hangar, which stands on the edge of the airstrip like a haunted sentinel. Its internal weathered walls are adorned with fading displays of its former glory. I could almost envision the ghosts of brave airmen who once called this place home, their spirits haunting the broken aircraft parts that clutter the area. Damaged parts are scattered on the ground, disused exhibits and equipment, remnants of a time long gone.

The musty fragrance of aged metal and dampness permeates the air, tangling with the distinct scent of dust and decay. The rusted remains of a crashed plane lay just beyond the hangar, a stark reminder of nature's relentless pursuit of destruction.

My senses are heightened as I strain to listen. The Australian Outback comes alive with a symphony of unseen creatures. Once more, their nocturnal calls carry on the sultry night air. The distant howls of dingoes echo through the darkness, a haunting melody that sends shivers down my spine. But beneath the lullaby of the wilderness, I sense a sinister energy lurking, waiting for its opportunity to strike. Every noise is a potential threat, each rustle in the bushes a harbinger of danger. We remain vigilant, our eyes scanning the landscape, alert to the shadows that lurk beyond our reach.

I sit on the cold concrete floor of the hangar, going through our plans for our imminent escape. Each step had been meticulously planned, every detail accounted for, but the uncertainty of the situation gnaws at my resolve. My eyes dart around, taking in the room and its occupants. The scene is set, the tension taut as a guitar string. Each team member plays their part, a well-oiled machine eager for action.

Derek, our communication expert, sits hunched over his radio, his brow furrowed in frustration. His hands move with urgency, manipulating the dials and switches to establish contact with the aircraft that is our ticket to escape, and whisk us away to safety.

His forehead drips with sweat, his breathing ragged. The soft glow of the radio's display casts a pallor upon his strained features, accentuating the tension etched in them. Static crackles in response, punctuated by the occasional broken transmission from other pilots, their voices distorted and faint, making them hard to hear. Derek understands that our lives depend on his ability to reach our only lifeline out of here.

George and Lucy, our team snipers, station themselves on opposite ends of the hangar, facing the approach roads, the guardians, and the silent sentinels in the night. Their eyes scan the darkness. With razor-sharp focus, they watch for any signs of danger from the drug cartel. Their rifles are steady, their fingers twitching, anticipating any conceivable threats. It is their job to ensure our escape remains unimpeded, to cut down any who dare to interfere. In the blackness, their eyes glint with a predatory hunger, ready to eliminate any potential attacks from the ruthless drug cartel that is hunting us.

Simon, a maestro of chaos, is crouched near the vehicles that have been our means of escape. He curses under his breath, the harsh syllables mingling with the symphony of the Outback's nightlife. I watch his hands move with precision, manipulating the intricate workings of the engine and stripping key components, rendering them inoperable, but in a way that if the aircraft doesn't show, he can put them back together in a short period of time. His expertise is evident in each stroke of his tools, ensuring that they will pose no danger of being tracked or commandeered by our pursuers.

Ana and James are sitting on some old cardboard, to protect themselves from the roughness of the oil-stained floor and broken glass.

The first signs of hesitant rays of dawn creep over the horizon and begin to penetrate the realm of darkness, casting mysterious shadows across the cracked concrete and rusted metal of Daly Waters Aerodrome, which lies shrouded in an eerie silence. The air is crisp, with a gentle breeze carrying the scent of eucalyptus and red dust.

My eyes strain against the gathering light, searching for any hints of movement of the aircraft high above the airfield, as it glides through the air with serene grace, throwing a faint shadow on the desolate landscape below. And then, like a spectre emerging from my darkest fears, the soft hum of the engine grows louder, echoing through the stillness of the early morning, until it engulfs my senses. It is a sound that carries promise and trepidation, a melody of anticipation hanging heavy in the air.

The sun paints the small aircraft in vivid colours as it comes onto the final approach, igniting the silver frame with a fiery glow. The ethereal glare of its landing lights gnawing away at the last remnants of our concealed haven, pierces through the dim light of dawn. The wings, outstretched like a bird in flight, shimmer as if reflecting the very essence of the dawn's radiance, as if to welcome the arriving aircraft.

Closer and closer, the aircraft drops with an almost cautious precision. The anticipation in the air is palpable, like a coiling spring ready to be released. The rhythmic thumping of my heart synchronises with the ever-louder whir of the engine, urging it nearer to its destination.

Distant birds chirp in celebration, their melodic trills punctuating the rising tension. The plane descends the last few feet with grace, its wheels grazing the uneven dirt runway, stirring up dust clouds in its wake. Derek's voice booms through my earpiece as he establishes contact with the pilot, his tone steady and calm, a testament to his expertise.

As the aircraft draws nearer, I can make out its details with increasing clarity. The rhythmic rotation of the propeller is reflected in the metal sheen of the engine, spinning effortlessly against the backdrop of the vast desert sky. The words emblazoned on its side, barely visible at this distance, promise both danger and hope.

The aircraft halts near the disused hangar. The engine's growl subsides to a hum, punctuated only by the crackling static from Derek's radio. Our rapid breaths break the silence, mingling in the heavy air.

As the engine winds down, the quietness is replaced by a newfound sense of liberation. We have completed this part of the rescue mission, and now, salvation awaits Ana and James. This once unforgiving prison, the Australian Outback, becomes a launching pad towards freedom.

The plane door creaks open, revealing a solitary figure stepping onto the airstrip. Shadows cloak his face, his features obscured by darkness. But his presence sends a shiver down my spine. As the stranger scans the area, his eyes dart from one patch of shadows to another, searching for any signs of danger.

One by one, our eyes lock on the person at the bottom of the steps, our training melding with instinct, analysing every move, every twitch like a hawk in the vast expanse of the bush, wary and keen.

My gut tightens, a knot of apprehension. This is the make-or-break moment, the catalyst that will shape the rest of the mission. I grip my rifle tighter, my palms slick with sweat. The stillness weighs on my shoulders, and I fight the urge to break cover and sprint towards the plane. But my experience tells me to remain concealed, so I stay hidden among this expansive land's foliage with the others, until Derek's voice pierces through the tension, signalling us to reveal ourselves and approach the aircraft.

We emerge from our positions, converging on the plane with military precision. As I step onto the aircraft, its interior hollow and comforting, the weight of the world rests on my shoulders. The engines roar back to life, the propellers slicing through the air with a sense of purpose.

Chapter Sixteen – New York

I climb into the right-hand seat of the cockpit of the light aircraft, next to the pilot and glance at the array of instruments on the dash, and remember most of them from my days learning to fly a few years back.

The early morning air is crisp and still, casting an ethereal glow over the Australian Outback. I fasten my seatbelt, sensing the subtle hum of the engine reverberating through the atmosphere, adding a sense of urgency to the stillness of the desert.

This is it, the moment we've been waiting for. I glance at the pilot, his steady hands gripping the controls. His eyes, focused and determined, his sunglassess reflect the rising sun's rays. A quiet confidence radiates from him, reassuring me we're safe for now.

With a gentle push on the throttle, the aircraft begins accelerating down the disused runway. The rubber tyres rattle over the rough ground, building speed. The motion pushes me back into my seat, and as we gain momentum, the horizon seems to stretch out before me, a canvas awaiting the artist's brush. The plane trembles with restrained power as if eager to take flight and explore the limitless expanse above.

At last, the wheels lift from the ground, and we are airborne. Gravity releases its grip on the aircraft, and the rumble gives way to the smooth hum of the engine, harmonising with my heartbeat. The morning light spills through the windshield, painting the cockpit with hues of gold, and throwing elongated dark areas over the instrument panel.

We climb steadily, reaching an altitude of 2,000 feet, where we level off. The vast expanse of the bush unfurls beneath us, revealing its raw beauty. The vastness extends in all directions, a tapestry of colours and textures. The ochre earth sprawls out like an artist's palette, dotted with patches of emerald green where rivers carve their path. Below, the sunlight caresses the land, casting long shadows that dance across the shifting topography.

My gaze shifts from the terrain to the team behind me. Lucy stares determinedly out the window, her lengthy hair catching the morning light. Simon, his robust features etched with a mix of exhaustion and relief, hugs his rifle. With a wiry build that belies his strength, Derek surveys the horizon with a calculated intensity. George wears a face of fierce determination that sets my mind at ease.

Between them are Ana and James, the two individuals we've just rescued from the clutches of the drug cartel. Ana's eyes are filled with gratitude and a hint of fear, and she holds James' hand. James, though just a young man, has a resilience beyond his years. Together, they embody the hope and innocence we've fought to protect.

I turn my attention back to the landscape below, the vastness of the bush stretching out into the distance. Birds of prey soar without effort on thermal updrafts, their wings outstretched as if embracing the heavens. I marvel at their grace, their mastery of the sky. Cool air rushes through the open windows, breathing life into my tired body. We're on our way to safety, but our journey is far from over.

"Hi, I'm Steve. Thanks for coming for us," I say, spinning in my seat to face the pilot.

"No problem. Eliza's parents are still relieved you got their daughter out of the clutches of the drug cartel. I'm Jack."

"Are we heading for Darwin Airport?" I enquire.

"We have been listening to the police radio. They have checkpoints everywhere, even at the airport, looking for the people who set off an explosion and left 20 people dead at the Burrow Creek Roadhouse. So, it wouldn't be safe for you. Instead, we are making our way to a small airfield called Emkaytee. We have a larger Global 7500 aircraft waiting to take you to Singapore. From here, you can catch a plane to anywhere."

"Sounds like some sort of a plan. Do you think we will have any issues in Singapore?"

"Nope. You should arrive by 18:00, and as we are landing at our private hangar, you will be driven straight to the steps of your aircraft."

Fifteen minutes into the flight, with none of the usual banter or slagging off coming from the rear, I turn around to see everyone fast asleep, apart from Ana, who is gazing out of the aircraft. The exhaustion of the last two weeks is taking its toll on everybody; me included.

As always, the brain is still in overdrive and running through the events; from arriving at Emkaytee and onward to Singapore, and wherever we end up dropping Ana and James off, and meeting up with Bear to collect the rest of the dosh.

I gaze out the window to my right as the light aircraft soars through the stunning azure sky. From an altitude of 2,000 feet, the Outback reveals itself with breathtaking glory as it unfolds beneath me. The sheer vastness of the landscape is staggering, as if the dense bush has painted a captivating masterpiece. The contrast between the vibrant hues and the endless blue is mesmerising. I can sense the energy of this place, a primal force that seems to run through my veins.

The sound of the engine hums in the background, harmonising with the symphony of nature below. Yet amidst this overwhelming sensory experience, my attention is captivated by the skilled pilot manoeuvring the aircraft. His finesse is awe-inspiring. Every twist of the plane is executed with graceful ease, dancing through the atmosphere as if weightless. Both hands guide the controls, maintaining a steady course towards Emkaytee.

"We will be at the airstrip in 10 minutes," says Jack, through my headphones.

"Roger that," I reply.

I turn to nudge Simon, who is the closest to me, "Wakey, wakey, we are almost at the landing strip. Wake the others."

Jack's eyes are laser-focused as we neared the Emkaytee airfield, scanning the horizon for the one-kilometre hard-packed sandy stretch of land that awaits us. With a calculated descent, the plane glides down to earth as if caressed by an invisible hand.

The moment of validity arrives, and the wheels contact the ground, eliciting a gentle thud—a testament to the pilot's exceptional ability to balance control and grace. Jack guides the aircraft along the compacted dirt with steady hands. He brings it to a graceful standstill in front of one of the hangars lining the runway's edge. Once the engines have stopped, I clamber out, standing a couple of feet away, waiting for the rest to join me and for Jack to explain what happens next.

Within a few minutes, we are being led into an enormous metal hangar. Inside is another larger aircraft with 'Global 7500' in big letters down the fuselage. In the corner is a bricked-off area with three large windows facing inwards.

The room is divided into two halves. The business and flight planning are to my left as I enter through the doorway. To my right are several sizeable green leather sofas, tables and a long teak bar lined with bottles of spirits. Up against the wall are two huge glass-fronted chillers. Both are full of expensive-looking wines and shelves of beer. Overhead, two ceiling fans are circulating the cold breeze from the wall-mounted air conditioning unit.

Plonk my arse down on a stool near the counter, after dropping my Bergen with the rest of the team's kit. At that moment, a familiar face enters the room. It's Bob, Eliza's dad.

"Glad to see you're all safe, and you have Ana and James," Bob says, walking over to the first of the two sofas where Ana has collapsed, taking a deep intake of free air.

"Yep, so far, a successful rescue. All we need now is a location to drop them," I reply, still eyeing up the beers.

"Talking of that, following a conversation with Bear, I was on the telephone with James' parents a few hours ago, shortly after we received your call about a pickup. They are in New York and asked if you could take James and Ana there. They will meet you in Hotel Edison in two days. Here is their phone number. Contact them once you arrive."

"Thanks, Bob, that saves Derek from contacting him. Can I grab one of those drinks in the chiller? Got a mouth like a camel's flip-flop.

"No problem, help yourselves. The staff have spread out some food for you as well," says Bob, pointing to the array of scran on the wooden table to the bar's left.

"Grab us all one as you're up, fat boy."

"Let me think about that, George... nope, get your own."

With still an hour before the flight is planned to leave, we permit ourselves a little time to relax. Drink a few cold drinks. We are too professional to allow our guard to drop too much. Even here, the cartel may have contacts at one of the other businesses located at the isolated airfield.

Sipping on my beer, still sitting on the stool at the bar, I scan the room, taking in the relaxing atmosphere. George and Simon are helping themselves to the food on offer while Derek is talking to James at the other end of the room. Lucy and Ana are slumped on one of the sofas, chatting away. It would appear on the surface we are all waiting for a flight in a business lounge at any airport in the world and not fleeing from a gunfight.

I glance down at my wristwatch. We still have 30 minutes before departure, so walk over to join Lucy and Ana.

"Don't know if you overheard what Bob said, but James' parents are in New York. We are heading to Singapore, where we can catch a flight to meet up with them."

"Excellent, I always wanted to go to New York. Maybe we can spend a few days checking the place out before returning to the UK," says Lucy.

"We could, I suppose. Let's see what happens when we drop off Ana and James," I say, looking at Ana.

It isn't long before Bob walks through the door, "Are you ready? The captain said he will be ready to leave in 20 minutes, so you must get on board."

Walk over to the pile of bags, pick up mine and Lucy's Bergens, and follow Bob out of the waiting area towards the aircraft. Behind me, the rest of the team is collecting their kit; apart from James and Ana, as they don't have any belongings, these were taken when they were handed over to the cartel.

As this is a private jet and there are no customs to deal with, there's no issues with taking our pistols on the jet, although we are still concealing them in case we run into any difficulties. Let's face it, Bob seems an OK type of guy, but when it comes to the crew of the jet, they are an unknown variable that my hypervigilance still doesn't trust yet.

As I step into the opulent interior of the Global 7500, I take a moment to take in the grandeur surrounding me. The aircraft is a vision of luxury, wrapped in a symphony of muted earth tones and tasteful accents. Crafted wood trim adorns the cabin, adding a touch of sophistication and warmth. The polished surfaces gleam under the soothing ambient lighting, casting a spellbinding glow that accentuates the magnificence of the surroundings, as though I have entered a personal sanctuary, insulated from the chaos of the world outside.

As I glance around, I detect the unique features that contribute to the overall grandeur of the jet. A sleek bar, designed with chrome, beckons me over from one corner. Crystal glasses sparkle in the soft light, inviting me to partake in a toast to the good life. A state-of-the-art entertainment system integrated into the cabin promises an immersive experience, capable of whisking me away to any part of the globe with the touch of a button.

Brough back to reality as George pushes past, "I'll have that seat. You and Lucy can have those two," he points to seats on my left facing each other, divided by a small wooden teak table.

"No problem, George, you lot can have that bank of four seats. They are closer to the drinks," comes the reply from Lucy, who is now sitting in the soft leather chair looking towards the back of the plane.

On the other side, Ana and James are seated in similar leatherbound chairs to mine. Once everyone has made themselves comfortable, a young woman in her early 30s appears from behind a blue velvet curtain carrying a tray of white flannels.

"Hi, I'm Lola-Mae. I will be taking care of you during the flight. If you need anything, just ask," as she hands out hot towels to freshen up.

"Could get use to this life," says Simon, stretching out and drinking a glass of champagne Lola-Mae just handed him.

"Better make the most of it then, Simon, as they would throw your scruffy sorry arse off any other private jet," comes the retort from Derek.

"As I always say, Derek... the second word is off. Try to guess the first one."

Not long after takeoff, I have a discussion with James. It turns out his father is a wealthy businessman who owns a chain of shops across America. They are opening a new flagship store in Manhattan. That is why they have asked us to go to New York.

When I return to my seat opposite Lucy, she is fast asleep. So, I spend some time watching a couple of movies until Lola-Mae comes around, passing me a sheet of cardboard on which is a lunch menu with a selection of freshly prepared food. She also gives me a mobile telephone.

"It's Bob, he wants to talk to you."

With the phone to my ear, "Hi Bob, is there an issue?" I ask, wondering why he has called me mid-flight.

"Not at all, Steve. Just a slight change of plan. We are in luck, a party of business people will join you in Singapore. They are travelling to San Francisco, therefore, paying the costs of this flight. So, no need to get off."

"Sounds awesome, but what about customs?" I reply.

"You will be landing at a private part of the airport, and as far as any of the airport staff are aware, the plane is empty and is picking four passengers up for their flight to the United States. The same applies when you land in San Francisco. Stay on board, and we will fly you to New York. You can leave via the domestic terminal, as your flight took off from another internal airport, so no Border Protection officials to worry about."

"Won't the flight plan have us landing in America along with the other people?"

"Let's put it this way. The Americans are too arrogant, hacking into the infrastructure, carrying out covert operations, and even assassinating people in other countries, that the idiots don't think other people will be doing the same to them. Once you take off from

Singapore, my people will change the flight details to only show the people joining you. So sit back and enjoy my plane."

"We owe you one, Bob," I say, putting the phone on the table and returning to the food menu.

The rest of the flight went without any problems. We picked up the people in Singapore. Three men and a woman, all dressed in grey suits. They sat at the aircraft's rear and mainly kept themselves to themselves. As Bob had explained, there were no issues in Singapore with officials. Our four business passengers alighted in San Francisco again with no government agencies coming on board.

We are now only 30 minutes away from John F. Kennedy International Airport. I have been through the domestic terminal at JFK a few years back, so know that once you collect your bags from the baggage conveyor, there are no police or others to deal with. We will pick up our Bergens when we land, from the plane's cargo hold before being driven to the main building. This means we can pass through without stopping, minimising any nosey person from Customs and Border Protection asking any stupid questions, like where we have come from.

I call the team to my seat, "We will be arriving soon, folks. You know as much as I do. We can't afford to let our guard down until we are back in England, after handing over Ana and James. So, suggest when we enter, we go in three separate groups, to help avoid any unwanted attention. Myself and Ana will go first, followed five minutes later by Simon and George. Behind them will be Lucy and James, if you bring up the rear, Derek. If anyone is stopped, the RV will be outside at the farmost end of the taxi rank."

"Do you want me to call the Edison Hotel and book us some rooms?" asks Derek.

"Good idea, mate."

As we step into the bustling domestic terminal at JFK Airport, the air buzzes with the soft hum of conversations, intermingling with the mechanical whir of baggage carts whizzing by. The scent of coffee and fast food wafts through the expanse of the hall, creating an odd mix of anxiety and familiarity.

No need to glance over to locate the rest, they are a team of skilled operatives. Ana walks beside me, her eyes scanning the crowd; even she understands how crucial it is to maintain a low profile, while we slip through the wave of passengers, blending seamlessly into the mass of humanity.

We soon come across the first obstacle that appears, in the form of an airport staff member blocking our path. A middle-aged man in a neon blue vest barks orders at a group of aimless travellers, his voice booming through the chaos. Carefully avoid eye contact as I swerve to the left, navigating around the airport employees.

Behind me, Simon and George weave their way through the terminal, their eyes flickering from one suspicious face to another. Lucy and James walk hand in hand, their voices just a quiet murmur as they skilfully evade the prying eyes of fellow passengers. We have all done this countless times, but the stakes are always high. The mission demands perfection; one slight misstep can mean the difference between success and utter disaster. Soon, the whole team slips seamlessly through the crowd, inching their way closer to the designated meeting point.

Outside the building Ana and I take a seat on one of the metal benches against the wall. In line with the taxis, wait for the rest to emerge onto the tarmac footpath that runs along the forward edge of the building. Finally, everyone is outside and standing near the waiting vehicles. From here, we plan to take separate cabs and meet at the Edison.

Stare out of the taxi as it darts in and out of the heavy traffic, making its way to the hotel, passing the different neighbourhoods that make up New York. Forty minutes pass before we pull up in front of the sliding glass doors flanked by two huge windows.

To my left, spread over the window in bold white letters, which stood out against the dark brown blinds on the inside, 'Friedmans', a restaurant of some sort. A similar decore is across the windowpane to the right of the door. This must be the bar, as the words 'The Rum House' are embossed on the glass.

I glance at Mickey. It is now 10 o'clock, plenty of time before we meet with James's parents, and we hand our rescued people over. As I'm about to go through the doors, two yellow taxis pull up alongside the curb of West 47th Street. The rest of the team have arrived.

On the other side of the door, a marbled floor stretches from one end of the hotel to the other. Off to my right is a bank of lifts and the entrance to The Rum House, via a single glass-fronted door. To my left, a clear window and an open door lead into Friedmans, with its laid-out tables and central bar and serving area.

Inside, the walls are adorned with vintage photographs, depicting moments frozen in time as if the restaurant has collected memories over the years. The warm, golden light filters through the extensive windows on two sides, flooding the space with a soft glow. Groups of people sit huddled together, their voices blending into a harmonious symphony. The smell of hot, buttered toast wafts through the air, mixing with the earthy fragrance of just-baked pastry. Plates clink as cutlery meets porcelain, punctuating the steady hum of conversation.

A little way into the hotel is a bustling foyer. The reception is ahead on the left. The air is filled with the intoxicating aroma of brewed coffee, from a machine situated on a small table at the entrance to the lobby, its aroma mingled with the subtle scent of polished wood. Soft chatter and laughter rise and fall like waves, melding with the clinking of glasses and the occasional clatter of luggage wheels on marble floors.

Behind the gleaming reception desk, the hotel staff navigate through a sea of guests, their hands and voices dancing in perfect sync. They wear neat, tailored uniforms, their badges glinting in the warm glow of hidden lights. Piles of key cards are organised, their metallic sheen reflecting the flickering candlelight that adorns the dark wooden counter.

Opposite is a reasonably-sized lobby. Leaning against the walls, ornate chairs and plush sofas, upholstered in shades of cream and gold, curve like a friendly embrace. Visitors fill these seats, their bodies sinking into the soft cushions. Some sip on cocktails, their glasses sweating dewdrops of condensation onto polished mahogany tables, while others engage in animated conversations, lost in a symphony of laughter and excitement.

Close to the lifts, a couple clings to each other, their fingers intertwined as they wait, their eyes radiating with anticipation. Close by, a traveller, his face weary with the weight of his journey. He sits on a sofa, his head drooping as he dozes off, lulled by the melodic tinkling of a grand piano that resonates from a nearby lounge.

Across from me, a little girl, her tiny hands entwined with her mother's, bounces on her toes, her eyes wide with wonder. She bobs her head with every word her mother speaks, her blonde curls dancing in perfect rhythm. A small smile graces my lips as I watch the innocence and joy emanating from that pure soul.

Above us, chandeliers cast prismatic rainbows on every surface, their countless crystals dangling like shards of frozen sunlight. The ceiling, a masterpiece of artistry, boasts celestial paintings that stretch towards infinity, capturing the alluring essence of the night sky.

The sounds of bustling receptionists, the rustling of papers, and the clacking of keyboards blend harmoniously with the melodies wafting from hidden speakers, creating a symphony of activity reverberating throughout the lobby.

Now standing in front of the desk with Derek, "Hi, I booked two doubles, one twin and a single in the name of Barker," says Derek, showing her the confirmation on his smartphone.

"One second, here is your reservation - four rooms for two nights with breakfast. And I see you have already paid," comes the reply from Tina, the receptionist.

"Where is breakfast served?" I ask, looking around, trying to spot a sign.

"In both Friedmans and Bond 45, which is towards the rear door," Tina points to her left down a long corridor.

She hands over seven room access keycards and vouchers, on which the name of the hotel is printed; if we present them to the restaurant staff, we get five dollars off our brekkie.

"Drop your stuff in your rooms, then assemble back up here in 20 minutes," I say, indicating to the lobby sitting area.

"Got a better idea. How about we meet inside the restaurant? I'm starving," says George, pointing at Friedmans.

"No change there then, George," states Derek, with a stupid grin spread across his face.

"You're the communication expert. What does this say," replies George, raising his middle finger.

We agree to meet in the restaurant and head for our rooms. After grabbing my room key, Lucy and I head to room 5500 on the fifth floor. I step into the hotel room, the first thing that strikes me is the whiteness of it all; the walls are painted a pristine white, gleaming under the warm glow of the overhead lights. It's a stark contrast to the darkness of the polished wood furniture. I walk further inside, allowing my eyes to explore the space.

To my left, two dark bedside cabinets stand tall on either side of the double bed, contrasting against the purity of the white walls. They possess an appearance of time gone by. Their rich brown hue adds a hint of sophistication to the room. On top of each cabinet, a small, delicate lamp emits a soft, golden glow, casting shadows in the corners.

Directly opposite the entrance is a wooden chest of drawers. Its frame looks solid, the grain visible to the touch. My attention is diverted by the door tucked away in the corner. Inside, a wardrobe stands tall, its doors boasting the same stark whiteness as the room. Within its vast domain, hangers and shelves lie empty.

Along the short corridor from the door to the main room is a white doorway — a gateway to the bathroom. I push it open. Continuing the same theme as the rest of the room, the walls are interrupted only by a sleek mirror hanging above the ceramic basin. The countertop is adorned with toiletries in small bottles. Stepping closer, I glimpse sight of the bathtub with a shower head protruding from the wall. An elegant, clear plastic panel surrounds the tub, offering protection while allowing a view of the room.

Back in the room, Lucy bounces up and down on the bed, "What are you doing, honey?" I say, a little confused.

"Just checking it for squeaks," comes the reply, as she winks at me.

I glance around the room, "That's rubbish, there is no brew-making kit; and they call this five-star. Considering this hotel is only 200 metres from Times Square, I would expect a lot more. Might as well go down and grab a drink from Friedmans," I say to Lucy.

When we enter the restaurant, the rest of the team already occupies a long table along the back wall. A waitress is topping up their coffee cups. The only two people missing are Ana and James. As I take a seat next to Simon, the young woman in her early 20s wearing a black skirt and a white blouse comes over with her notepad, her pen, ready to take an order.

"What can I fetch you, folks?" through a forced smile that says I hate this job, but it pays the bills.

George jumps straight in with, "I'll have scrambled eggs on toast with a side of beans, mushroom and bacon."

"Sounds good to me. I'll have the same."

"Me too," says Simon.

"Better make that five, and can I get two coffees, please," I say, putting down the menu.

A few minutes later, James and Ana come through the door, looking around before spotting us and coming over. She looks different now, as freedom hangs well with her. A big smile is across her face, her hair, long and black, falling onto her shoulders.

Once we have all finished eating, "The meeting with James' parents and Bear is at 14:00 in here. The time now is 12:00. So Lucy and Ana will take up a position at that end of the restaurant," I say in a quiet voice, as whispering in this environment would appear out of place. Plus, for all we know, we could have been followed to the hotel and someone is trying listen in on our coversation. Let's face facts: drug cartels have their people and connections everywhere.

I point to a table by the window. "James and myself will be at this one, or close to it if the table is already occupied. Simon will be observing the door from inside the lobby. George will be outside on the street..." I'm interrupted by George.

"Why am I the one out on the street in the cold whilst you numpties are sat in here drinking beer."

"Simple, short arse, you can hide in a crowd," Simon says, after taking a swig of his brew.

"Maybe you should be the one on the street, as you can see over the heads of everyone, you lanky streak of piss," retorts George.

"As I was saying, Derek will be sitting on one of the sofas at the end of the corridor leading onto West 46th Street. Once any of you spot James and Bear coming into the hotel, use your earpiece radios and let the rest of us know."

I spend the next five minutes going through the handover procedure and, of course, collecting the money still owed to us, and details of an emergency RV if things don't go to plan, which will be on the first floor of the M&M store on Times Square.

"If nobody has any questions, be in your position by 13:45. Ana, you stay with Lucy and me while James remains with Simon. If they move, you move. I would hate for anything to go wrong this late in the mission."

Chapter Seventeen – Drop-Off

Dead on 13:45, I enter the restaurant, with James following a few feet behind me. On entering, my eyes dart around the room. The place is full of a different type of clientele than at breakfast. Gone are the holidaymakers, who are more than likely exploring all the tourist joints of New York. Conversations compete with the clattering of metal-eating implements on china plates. The aroma of freshly brewed coffee battles for supremacy over hot pastries straight from the oven, to overpower your sense of smell.

A woman in her mid-20s stops us a few feet from the door. "Good afternoon. Would you like a table, or would you prefer to sit at the bar?" she asks, through a practised smile.

"A table for two, please, at the rear of the room," I point to the back of the place.

Without saying another word, the young lady picks up two menus from the counter and walks around the seated diners towards the back. Shit, the one we want and the ones on either side are occupied. I started formulating a quick alternative plan when two people stand up, throw a couple of dollars down and walk out of the restaurant. Before any other sneaky buggers grab the table, I plonk my arse down on the red leather bench that runs the whole length of the back wall. James does the same.

"Here are the menus. I'll be back in a few minutes to take your order," says the waitress, in a bored-sounding voice.

While she's gone, I turn my attention to the people in the room. Give each one a short once-over, looking for tell-tale signs that indicate the diners are more than innocent bystanders enjoying a business meeting or escaping their mundane jobs for lunch.

I've cleared most of the room, when Lucy and Ana enter the restaurant and occupy a table close to the window. At this point, it's best everyone doesn't make the connection. So, with a gentle nod, something that only the trained person would notice, I acknowledge I've seen them walk in.

My gaze runs past Lucy and onto the people sitting on the middle table of four, that line the enormous window overlooking the road. Out of the corner of my eye, I watch as Lucy picks up the menu, ensuring she holds the thumb of her left hand up along the edge of the card; she's seen us.

Five minutes later, there is a slight vibration in my ear as the radio comes to life.

"ST, in position."

Simon is somewhere in the lobby, watching the doorway that leads onto West 47th Street. It's not long before Derek in the corridor checks in. One minute passes, and the earpiece vibrates again.

"GD, outside in the cold," says George, with a pissed-off tone to his voice.

"Stop moaning. You have enough fat to keep a seal warm," comes the instant reply from Derek.

Great, we are all ready. Not only will we witness James' father and Bear entering, we will also know if they are alone or have brought someone else along. Plus, the boys will remain in situ as a safeguard the whole time the handover takes place, to ensure any of Arons's people did not follow Bear and John into the hotel.

I glance down at Mickey on my wrist. The time now is 14:05. They are late. The waitress comes over, holding a flask of coffee. She refills our mugs and places two loaded sub sandwiches on the table. I am not hungry, but we must blend into our surroundings to avoid standing out in a crowd.

Another five minutes pass before I receive the message we have all been waiting for.

"All call signs, this is DR. Targets acquired, and they are not alone. Heading your way."

I raise my mobile phone to my left ear in the pretence I'm taking a call. But this is a decoy for me using my radio.

"DR, roger that."

"The two men have passed my location," comes Simon's voice over the airwaves.

This is a critical stage and could still all go wrong. Prior to the meeting, Lucy and I spent time with Ana, making it clear how important it is for her not to jump up and run over to anyone she might recognise coming through the door, even though it's been a long time since she last saw them.

It would be hard for her, as she didn't know if she would ever meet them again. As for James, he is easy to control as he's next to me. If he tries to get up, I will force him back into his seat.

Scrutinise the situation as the waitress who greeted us talks to Bear and another man — more than probably James' father — and brings them to my table. If this is the father, he will have recognised James sitting at the back of the room. I start to stand up, when George's voice breaks through the airwaves.

"We might have an issue. The target was being followed. They've stopped across the road from the hotel and are now loitering in the doorway of the Richard Rogers Theatre."

"ST and DR, assist GD and neutralise the threat. out," I transmit via the radio, once more using the phone as a decoy.

Seconds later, standing before me at the table are three individuals. Two of the men are dressed in impeccably tailored grey business suits and exude an undeniable air of authority and power. Both stand with confidence, their facial expressions giving away nothing of their intentions.

But it is the third figure that catches my attention. He stands out like a sore neck in his casual attire. The green polo shirt strains against the bulge of the man's protruding beer gut, a stark juxtaposition to the dapper appearances of his companions. His presence sparking a mix of curiosity and wariness within me. No doubt this person likes a drink, and with equal measures, a hatred of any physical exercise, from his appearance. But who am I to judge?

Standing tall amidst this formidable gathering, a towering figure with short brown hair and broad shoulders emits an air of quiet strength, as he surveys the room and looks me up and down. His gaze is a fusion of pride, relief, and overwhelming emotions. I glimpse the weight of our assignment in his eyes as he holds out his right arm, ready to shake my hand.

Next to him is Bear, who I recognise from our initial meeting, our indispensable link to the concerned parents of the rescued hostages. And, of course, the rest of the million dollars still owed to us for the mission.

"Nice to meet you at last. My name is John; I'm James' father. I believe you already know Bear, and this fine gentleman is Ronaldo, Ana's dad. He insisted he came to pick up Ana."

I turn to face John, "Hi, I'm Steve. As you can see here, James is alive and unharmed, as is Ana…" I'm interrupted by Ronaldo, eager to catch sight of his beloved daughter.

"Where is Ana? Is she here? I want to see her," declares Ronaldo, in an excited sort of way.

"I'll let you know the answer to that question once we have the business out of the way," I reply.

My eyes flicker towards the window for a nanosecond, where, amidst the commotion and the scent of sizzling culinary delights that perfume the air, intermingling with the clinking of glasses and the hushed conversations of diners, Lucy and Ana's eyes are fixed on the events unfolding at my table.

Through the symphony of sounds—the clatter of cutlery, the murmurs of conversation, Ana's brown eyes gleam with a steely determination. Her gaze meets mine, a silent exchange of an unspoken understanding of the situation, her face etched with the scars of her harrowing ordeal. Her eyes flick between us and our companions, eager to run over and hug her father.

With my focus back on the people sitting on the other side of the table,

"OK, gents, down to business. We have freed Ana and James, plus Eliza and Ralph, all uninjured. So, down to the rest of the dosh for the job. You have my bank account number. So once you send the funds, we will hand over Ana and James."

Bear slips his right hand into his jacket. I tense up, my hand on my pistol, which is resting on the chair behind my back. My eyes fix on Bear as he removes his hand with a slow, gradual motion as if he is teasing me, and pulls out his phone.

"I'll transfer the money over now. Plus the extra 50,000 you requested for having to change continents," Bear begins tapping on the screen of his smartphone.

Once more, I glance toward Lucy, trying to make my movement undetectable as though I am diverting my eyes away from Bear's telephone. Over near the window, Lucy takes her mobile out and starts to tap away. I don't need to know what she is doing, I already know.

After the incident with Henry, after the job on St Halb, we altered how we received payment. She will divide what is left of the money after deductions for costs and transfer funds into each team member's accounts. This was done for several reasons. First, we do not have a single bank account with a considerable amount of cash. Second, the business account will be empty if the employer stops or recalls the money for any reason. Plus, of course, everyone gets paid straight away.

Keep John, Bear and Ronaldo in conversation while I wait for Lucy to signal that all funds have been transferred. In this instance, it will be her letting Ana come over and be reunited with her father.

"First time I've been on a private jet. All thanks to Bob, who appears to be a nice person."

I keep the focus of the three people sitting opposite me, and not on what is going on behind them.

"I've known Bob for a long time. He is a good guy and can be trusted most of the time."

Now curious. "What do you mean, most of the time, John?"

"Let's put it this way, Steve. That aircraft of his is expensive to run and maintain. So, he offsets some of the cost by importing stolen artwork into the United States. He probably smuggled several pieces of art onboard with you. Suppose the plane had been boarded, he would have denied any knowledge and blamed it on whoever was flying at the time. On your trip here, it would be on you."

"That's interesting, John. He forgot to mention that bit of information."

But in the back of my mind, I'm thinking, we are here, so who gives a shit what he gets up to. Moments later, Lucy leans into Ana and whispers in her ear.

"Go on, your dad is waiting."

Without saying a word, Ana rises from her seat. Her every movement teems with fervent anticipation. Her eyes, wide with hope, flicker with a newfound light as she glides across the busy floor of Friedmans restaurant. Her delicate footsteps hasten, creating a soft melody that crescendos in perfect harmony with the symphony of clinking cutlery and lively conversations.

Through the crowds of joyful diners, her slender figure navigates the space as her ebony hair cascades down her back, their strands swaying with each purposeful stride. The world surrounding her, bustling and alive, vanishes into a blur as she approaches my table.

As she gets close. I sense the palpable tension between a young lady yearning for her father's tender embrace and a father longing to envelop his daughter in his protective arms once more. It is a moment suspended in time, where every beat of their hearts propels them closer.

As Ana reaches the table, time stands still. The crescendo achieves its peak, intertwining with the rhythm of her pulsating heartbeat. The world fades into the background, leaving only their reunion to capture our collective consciousness.

Ana's eyes sparkle with a blend of relief, gratitude, and sheer unadulterated joy. She throws her arms around Ronaldo in one seamless motion, and he folds her into his embrace. As they come together, I detect a deep connection built on unconditional love.

In that moment, as I witness their profound love, I am reminded of life's fragility and beauty. My thoughts divert to my children back in England. What I would do, and the people I would kill if they ever got into this predicament flash in my mind. A strange emotion comes over me for the first time in a long time: empathy; a stark contrast of fear and hope, despair and redemption, Ana and the others have been rescued from.

While I watch, a voice vibrates in my ear, "S3, this is GD, threat neutralised." It is George from across the road.

"Do not know if James told you, we are opening a store here in New York today, so we will have to leave you. Again, thank you and your team, sure they will be observing the meeting from somewhere, For bringing James back alive and unharmed and the rest of the hostages, you are welcome to attend if you like?" says John, standing up from the table.

"Thanks for the offer, but we have things to organise." I stand up and shake everybody's hand.

When they have all vacated the restaurant, I'm joined by Lucy, who sits beside me on the red leather bench.

"That went better than I thought it might, Steve."

"Sure did, Lucy. It's time to call the boys back, once they have confirmed that John and his team have gone and not left behind any nasty surprises for us."

Push the transmit button in the centre of the earpiece radio with the index finger of my right hand.

"All call signs, this is S3, RV in Bond 45 near the rear door of the hotel after all tasks complete, out."

With the bill for the drinks paid and a ten-dollar tip placed under a glass on the table, Lucy and I leave and walk through the hotel past the bustling reception area, weaving our way through the hoards of happy holidaymakers to the entrance to Bond 45.

The layout has the same vibe as the Friedmans, with a central bar and tables packed with diners. Conversations mixed with the aroma of freshly brewed coffee and baked pastries that circulate the place—enticing people to sample their delights.

A few empty tables run along the back to the left of the doorway. Out of habit, I sit with my back to the wall. This is something my

PTSD always keeps me doing, so nobody can creep up and take me by surprise from the rear. It isn't long before a young waiter arrives and takes our order.

"Five large beers, please."

Trying my best to confuse the man standing in front of me, who, by his appearance, is trying to divide five into two, I could tell him we have friends joining us, but it is more fun to scrutinise his contorted face.

The boys must have smelled the beers as they are placed on the table. They walk through the door and join Lucy and me. By the time the man returns, hoping to take a food order, we have downed the beers.

"Better make that five more," Lucy announces, handing him her glass.

"Any idea who the people who followed Bear and his cohort are, George? Plus, did you discover anything on them that may be useful?"

"No clue, Steve, but they were not your normal hired thugs, as I couldn't find anything on them. At least we didn't come across a damn envelope with a blue stripe, so nothing interesting. So what's the plan now, boss?"

"Before we do anything else, George, can you book our flights home for tomorrow morning, please, Simon?"

"Any preference in airlines or class of seats?"

"I've left enough money in the account for business class back. Plus, the money for the job is already in your bank accounts," states Lucy.

"Five non-cattle class flights coming up," Simon taps away on his smartphone.

With plane tickets booked and the beers flowing, we spend the next two hours winding down from the mission, letting the tension we have all held since first landing on Saint Ann escape. A collective weight being lifted from our shoulders as much as we could, as the assignment isn't over until we are back home. Something our military careers taught us. Too many people have been killed when they relaxed too soon.

"Why not sort our equipment out? We can meet back here at 19:00, as I want to visit Times Square at night," says Lucy.

"Sounds good to me. See you all in the reception later," Derek declares, heading for the door, followed by Simon and George.

Back in Lucy's and my room, I double-check my kit is ready to go before walking to the bathroom to join Lucy. As I step into the warm embrace of the shower, steam envelops my body and obscures the view outside. The droplets cascade over my skin, each tiny drop acting like a gentle caress, igniting my senses. I close my eyes, surrendering to the sensation of rejuvenation.

The rhythmic sound of the water hitting the tiles creates a soothing symphony, drowning out the noise of the bustling activity beyond the confines of the room. Its cadence becomes a backdrop to the intimacy that unfolds in this sacred space.

I reach out my hand, discovering the wet smoothness of the tiles beneath my fingertips. They provide stability, grounding me as my world revolves around this single moment. The water dances in sparkling reflections on the walls, adding a mesmerising visual layer to the experience like shimmering diamonds.

As the steam engulfs us, I take a deep breath, the air heavy with the scent of lavender from the fragrant soap Lucy insisted on buying. It lingers in my nostrils, mingling with the damp earthiness of the steam, transporting me to a realm of tranquillity. The scent wraps about me like a comforting embrace, heightening my connection to Lucy.

I lean forward, closing the space between us, sensing her soft skin under my fingertips. The heat of the water amplifies the electric intensity of her touch, sending shivers coursing through my body. Our bodies merge like two puzzle pieces, finding their perfect fit, and the sensation is overpowering.

Lucy leans into me, her head resting on my shoulder as I whisper, "Sorry, honey, maybe later, as you want to visit Times Square."

"OK, but I'm holding you to that," through a seductive smile.

By the time we arrive in the lobby, Derek and George are already there, sitting at the rear on a soft fabric-covered sofa, each drinking beer from a glass.

"Where is the recce troop, lost again?"

A voice behind me shouts out. "I fucking heard that, you green numpty."

"Great, now Simon is here. Let's go and find out what all the fuss is about, regarding a street full of advertisements," I say, walking towards the exit.

As we leave the elegant Edison Hotel's revolving doors, Times Square's bright lights greet us like old friends. The night sky above is alight with a thousand colours, reflecting off the towering 3D screens showcasing lifelike animals leaping from the screens at us. It's a scene straight out of a futuristic movie, an electrifying blend of fantasy and reality.

As we stride onto the cracked pavement, we are surrounded by a sea of people swarming like ants. We forge ahead, making our way to the centre of the pedestrian area, weaving through the pulsating crowds. Every step is like a negotiation; we push through with precision and caution, always aware of potential threats lurking in the shadows.

Tension hangs in the air, intensifying the vibrant atmosphere. Everyone's heard of the criminal gangs that call Times Square their territory, rulers of the neon jungle — the adrenaline courses through my veins, heightening my senses to a state of hypervigilance. Out of habit, my eyes dart from side to side, scanning for suspicious figures. At the same time, my ears strain to pick up the slightest irregularities amidst the cacophony of honking cars and chatter.

As we navigate the labyrinthine maze of bodies, everyone is looking for any indications of the drug cartel; like whispers in the wind, a discarded cigarette butt smouldering near a graffiti-covered wall, a quick flash of a familiar tattoo on a passerby's wrist. My heart races, my eyes narrow in suspicion, and my mind subconsciously calculates possible escape routes.

The bustling streets are a sensory overkill, assaulting me with their symphony. Horns blare with anger, intertwining with the hum of the neon signs flickering above us. The sharp scent of roasted pretzels mingles with the whiff of exhaust fumes, creating a paradoxical mixture of hunger and nausea.

An array of people dressed in an assortment of characters from movies mingle in the crowd. A question leaps to the front of my brain. Who and what is under the costume? It is ideal place to hide if you are a member of some organised crime gang. Out of the corner of my eye, I detect one of the idiots outfitted in a British guard's uniform.

"George, look over there; you have a twin," laughing out loud.

"You know what you can do, arsehole, and there is your brother, Steve," replies George, pointing at a giant gorilla.

"You're right. Help me to take it back to the Empire State Building down the road. I'll let you stand guard in the doorway."

"Fuck off, you green numpty."

As we walk around admiring the sights, I can't shake off the sense that we are being watched by unseen predators scrutinising our every move. A bead of sweat trickles down my temple. It is a testament to the weight of the situation we find ourselves in.

Suddenly, a commotion breaks through the clamour, slicing through the tension like a knife. A scuffle erupts a mere few steps ahead. The shoving and shouting are a vivid testimony to the danger that lurks underneath the bright lights. We freeze, gazes locked on the unfolding chaos. It could be a trap, a diversion to distract us from an imminent threat.

The crowd parts for a moment, revealing a glimpse of a shadowy figure escaping into an alley. Was it one of the cartel's men? Simon and George exchange wordless glances, determination etching lines into their faces. Times Square may glitter with superficial beauty, but beneath the vibrant façade is a world of savagery, waiting for an opportunity to pounce.

Despite this, we spend the next couple of hours walking around and visiting the many shops that line the streets, buying tacky souvenirs for families back in England. By 22:00, we have all had enough of this sightseeing malarky and head back to Bond 45 for a few nightcaps.

Once more, the drinks flow, with everyone letting their guard slip a little and enjoying the moment. Forgetting about the mission we have just completed and the people we killed along the way until 01:00, when the barman insists we leave because the place is closing. With my body telling me I'm a little tipsy, I turn to Lucy, who is also somewhat drunk.

"Come on, honey, let's go to our room. I made you a promise earlier."

"Sounds good to me," comes the reply.

After agreeing to meet at Friedmans at 07:00 for breakfast, we all head for the elevators tucked in down a small corridor straight across from the door of the bar. A few minutes later, I fumble with the hotel room key, my fingertips grazed by the cold metal before finding the slot. The door swings open, revealing a sanctuary cloaked in soft golden light, casting playful shadows across the room. As we step inside, urban noises fade away, leaving an air of tranquillity that soothes my weary mind.

The quiet hum of the air conditioner punctuates the silence, a soothing lullaby that tugs at my tired eyelids. I glance at Lucy, her eyes reflecting the shared weariness we both share. A silent agreement that sleep is the only respite our exhausted bodies crave, we exchange a knowing smile, our lips curving upward in unspoken understanding.

We glide towards the inviting bed, its vastness seeming to swallow us whole. The plush mattress engulfs us, supporting our weary frames as we settle into its embrace. A gentle sigh escapes Lucy's lips, a soft melody that harmonises with the distant rustling of the curtains and the steady rhythm of our breaths.

Chapter Eighteen – Journey Home

The sound of Reveille playing at full volume on my phone wakes me from my slumber. At least I'd remembered to set the alarm last night before hitting the land of nod. I glance over to the other side of the bed. Lucy is starting to stir.

"Better get up, honey, it's 06:00," slipping my legs out from under the quilt and landing them on the floor.

"Right behind you, Steve."

After a quick shower, I search the room for a brew-making kit before the brain kicks in and reminds me there isn't one. I need my morning gallon of roasted coffee. So, as soon as Lucy is ready, we head down to the restaurant for breakfast and the all-important beverage. We are the first to arrive, so take up the same table at the back of the room as we had used for the meeting yesterday.

Soon, the waitress, a young black woman in her mid-20s dressed in the company uniform, comes over holding a flask.

"Would you like coffee?" she asks.

"Yes, please," turning Lucy's and my mugs over.

As I sip on the nectar of life, I take in the sights and sounds of the restaurant as it starts to fill up. The chatter of early risers discussing the day ahead. The clinking of cutlery striking the plates with the faint noise of the traffic passing by the window. All wrapped in the scent of fresh brewed coffee and pastries that hang in the air like an overcoat.

I'm brought back to reality by the words, "Morning, fat boy," from Simon, who is sitting down at the table next to me.

"Glad you could be bothered to join us, you lanky streak of piss. How's your head?"

"Like the gorilla broke into my room last night and shit in my mouth and whacked me over the head for good measure."

"Yep, I know that feeling," I reply.

Once Marion, the waitress, comes back, we all order breakfast of scrambled eggs on toast with a side order of sausages and bacon with plenty of coffee and orange juice before our attention turns to the route home.

"I've booked us flights with British Airways leaving at 12:00. Suggest we leave straight after we finish here," says Simon, after finishing a mouthful of bacon.

"I'll book us a couple of taxis from the reception desk for 08:30," says Derek, after stuffing his face with a loaded fork of egg and toast.

With food out of the way and all bags collected from the rooms, we clamber into the two yellow New York taxis and head for JFK airport.

Once we arrive, we jump out of the two vibrant yellow cabs. Our hearts are pounding with the excitement of heading home after a successful mission. The journey has been intense, filled with danger and pulse-racing action. We make our way towards the British Airways check-in desk.

With our business class booking, we navigate through the bustling terminal. Each step is calculated. Our senses are heightened, attuned to the slightest trace of the infamous drug cartel we rescued hostages from.

The air is thick with the promise of departure. It crackles and hums with the energy of a thousand stories unfolding at the same time. The aroma of freshly brewed coffee mingles with the scent of jet fuel, a heady mix that invigorates us and heightens our senses.

We approach the check-in, and relief washes over us as we witness the short queue for the business check-in desk. We exchange a glance of gratitude, knowing that luck has favoured us in this crucial moment. We maintain composure, concealing the truth of the danger lurking in the shadows.

As we near the counter, I hear the gentle hum of voices mixed with the clatter of keyboards and the distant buzz of the intercom. People mill around us, their hurried footsteps blending with the murmurs of conversation; the terminal, a sea of faces and emotions, swarms with life.

We reach the desk, and the receptionist meets us with an air of professionalism. I sense a whispered sigh escape my lips as the tension is lifted for that short moment. Lucy's grip on my arm tightens, her eyes glimmering with exhaustion and triumph.

The check-in clerk smiles, oblivious to the chaos we have just emerged from. Her voice, soft and serene, evokes a feeling of calm. She takes our passports with practised efficiency and begins to process them. My hands begin to sweat with nervous energy. We might have landed in New York from San Francisco, but there is no record of us entering America. If she does start to ask awkward questions, I've already decided on a course of action.

After what John told us about Bob, I'm prepared to throw him under the proverbial bus. Explain as it was a private airline bringing us from Singapore, we believed he'd taken care of everything. I glance back at the others, each with their battle scars, each carrying the weight of this shared experience.

As we walk from the check-in desk, a renewed sense of purpose fills our stride. Once imposing and daunting, the terminal appears more diminutive and manageable, but we are not safe yet. Our adventure is far from over. We still need to board the plane and navigate customs at London Heathrow.

A quick look at the flight departures noticeboard confirms our gate number. When we arrive, airline staff are checking boarding cards and passports before letting travellers into another smaller room, bordered on three sides with floor-to-ceiling windows.

Inside, people are trying to occupy the chairs closest to the door leading down to the ramp and onto the plane. I can't see the point of this. Boarding is always carried out by the group number on your ticket. Head for the seats at the back of the room. Twenty minutes later, the voice in the ceiling announces they are starting to board business class passengers.

Turn to the others. "You lot ready?"

"Sure am," says George, heading to the aircraft.

Once onboard the British Airways aircraft, the cabin exudes an air of sophistication. Warm ambient lighting illuminates the spacious area ahead. I'm immediately drawn to the plush fabric seats. Their rich blue colour offers a sense of elegance and luxury. The cushioning seems to envelop my body as I sink into the seat, caressing me gently. It's like falling into a cloud, a haven that promises hours of uninterrupted relaxation.

To my left, Lucy settles into her seat with a contented sigh, her expressions mirroring my delight. To my right across the aisle, Simon, Derek, and George recline in theirs.

Around us, fellow passengers are also settling in for the flight. Their hushed conversations and occasional laughter create a pleasant background hum. A soft melody wafts through the cabin, enhancing the ambience.

The air hostess glides with grace and style towards us, embodying elegance and professionalism. Her immaculate uniform, adorned with the company logo, displays a subtle insignia of quality. She carries a tray of hot towels, their gentle steam rising towards the ceiling.

Another person comes over to my seat with a glass of champagne, its effervescence dancing in the crystal-clear flute. The golden liquid cascades, overflowing with bubbles that shimmer and sparkle like miniature stars captured in a glass.

The air hostess, ever attentive, moves through the cabin, attending to each passenger's every need. Her demeanour radiates warmth and genuine care, offering a glimpse into the exceptional service that awaits us. Her every movement, a graceful ballet performed with impeccable precision, further enhances the refinement surrounding us.

The flight to London Heathrow is only a short seven hours. For the first time since we met with Bear in San Juan, we can relax even if someone from the cartel did board the plane. Nothing could happen until we arrive at Heathrow.

Like the rest of the team, while away the hours, with a combination of sleeping, watching movies, eating and, of course, the occasional drinks brought to me by the lovely hostess.

The aircraft starts its descent into London on time, and by 19:00, we are walking up the covered walkway into Terminal 5.

The scene that unfolds before me is pure chaos, as we step out of the walkway and onto the vast hallways and corridors that lead to customs. The air at Heathrow Airport is alive with a frenzy of voices in different languages; the sound of luggage wheels screeching against the tiled floors and the occasional blaring of announcements over the intercom. It's a symphony of disarray, and I am just another player in this chaotic orchestra.

As I approach the control point, I have to squeeze through a never-ending sea of people. The heat of their bodies radiates through the sheer number of them — beads of sweat form on my forehead. There is a sense of urgency in the air, as if we are racing against time. The queue moves slowly, the line curling and twisting like a snake, making progress almost impossible. This is made worse by the electronic passport machines being out of service.

I glance to my left, catching a glimpse of Lucy. She clutches her passport, her knuckles turning white from holding it too tight. Her eyes dart from side to side, scanning the crowd for any signs of trouble. We exchange a nervous smile, a knowing look that we are in this together. We have done this before, but the stakes are higher now.

George and Simon are just behind me in the queue, about 10 people away. George checks his wristwatch every few seconds, a reminder of the precious minutes ticking by. His eyes dart back and forth between the clock and the control officer, willing the line to move faster.

Finally, it's Lucy's and my turn. She hands me her passport, and I hand both to the officer, trying to look calm and relaxed. He scans it, his eyes lingering on my face for an agonising second longer than necessary. Panic threatens to overwhelm me, but I keep my cool. It's all about appearances.

Derek is a little way back. Once I'm through, I stand at the entrance leading down to the escalators that go down to the baggage carousels, and monitor passport control as the others come through without any issues.

Phase one is complete—time to move on to baggage reclaim. When we arrive, the carousel is packed with luggage from multiple flights, like a carousel of lost souls. Each bag that comes into view is met with anticipation and dread. Like everyone who flies, we go through the anxious moments of wondering if our luggage will be there.

Soon, I sigh with relief as our bags come out of the hole at the end of the conveyor, like the rest of the team. I leave my bag to go for a ride around a couple of times to ensure nobody is watching or paying attention to my bag. After the third time around, I walk over to the belt from near the carousel behind me, where I've been watching from.

Once everyone has their luggage in hand, we navigate through the hordes of people to the entrance to Customs at the far end of the hall, keeping a low profile. The scent of coffee lingers in the air, mixing with the perfume and cologne of the passengers, creating a heady and almost suffocating odour. The movement of bodies is a dance that we must navigate with precision, avoiding any bumps or brushes that might draw unwanted attention.

As we approach Customs, fear clutches at my heart. The officers stand tall and imposing, their eyes trained on each passerby, searching for any sign of deception. I hold my breath as I pass through, but they barely give me a second glance. I glance back to catch sight of Lucy, Simon, and Derek, who have all passed through. At one of the tables, George is opening his carry-on to a customs officer who has stopped him.

Rather than stop, we head for the arranged rendezvous point, Caffé Nero, at the far end of the terminal and wait for George.

"You getting the drinks in, Steve?" says Simon, plonking his butt down at one of the free tables.

"Yeah, no problem. I wonder what happened to George?" I say, placing my case close to where Derek is sitting with a stupid grin.

"Remember after the last mission when George told Customs I had something in my bags?"

"What the fuck did you do, Derek?" asks Simon.

"Well, as they say, revenge is best served cold. I would love to see his face when he tries to explain the arse probe I slipped in his bag before we left New York."

Ten minutes pass before a red-faced George appears in the café and throws his Bergen on the floor.

"OK, which of you bastards placed this in my bag? I bet it was you, Simon," George holds out the probe.

"Don't fucking blame me."

After we have all stopped laughing at George's expense, Derek owns up, "Revenge is a bitch, hey, George!"

"While you lot finish your brews, I'll get our transport for the way back to Southampton," I say, standing up.

Not wanting to leave any type of trail of our whereabouts once we leave the airport, I purchase five National Express coach tickets with cash. From there, Simon and George will go their separate ways; as Derek isn't flying back to St Halb for a few days, he is returning to my place with Lucy and me.

Two and a half hours later, the coach pulls into Southampton bus station.

"OK, you two idiots, fuck off, and I'll be in contact next week to arrange a piss-up," I say, as Simon and George clamber into a taxi to the station to catch a train home.

It is only a short distance from here to the ferry, so we all walk, rather than grab a taxi. Inside the terminal, people sit around the few seats the company left when they turned the establishment into an automated service area. Gone is the interaction with the staff when booking a crossing. In their place are two bright red ticket machines, standing faceless against the far wall close to several vending machines. The only human presence is a female behind the counter of the shop-come-café.

By the time I've purchased three tickets, the Osprey pulls into port, so head towards the large metal gate at the end of the building and wait for the attendants to open it to allow people to get off before we can get on board.

As we step onto the busy car ferry at Southampton, the air is thick with anticipation and the bustling energy of fellow passengers. The ship's horn sounds, punctuating the chatter with a sense of urgency. The vibrations rumble through the soles of my shoes, and I feel a jolt of expectation surge through me. It's time to set sail.

Moving to the outer deck, I look towards the City and Mayflower terminals as several cruise liners edge closer to the harbour wall. The water is a kaleidoscope of greens, reflecting the clear sky above. Seagulls dance in the updrafts, their high-pitched cries blend harmoniously with the gentle waves lapping against the ferry's hull. I lean on the railing next to Lucy and Derek. The cool metal presses into my palms as I take in the magnificent vista before me.

As the ship cuts through the sea, the wind tousles Lucy's long hair, and I can taste the ocean on my lips. It's a salty tang that invigorates me, heightening my senses. I monitor the churning water behind us, like white foamy trails that mark our passage.

As we approach Cowes, the atmosphere on board turns electric. Passengers gather near the railings, cameras poised to capture the first glimpse of the charming town. The ferry slips into the dock, and the engine's roar fades into the background, replaced by a symphony of excited chatter and the clatter of footsteps.

Outside the East Cowes terminal, a line of taxis are parked along the edge of the railing on the other side of the road, waiting for weary travellers. We walk over and clamber into one.

"Good evening. Parkdean Resorts, Shanklin, please," I say, after I've fastened the front passenger seatbelt.

"No problem, you travel far?" the driver enquires.

"Not really, just back off holiday in the north," I lie.

We arrive at the gravel car park across from my lodge within 30 minutes. Once out of the vehicle, we wait until the taxi disappears back up the hill.

"If you stay here with the bags, Lucy, Derek and I will go check the tell-tails I placed around the lodge before we departed for the cruise. Want to make sure we are not walking into any type of trap," I say, pointing for Derek to go one way while I go the other.

As I make my way around, I spot something that makes me stop in my tracks. The grass beneath the kitchen window has been trampled underfoot. Look up. The hair I placed between the window and the frame blows about in the wind. Someone's been inside or tried to. Moments later, Derek appears from the back.

"All clear, my side."

Without saying a word, I point to where the plastic tape is still attached before making my way to the door. This also has been opened.

"Derek, come with me to the back. I may need help to peer through the kitchen window. Want to see if there is something behind the door."

Derek leans back on the lodge, trying not to make a noise. He clasps both hands and then lowers them to a height where I can put my right foot in them. I bounce a few times with my other leg, then jump and haul myself up to peek inside. From my vantage point, I can't see anything out of place. There is no trip wire to the front door that, when opened, sets a shot off into any unsuspecting person who opens the door.

"Appears clear, Derek. Go and fetch Lucy," I say, returning to the entrance.

Position my left hand on the door handle before inserting the key. I turn the key in the lock in a slow, quiet motion. Wait five seconds before pulling the door ajar a few inches. Move to the side and inspect around all the edges for anything connected. There isn't any, so I pull the door open an inch at a time and walk inside.

I carry out the same procedure in all the rooms. They are all clear. Nothing out of the ordinary apart from the main bedroom, where some of my clothes from the wardrobe are slung across the bed. With the lodge cleared, I open the door and call Lucy and Derek to join me.

"Find anything that shouldn't be there, Steve?" Lucy asks.

"Nope, all I can think of is the park maintenance team's been in for something while we've been away."

A habit I picked up in the army is not to leave your kit festering in your bag for the day. Deal with your dirty equipment straight away. So, I spend the next half an hour sorting my stuff.

Lucy and Derek do the same, before Derek slumps into a well-worn armchair. An audible sigh escapes his lips. Lucy collapses onto the sofa, her eyes fixed on the flickering flames of the gas fire. She turned it on to heat the place and remove the damp odour that hung in the air like a dead rat on a string.

I take a deep breath, taking in the scene. The lodge has witnessed our victories and failures with its rustic charm, offering relief and refuge when needed.

As I sink into a worn couch, the sense of well-being envelops me, wrapping me in its warm embrace. It's as if, at this moment, time itself stands still, and the world outside ceases to exist. I'm reminded of the true meaning of coming home, of finding solace in the familiar and sharing the weight of our burdens with those who understand.

We sit in silence for a few minutes, the fire crackling and coffee brewing. We take comfort in the warmth of our triumph, and the bond between the team has grown stronger amidst the chaos.

We've been busy doing nothing besides drinking a brew and chatting about anything but the mission when my phone in the dining area starts playing my ringtone, 'I am ninety-fifth'.

"Lucy, as you're up, can you see who's calling?"

Lucy walks over to the table, picks up the smartphone and reads the name on the screen. "It's Simon. Shall I answer it?"

"Better see what the idiot wants. He probably got lost on the way home," I joke.

"Hi Simon, It's Lucy. What's the problem."

After a short conversation, Lucy replaces the telephone on the table and joins me on the sofa.

"What did Simon have to say?"

"Nothing much. Someone called him a few minutes ago and said they have a job we might be interested in."

Glossary

Dhobi Dust	Washing Powder
Mickey	Cheap Wristwatch
Egg Banjo	Egg Sandwich
PAYG	Pay As You Go
Chimp	Mind / Anger Management programme used in the treatment of PTSD
Call Sign TS	Tanky Simon
Call Sign GD	George Dog
Call Sign S3	Steve 3(RGJ)
Escaped Librarian	A term used in the treatment of PTSD
Donkey Walloper	Tank Driver
Click	Kilometre
OP	Observation Post
Polo Donkey	Horse/Donkey
RV	Rendezvous – Meeting Point
Bergen	Backpack
Stag	Sentry Duty
Shanks Pony	Walking
Pit	Bed
Grunt	Ground Reconnaissance Untrainable
SLR	Self Loading Rifle
LZ	Landing Zone

For more information about our books or services, please visit

www.green-cat.shop

www.ingramcontent.com/pod-product-compliance
Lightning Source LLC
Chambersburg PA
CBHW070559260626
47161CB00002B/658